PROBY AND ME

PROBY AND ME

A HOWLING TALE
OF A FALLING STAR

MJ CORNWALL

Printed by BookPOD

First published 2023

ISBN: 978-0-6454923-2-3 (paperback)

ISBN: 978-0-6454923-3-0 (ebook)

Front cover and internal photos: Tony Mott

Cover design: Louise Cornwall

NATIONAL LIBRARY OF AUSTRALIA

A catalogue record for this book is available from the National Library of Australia

For Duncan Stewart

AUTHOR'S NOTE

This story is peppered with the vernacular from times past, pertaining to gender, cultural background, sexuality and related phenomena. These terms are now regarded, rightly so, as offensive and unacceptable.

The author begs the reader's understanding that such language is used here for no other reason than to portray people and culture as they were, to afford insight into that world and those mindsets.

There are also references to predatory sexual behaviours and to domestic violence. Again, these are not intended in any way to encourage, enable, or normalise such practices, nor to offer agency for apologists. They serve only to provide a full and frank picture of the way it was in those places and times.

And in what business is there not humbug?

– PT Barnum

He never settled till I got him to the pub of a morning.

'John Wesley Hardin,' he says. 'Y'all heard of him?'

I had. The outlaw. The Bob Dylan album.

'My great-grandfather.'

Geez, Proby. Ace it up, I thought. But it checked out later...

'His first kill at fifteen, Brett. A freed slave who taunted him. Then three Union troopers after him for it.'

I didn't recall this from Dylan's account.

'Wes criss-crossed Texas to evade capture. Showdowns unavoidable. Shot a man's eye out for a bottle of creek-brewed liquor on a bet. Dropped a black boy in Leon County. And some jackfly who had at him for cheating at cards. In Limestone County, one in a tussle at the travelling circus. Then, a hooker's pimp. A spat over the fee.'

He took a pull on his stubby. Warm. *Works better that way, Brett.*

'But they corralled him in Waco. Just seventeen, he shot a marshal in a barbershop there. In the log jail, acquired a handgun somehow. En route to trial, despatched his escorts.'

He tilted his head back. Raised those reach for the sky eyebrows.

'I look just like ol' Wes,' he said. 'Think like him too.'

'His cousins found him a way out, Wes now with a price on his head. Hired on as a trail boss. Herd bound for Abilene, Kansas. On the drive, a dispute with *los trios amigos* Mexicans over a game of three card monte. Wes, well, he ended it. Then a to-do with a Mex herd tailgating his. A gunfight ensues. Three fewer *vaqueros* in the saddle come sundown. Further on, Wes greased two injuns trying to steal beeves.

The town marshal for Abilene knew not Wes was a fugitive, but liked him not anyway. So bid Wes surrender his irons. Only gun alive who could outdraw him, this Wild Bill Hickok, so Wes complied.'

He eyed his beer and Clyde and me. *Running on empty here.*

'Genius and alcohol, boys. They go hand in hand.'

Clyde moved to the bar.

'They grew to be amigos. Then one night, disturbed by snoring, Wes fired shots through his bunkhouse wall. Hit the offending party in the head. As Bill and his constables made for the disturbance, Wes hid in a haystack. Then lit out for Texas.

Two Texas Special Police rode out when word came he was back. One returned. A coloured posse from Austin came back three men light. And in Corpus Christi, a Mex bit the dust. Their quest for bounty, foiled by his moxie with the double draw.'

Hardin then near died, said Proby.

'A set-to. Poker game. Wes, gut-shot. Turned himself in for medical palliation, believing his end near. Yet he healed. So some tin star charged him for a string of homicides. A hacksaw dropped through the bars, by brother Jim or a cousin most like, brought means to cheat the hangman.

In Comanche, Texas, Wes plugged a deputy, name of Webb. A lynch mob assembled. Hardin's brother and two cousins by now locked up here on other warrants. This Webb popular in these parts. So those bible 'n' ropers hanged 'em all three when Wes gave them the slip. He was collared in Mobile, Alabama. Broke out again but was cornered on a train in Pensacola, Florida.

Served sixteen years. Studied on law. On his release, passed the bar exam. Lettered now. Yet unchanged.

In El Paso, he pistol-whipped a fella objected to Wes cavorting with his wife. So that pup's daddy dog-shot Wes in the head as he gamed at dice in the Acme Saloon.'

Proby clinked his beer on ours and raised it high.

'I see much of myself in that man.'

So would we in time.

CHAPTER ONE

His first days among us, we thought he was making it all up, but when we jerried he wasn't, we saw just how much trouble we were in.

Look, it won't make no sense without some backstory. It was the Hopetoun Hotel. Year of '89. My local. My birthday. Fifth November. Proby's next day. Never seen him live. Never had the chance. All of us, fans. Bigtime. He'd left a mighty body of work. But long gone and forever, it seemed. And I've just blown a pubful of minds with my news.

Out on the trawl that day. Vinyl bins. *Bang*. Twelve-inch single. *New release*. Proby doing Prince. *Sign O' The Times*. I can't hardly believe it. *He's alive*.

'Brett! Where to for afters when they chuck us out of here?'

I lived close by. Clyde Bramley, late of the Hoodoo Gurus, next door. So I said how about back to his, a bunch of takeaways, this mob here, and play PJ Proby and nothing else?

'A singularity of a playlist, my man.'

The fun lovers. Clyde. The formidable Janine Hall. Rob Younger, once were Radio Birdman, now New Christs. Caroline, my by now kind-of ex. Long story. And Sally Geschmay, housemate. Spencer Jones, he of the Johnnys and Beasts of Bourbon. Speedy, roadie for both. Others. Proby tragics all.

'Oorooski, fun lovers! There's an address on the cover.'

I reef out the disc. Savoy Records. Manchester. *And that's how it started*.

'Hey! We could tour Proby out here!'

I forget who. Copious beers and ganja on the swirl. Then this from Clyde.

'I could cover airfares and some expenses.'

Yeah, I know. But despite the sound of it, not my first go at this. I'd booked and toured, local and beyond. Ran the Newtown Hotel, the Leichhardt, Max's Petersham Inn. Put on Bo Diddley, the Troggs, Billy Joe Shaver, Tav Falco's Panther Burns. Chris Bailey from The Saints. Hard cases too. Stevie Wright with Hard Rain. X with Ian Rilen on board. So...

I trailed the phone away from the mob. Shut the door. ISD operator finds the number off the address I supply from the record cover. Easy as.

'We specialise in stuff that gets banned,' he says, 'to generate sales.'

After midnight here. Ten AM in Manchester. This joker David Britton runs Savoy Books. Proby, he reckons, lives in Bolton, just out of town.

Target sighted.

'Oh, goodo. Mate, I'd like to tour him out here. Would it...?'

'Oh.' A pause. 'Um, listen, mate. He's a bit hard to work with, like.'

'I am aware of that, my man. Saw your record cover notes. But you're making music with him. So it might be possible.'

'Well, like, he doesn't have a phone, man.'

Oh. Dude don't have a phone. A bit off the charts, but, you know, missionary zeal...

'Listen. Here's me number. Tell him give us a ring. I know it's his birthday today and...'

'Aye,' he said, 'it is. Well, I'd be surprised, like, if he doesn't turn up here, man. For a present off me, right?'

He don't sound chuffed at the prospect. A red flag, sure. But...

Back at the party, I told 'em all about it. Great happiness.

*

Last night's memories roll and tumble in. *Oh, fuck, did I really do tha…*A moment's ice in the guts. Then dismissed it. Went and drove a taxi shift. Been out of the music game and shall we say other interests for a bit. Had my reasons. Chose to forget about it.

I hadn't hardly got to sleep. *Who the fuck?* Then I went *Proby!* That's freakin' *Proby!* I bounce down the stairs in the dark, make for the ringing phone. This scuzzy share house, they'll start up any minute. *Fuck, Brett, this hour o' the nigh…* Ne'er do-wells. None of 'em had a job. But they'd whinge anyway. I grab it. Croak *how do.*

'Will you take a reverse charges call from a Mr PJ Proby?'

'Will I *what!*'

It's four in the morning like the Faron Young song.

'PJ Proby here.'

'Proby! It's you! Brett's the name. Happy birthday.'

'Ah, thank ya.'

ISD call. Pricey. I got right to it.

'Listen, I'm a booker. Got a backer.'

Well, Clyde did say…

'Can you get me on *Neighbours?*'

Eh? Oh. The TV show.

'Well, ah, PJ,…'

'Call me Jim!'

'Well, *Neighbours*…ah, not really my field, Jim, but I mean, I'll make any enquiries I can.'

Anything to get him on a plane.

'Listen. I'm gettin' older. I don't expect a part as a leading man. Maybe the leading man's father. I come from a theatrical background and…'

'Yeah, well, leave that with me, my man. I will most def look into it.'

Pig's arse I would. But you know, whatever it takes…

'Now,' I said. 'A tour.'

Silence. Then this.

'I only do dinner and a show. Cabaret. Orchestra that can read music.'

Orchestra?

'I got charts. Y'all bring that orchestra to this dance, I'd be interested...'

Cabaret. I'd envisaged rock venues. Five piece band. Still, well, ...

'Alright, fine and dandy. Now. Have you still got it, Jim?'

'Have I still *got* it?'

Out it came. That voice.

'The most beautiful sound in a single word...'

I get a vision. Derro in a phone box in the snow. Some shiver me timbers in a brown paper bag, rippin' up on *Maria*. It's spot on! I want to wake up the mob here. *Listen, you ferals, you won't believe this...* Took a sec to get me breath when he stopped.

'So you can still sing,' I managed.

'Of *course* I can still sing!'

'But you ain't got a phone.'

'No, I don't got a dadgum phone.'

I can't do nothing without Clyde has a word.

'Now, Jim, we are serious. But you gotta ring back same time tomorrow.'

'Alright, pilgrim.'

No further questions, your honour. My first mistake.

*

The way past midnight hour. Phoneside vigil. Rip the scab off another longneck...and it rings! Right, *bang.*

'Hi, PJ. It's Clyde, Brett's partner here.'

'Call me Jim!'

'Righteo, Jim. Where you ringing from?'

'Oh. My neighbour's.'

'Can you put him on?'

They're on a houso estate. He looks after Proby. Far as that's possible, he says.

'Not a fan, me,' he tells Clyde. 'But know who he is, right.'

'Don't mind using your phone as a contact?'

'No, man. Jim gets an earn out o' this, like, it's good for everyone, right?'

'Okay, straight up. I send a ticket, could you get him on a plane?'

Dude's away from the phone for a while. Quite a while. Conferring with Proby. I'm thinking, well, it's not that hard of a question. I'd learn later on, this dance of the brolgas caper, standard operational with the Proby. I shoot Clyde a query look. Just as the neighbour comes back on.

'Yeah, mate.' Dry, metal. Via satellite. 'I can do that.'

So. A head on the ground who can get him in the air. And Proby's had his power and water cut off, he tells us. No wonder he's keen. *Looking good, my man.*

We send the ticket. Hard copy. To the neighbour. Not Proby. No cash. No cheques. He was big as the Beatles for a flash of rock 'n'roll time. Spent like it too. Odds on, he'd repurpose this for *some kinda fun.* Told you I'd toured people.

'I will not do this tour if not. Do you understand?'

Proby calls next night. Must come *now* or not at all. Don't say why. Don't have to. About to be tipped out of the houso, my short-priced favourite. Nowhere to go. Nowhere but *here.*

'We can't book a three-state tour to start in three weeks,' says Clyde.

'So we get him early. A pile of promo. In the flesh. On TV, radio,...'

'Live and dangerous.' *Yeah, that'll work,* he nods.

'More time,' I say. 'To wrangle a band. To rehearse. Do some secret pre-tour gigs. Sellouts, every time. Why not?'

Why not? Well. How were we to know?

CHAPTER TWO

Tours. A bit to it. Work visas. Line up a circuit booker, to get your act into the best joints. Clear it with the unions. Ground transport. Accom. Sound, lighting, rigs and crews. Promo. Square what has to be squared and the truth is what you make it.

But I had skills, learned hard. Booking Max's Petersham Inn for one. Manager there, Uncle Dunc. Liked it out of control. Five-band thrash bills. His 'Free Beers For Nudes' night with Tex Perkins. Fred Negro with I Spit On Your Gravy, Fred dancing naked, *genuine fuckwit* painted on his back. One-gig maddie outfits like Chainsaw Sprocket Knucklehead Tank. Or the Cosmic Psychos any time. For Dunc, if it wasn't mayhem it wasn't goin' off.

And some of the punters. If they played up, belt these rowdies with an iron bar and they'd laugh as blood ran down their face.

I think you need a bigger bar, mate.

Dull moments, mighty few. Armed holdups. The night the joint set itself on fire. The pet pig up on the roof. Other stuff. So. Up for anything the Proby drops on us. Or thought I was.

'Never mind how, my man. Clean enough.'

I had contacts in government, I told Clyde. Proby, a history of deportations from the UK. So a visa, tricky. But I got it, *bang.* The company name we registered said it all. *Wild Turkey Tours.*

'Alright,' said Clyde. 'Where we gonna put him on?'

'Nini,' I said, 'what about your mob? Your hat acts?'

Enter Janine Hall. This agency she was offsiding at, BBC, had a circuit. Toured these alt-country carnies from the US. Townes Van Zandt, Kinky Friedman, Lucinda Williams. Mid-sized joints. Just right.

'I can ask, Brettski.'

Nini. Bass player. The Saints, Weddings Parties Anything. Others. She set up a sitdown.

'Proby! A deadset goer.'

They're impressed.

'But all our rooms, booked up, matey. Months ahead. But listen, I'd go bigger than us anyway.'

'I could be persuaded, my man. What's the story?'

'Clubs. *Real* money.'

His offsider chimes in.

'Proby's old school fan base, china. From back then.'

Leans back in his chair.

'They saw him here in the 60s when they were kids. So you pull your own mob from the rock pubs, plus these foggies. Double your crowd.'

'Triple it,' says his mate.

'Well,' says Clyde. 'Dinner and a show. That's what the man said.'

'Truly? You guys got PJ *Proby*?'

'Too right we have,' says Clyde down the phone.

'Oh! Come in and see me!'

The BBC mob slung us this contact. Clubland booker. His tail, waggin' ten to the ton.

We drive over the Harbour Bridge. The setup, a luxed-up lair. Straight outta *Boogie Nights*. Shag pile. Red leather. Vamp on the desk. *He's expecting you, boys.*

'So you've got *Proby*, fellas.'

The vibe, the usual go with these wombats. He's a used car shonk and we're a head in the yard. But not to worry. *Been here before.* I rip into it. Embellishment as required, that I've toured OS acts before. And well across the dealio.

'And I was in the Hoodoo Gurus,' says Clyde.

'Truly?'

'Played the clubs. Know 'em well.' Smiles. 'And the take you could expect off the door.'

Dude gets the message. Sort of.

'You're talking real money here,' he says. 'Five large a pop.'

I think you mean ten large, my man.

'You boys sound like you know where.'

He don't drop no names on us, of course. Lest we stick our beaks in on his action. I'd say Rooty Hill RSL, Revesby Workers. Penrith Panthers. Their equivalents interstate.

'Well,' I lied, 'he's got most of next year booked. March onwards. Europe and whatnot. Can we sort it quick smart? So he don't get away from us..'

'Done. Late Jan, early Feb. Best time of year in fact.'

We stroll out on a cloud. *Too easy, my man.* And it was. At first.

'If not, this here tour is in jeopardy.'

Proby calls. Munted. Lays a rave on me. Wants five-star hotels. Driver and Roller. A *valet.*

'Now listen, Jim,' I said, 'hold the phone. We're not rich. But big fans. We want a tour where we all get *paid.* Including you. So for now, those days, goneski for you. And your plane ticket if this keeps up.'

Dead air for a sec. Then this.

'Brett. A guitar and toothbrush is all I need. A *git-tar* and a toothbrush. Let's go pickin'!'

Then he starts singin' *On The Road Again. Yeah, righteo, Proby.* A victory. Ahead, other outcomes.

CHAPTER THREE

'Daddy was a banker.'

I've pulled Proby day care. Cricketer's Arms, Surry Hills.

'He left school at fourteen, Brett. First job a janitor. Same bank where he rose to be vice-chairman. Houston, I got born. Nineteen and thirty-eight. Home, close as gets to call it mansion. Help and chauffeur, coloured. So, too, my nanny.

My mama's people owned the first private correctional facility in Texas. On one occasion, I'm gone contrary. Grandpa scooped me up, a boy but three. Strapped me into Old Sparky. The electric chair. One of my exes told the press about it.'

He took a drink.

'Said it was a shame he didn't turn it on.'

'My mama used to dress me all in white. Her boychild angel. She'd hankered to join the circus, she and her brothers. But my grandma, she'd go down there. Yank them out by their ears. A scarlet business, she said. All whores and pimps. And she was entirely right!'

Bert Newton morning show on a screen behind Proby's head. I'm wondering how to get him on as a guest.

'Mama. Those looks. Couldn't walk past a mirror. Not much impressed by anybody. Even meeting Presley.'

Pressley he pronounced it.

'Too impressed with herself.'

I can see where you get it from, I almost said out loud.

'Daddy loved hunting. Elk, stags, red deer. I went out too from age five or six. Took an early fancy to firearms. And daddy and mama had these Texas cookouts. So hot, they give children beer. I'd take a few sips, get giddy, run around. They'd say, oh my, isn't he cute, give him another,' he said. Hoisted his drink.

'How all *that* speedway got started.'

'Mama had lover men. Her most favoured, our family doctor, Alan Moers. Prodigious taste for liquor. We'd go sailing in the Gulf of Mexico, he'd fall overboard. One time, a gas stove at home caught fire. He peed on it to put it out. Anyways, in time, by this freewheeler, mama's with child. Little Betty lived with us, as my full sister. All knew this to be a falsehood. All but me.

Mama taught me Stephen Foster songs. *Shenandoah, My Old Kentucky Home.* Had me sing for visitors. And the mailman. They too perhaps enjoyed intimate liaison. Me, gussied up in white. So scared I hid in a broom closet by the front door, Brett. Sang from in there.'

Liquor and firearms. They'd inform a deal of what followed.

'Seven years old. A snowball fight with uncle Dan and my cousins. I'm hit upside the head. Hey presto, deaf in one ear. Hence the finger in there, my hand cupped behind it when I sing. To hear myself over the band. And the squealin' *chiquitas*. Oh, yeah. I came to know numbers of them, very well...'

The sixties. Brutal appetites. His. All of 'em. More I heard, less I wanted to.

'I was maybe three or four. My first record. Music stores in Houston had these booths. Dime in a slot. They'd cut a disc. Uncle Dan wanted to surprise my mama. Bribed me. A stick of gum. *Sing into that thing there, Jimmy.* I piped out *Roll Out The Barrel.* Got me bedazzled. Dreams of being a singin' movie actor.'

On the pub TV now, morning news. Humans laying into the Berlin Wall. Hammers, chisels, picks.

'At home, Brett, I was bounced between my parents' and uncle Dan's. Then mama said she's leaving. Daddy racked three slugs into a 300 Savage rifle. *One for each of us,* he hollered. He was overpowered by uncle Dan.'

Ain't no fun watching a human out to quicken their own end, slow but sure, no risk. To just that, I twigged I was bearing witness. And learning why they're on that road gives you the dry horrors.

'My parents divorced. Mama wed Moers. Took Betty. So I'm alone with a man of sore temper, his armoury at footfall's reach. The court told *me* to decide who I'd live with. Daddy, not pleased at my choice. Court officers had to restrain him.

So they declared *neither* parent fit and proper. Made me a ward of the state. Daddy's told he must provide for me. So next stop, hello, San Marcos Baptist Military Academy, San Antone. I'd picked wrong. So must be punished.

You are nine years old now. You are a man, Jim. We drove there in daddy's Hudson Hornet. He showed me how to make a hospital corner with a bedsheet in the barracks. Then was gone.' His eyes glistening now.

'Yeah. The higher powers of gavel and gown, Brett. We'd come to be well acquainted.'

CHAPTER FOUR

'**I** must be able to cook. I love cookin'!'
This when we call to check the ticket showed up. Meantime,
our tour booker assures us deals are going down. Well, his front of
house does. Default blowoff. *He's in a meeting.*

'My money's on he's playing his venues off against each other,' I tell
Clyde.' Stock standard swifty.'

An auction we won't be told about. Slurp himself a skim off the top.
Such is the game and its players.

For Proby's must-have kitchen, a semi-furnished flat. Womerah Ave,
Darlo. Three month lease. Its condition, well, mindful of our budget.

'I mean, we've all lived in worse,' said Clyde.

'Yeah,' I said. 'And so's *he!*'

'A bit out of our field, you know?' says Clyde.

Proby's not getting no orchestra. But wants players who can read.
So. Scope around. Maybe these cats from the *Midday Show*. Geoff
Harvey's Channel Nine outfit. Or pit bands from those fruity musicals
of which Sydney is so fond. Six, seven players. Couple of horns. Can't be
that hard. Well. Turns out that was the easy bit.

He'd worked with Ignatius Jones. Or Iggy's sister, Monica Trapaga. Or
maybe both.

Piano player. Clyde got the big tip from someone in that zone.

'Snazzy,' says Clyde on the drive to Double Bay. 'Must be doing
something right.'

'Snakes in his kick and a mouthful of gold teeth, bwana,' I say. 'I
don't know no piano players who can afford to live around here.'

'Musicians, come to that,' he says.

Dude's cordial enough. Clyde flips him a cassette. Proby's hits. We shake on a fee. Leave him with the brief. Find a band. Write 'em charts. A sweetener up front. Here's gold for thy pains, my man.

CHAPTER FIVE

'So at age nine,' says Proby, 'they threw me a steel helmet and M1 rifle.'

Same shit, different pub. Today, the Bat And Ball, Redfern.

'It starts at 0550 hours. We cadets don't get up just yet, but the upperclassmen, already out in the quadrangle. Bells clang. Buglers blow reveille. Other boys rap on drums. I learned to play 'em there too.

Lights come on. We plebes get up. Full dress uniform. Got but ten minutes. Thirty licks of the belt if you're tardy. First formation. Back to the dorm. Make beds. Mess call. Inspection by First Classman, twelve to your nine or ten.

Mess hall, you sit *at attention*. Or your chow is taken from you. *Pass out your plate.* At 0700, clean the dorm. While we're in class from 800, barracks inspection. If not immaculate, the belt awaits.

At lunch, you pick up a forkful of food. Raise and extend it regulation length from your face, to your mouth. Then lower fork to plate. Or you don't eat.

Class dismissed, 1500 hours. For drill. Or sports. Football. Boxing. I got good at both. It's that or get beat up every day.

Preferred my parents not visit. I'd weep when they left. All these Texan boys would see me go sissy. Yet summer vacation I came to dread. Weekdays with mama, weekends daddy. I toted messages between 'em like a dadgum pigeon as they no longer spoke.'

His bevvies, beer and house white, empty again. Flashes me a faceful of panic. No stars in his eyes now. Drowned years back in sour mash tears.

CHAPTER SIX

'Sorry, boys. I wish you'd told me.'
'Told you what?'
'Proby. He's poison.'
'Says who?'
'These club managers. I cannot even open up a dialogue. They don't want to know.'

Had to wonder why. Found out soon enough.

'So youse have got *Proby!* Choice! I'm a *huge* fan.'

Hopetoun Hotel. Spencer Jones comes across me and Clyde, still dazed at today's news. Best keep it *schtum,* we've agreed.

'Flying in tomorrow, as it happens,' says Clyde.

'Oh! Can I come? Man, he could shit in a bag and I'd like it.'

*

Gun shops. Porno pits. Pawnbrokers. The Paris end of George Street. Clyde's booked Proby into that three-star there. The Southern Cross. Two nights. Can't drop him into the Darlo flop jetlagged. Want him to come up smilin' for rehearsals. Keep him need to know on the gig sitch, we decide. As in he don't need to know there ain't any.

Clyde's ride, his just-bought white 1966 Daimler Jag. Sally Geschmay from mine joins us. We make for the airport.

'That'll be him!'

Spencer clocks him first. Grey beard. A black John B Stetson. Guitar case. And baggage trolleys piled moon-high.

'You must be Proby!'

His eyes dart our way.

'Eh, Jim.'

I wave at all his bags and cases.

'You said alls you need's a guitar and a toothbrush, my man!'

He gives me a face I'd come to know well.

'I lie.'

I turn to Clyde, laughing it off.

'Take note, Clyde. We could be in trouble!'

Thought he was joking. That would change.

Clyde's Jag a stylish carriage for our star, to be sure. But not a ton of space. Limitations as both bulk freight and people mover. So Proby's freakin' hillsides of luggage, we cram all that and me into a taxi.

At the Southern Cross, we hit the bar. Proby on Proby. He's done it all. Bar murder.

Far as we know.

*

'I'm not doin' anything, y'all. That dadgum flight screwed me. Need five days. Seven.'

Two days on. We tip him into his flat. He's crook as. Pulls a sit-down strike. Tomorrow's rehearsal, blown out. We let him call it. Lest he starts asking about gigs.

'Why have I been *abandoned?*'

Darlo, next day. Turns out he's lobbed here penniless. No walking round money. He's knocked over the slab of Reschs and the cask of rough white he stuck his hand up for yesterday. And now he wants an all-day drinkin' buddy is the mail.

He don't go out on his own, he says. Never has. I cop a squiz at an open suitcase. Little brown bottles. Cartons of 'em. Pharma. Benzos, moggies, vallies. Then *this*.

'There must never be less than half a gallon of wine here, Brett. And two six packs of beer. I come home to but *ten* beers, well, y'all will have to go out and get *more* ...'

He stops. Lost in the ozone. Then remembers.

'Some dadgum bourbon, too.'

'No, no, no. I wanna ride in the – how do y'all say it- *Howden?*'

Turns out Proby don't much fancy the Jag, to its owner's disappointment. Prefers my Kingswood wagon. The *Kingsmont,* he says. And that's how it went, whole time he was here. Don't ask me. It's a shitheap. Borrowed from a mate who's in the States. All rust, bullbar and Queensland plates. Whip aerial. Ten kinds of cop magnet.

'It's like a Chev,' I explain as we drive to the pub. GMH, I say, the Aussie take on General Motors. He starts up a rave about an ex-wife. Heiress to the Buick fortune.

'Cadillacs for n....rs.' His thoughts on the make. *Spare me days.* From Texas, you say.

So, then. The Hoey. The whole day. Wild tales cascade from him. I freight him home round sundown. Stand watch till he spirals into rummy's repose. Left him a stack of fresh takeaways. He'd be right. Peace in the valley.

'I ain't livin' *here! I* am on *tour!* I do *not* do house domestics. I am an artist and should be exempt from *shit.'*

Next morning, Clyde reminds him, softly softly, why he's here. That kitchen he demanded.

'*No. No. No.* I want to cook, but not like *this.'*

It weren't no request.

'How about that, Jim? On a clear day you can see New Zealand, my man.'

Serviced apartment. Bondi. Campbell Parade. Clyde's left his gold Amex with reception. For the rent. And Proby's use. *But call me first if it's something big,* he tells them. Wise, as it turns out.

CHAPTER SEVEN

'**B**rett, I've spent more time with you than anyone, ever. Even my wives.'
       I could believe it. Dude didn't mingle. Held court. Delivered monologues. I'll say one thing. He don't do dullsville.

'The reason I am fearless, I shirk no challenge, is military school.'
    On the pub tellies, Australia v Pakistan. Test match. Blue silk Sydney day.
    'The academy came to be my family, Brett. Even vacation one year. Took a course. Culver Naval Academy, South Bend, Indiana. There, my eyes fell on these pictures in the books. Eighteenth century swabbies. Ponytails. Knee high breeches. Loose fitting shirts. Came a notion. Singing star. Pirate's garb and the pipes of Caruso.

Now mama made me sing and I didn't care for it. But at age ten, I discovered that you could make money off of it. She took me to this club. The Hitching Post in Houston. Talent quest. Guess who won. Did a local TV show too. *Rocket To Stardom.*'
    His face fell now.
    'A dadgum setup. Rigged.'
    'Always is, Proby.'
    'You are so right, Clyde. Now this kid who sang at the Post, Tommy Sands, was a teenage star around Texas. On the radio too, Biff Collie's *Crackerbarrel Corner*. I took to pallin' round with him. Yeah. That club. Possum played there, George Jones. Ernest Tubb. Tennessee Ernie Ford. They'd get me up to sing. And I saw Elvis here with his Blue Moon Boys. Scotty, Bill, DJ.'
    Fuck me. This was some honky tonk.

'And this led to more. Other joints round Houston. The Eagles Hall, the South Maine Old Spanish Trail. Now Colonel Parker, he's wranglin' Hank Snow, Ernest Tubb and Tommy. Fixin' to take me on too, he claims. Then one day, he calls.

'Now, this boy is like to occupy all my hours, Jim, so I am sorry to haff to tell you,...'

Yeah. We but piggy banks to the Colonel. Presley, an all day all night cash machine. Oh, and about Elvis, Brett. We're family.'

You gotta be shittin' me, Proby. He must've seen my face.

'Sure as hell awaits. Cousins. His mama Gladys, see, her name was Smith. My real name too. Now you can say every third cracker east of the Pecos goes by it. But look at the pictures of us all.'

Yeah. Possible. I mean, these hoedads known to marry their cousins at twelve.

'Tommy got me on the Biff Collie show. So scared I'm shakin'. And at the Post, those country stars saw me in the same state. So they'd buy me beer. Bein' I'm but ten, I neck 'em behind the stage, out of sight. Fear begone!'

He raised up his beer. And his wine.

'The genesis, those days. Of a lifetime's true love.'

CHAPTER EIGHT

Daily Probywatch routine now. Dayful of pub. Ship him home. Linger like a green-arsed fly for the coma to hit. Shoot through. Back there nine of a morning. *Half past beer* he called it.

'I will box any stallion and pleasure any filly who'd have it so,' he says next day. So now it's the fit and well Proby. Curious about certain matters.

'Still being finalised, Jim,' my reply. He don't need to hear Clyde's news. All the big circuit pubs we reckon he'd go good, Clyde's called round. They're booked solid. Months out. So. Plans A and B, cactus. Plan C, yet to show itself.

'Can you fetch me a nurse, Brett? I'm took *poorly.*'

This, the day after. Guzzles like he does, but can't suss why he's got no go in him.

'I need some of those vitamin energy shots.'

Hospital-grade speed. Squirt that into him, you'll need a whip and a net. A better idea presents itself.

'Can you start today, Nini?'

Janine Hall saw Proby live in NZ as a schoolie, back in '66. She's observed our talent's unfortunate disposition and made a suggestion. Now she swept into the Hoey. Worked her voodoo. Massaged him. Cooed sweet nothings. Whispered him back to the cradle. He's just about got his thumb crammed in his gob by the time she's done. A deadset *nanny.* We put her on the payroll.

Nini. From down the deep end. Gone now. Like too many others.

'For a room read on industry and punter interest'.

Clyde's lined up the Hoey to host. Proby still won't rehearse, *I am taken unwell,* so we bung on a meet and greet. I mean, he's not too ratshit to sit in a pub all day. So, an informal presser. A reception. Get the word out. Make him earn these bar and accom bills. *Rock 'n' rollers, meet The Probes.*

At Bondi, brekky. He's already necked a warm moselle when I rock up. Now, a warm VB. Rough as, but on his feet. Then he takes his beer into the *shower.* A first for me, and I like a drink, but…Out of the bathroom, he rips the scab off a freshie. *Pfffzzzt.*

'Righto, Proby. We're going to meet a few people.'

'*Oh.* Better grab a six pack, Brett.'

'We're going to a pub, Jim. Ain't far.'

'I cannot ride in this vehicle, this *Kingshood,* until…'

'Five minute drive this time of day. Take a traveller from them ones there. I even warmed 'em up for ya.'

Three of them. Kitchen bench, placed to catch the sun through the window. But his hand splays out, *stop.*

'Brett. *What if the car breaks down?*'

Yeah. *Bang.* That was the moment. *Right then.* When I went *oh hell* in the caverns of my mind. Look, the joys of the drink, not an undiscovered country to me. Can relate to a whole pile of stuff, but this…

'Listen, on the way, we'll stop at a bottlo and…'

Talk him down. He'll live.

'No, Brett. *No.* I don't believe you *heard* me.'

He's next door to shakin'. I shank it round the corner on me own. He can't leave them three beers unminded. Wants VB. Already telegraphed his dislike for Reschs. The least of his sins. Well,…

*

'Brettski!'

'How do, fun lovers. This is our man PJ Proby!'

'Call me Jim!'

Mixed bag here. Heads from Clyde's alma mater, the Hoodoo Gurus. Rob Younger and crew. Spencer Jones. Nini. My housemate Sally G. Speedy the roadie. Assorted Beasts Of Bourbon and Johnnys. JJJ DJs like Biggsy. The music press, *Drum Media,* all them. Best of all, some gig bookers.

We shoved some tables together. Clyde directing traffic. Nini at Proby's flank, doing the subliminals. Local legends came and went. A lot of heads and interest. A bright flag for our enterprise.

'There's a place, a-for us, some-a-where, a place for us...'

The pub buzz *stops dead.*

'Holy *fuck*. What was *that?*'

Now and then he'd rise in his place. Sing a phrase or two. It turned heads. But he refused to work the room. They had to come to him. He went long and loud on all those who'd trashed his career. No crowned head of pop left unspiked. A long and winding shit list.

'Forget the circuits. We'll book it ourselves, my man,' says Clyde. 'Out of town tryout first. Say, Newie.'

Plan C in the house. He meant Newcastle.

'Then, one big room in Sydney. A showcase. Hire it if we have to.'

'One show? Proby's not gonna be ...'

'Brett. He's got no return ticket.'

Made sense. Get all the bookers in for a squiz. Promo the fuck out of it. A packed house. They see a big drink in doing more. Don't matter when. The Proby's homeless. We got him chained to a stake.

'We're doin' *American Trilogy.'*

'Listen, Proby,' I say. 'We're not in America. We're in Australia.'

'We know Elvis did it,' says Clyde. 'We're Elvis fans. We get it.'

'But it don't mean a thing here, Jim. Might not go over so good...'

We're trying to organise a set list with this peanut.

'We're doin' it. I had a lot of success with it. A show in the West End'.

Yeah, right. *That* show in the West End. *Elvis:The Musical.* Proby, speared five nights in. Why, well, we'll get to that.

.

CHAPTER NINE

'My daddy said no more money for military schools. So now, Lamar High School in Houston. Fistfights. Drink. I raised Cain and hell. So he backslid. Next stop, Western Military Academy, Alton, Illnois.

Played a lot of football there. Boxing. First car wreck too. Almost scalped. Bandage round my head. Fetched me the cast of a Comanche brave. Scars and shiners most all the time, Brett. Our coaches, boy howdy. Get beat up out there, they'd send you back on right quick. Painkillers.'

Bang. The pills in his suitcase. Dished out like lollies back then. Odds on, a popper for yonks. Never had a chance.

'My third year there, I acquired a guitar. Sang at prom nights. School concerts. I set to dreaming. Graduation couldn't come swift enough, Brett.

A mess of scholarships on offer. University of Miami, to play football. Helen Hayes Drama School, NYC. Naval Academy. West Point.'

Drama school? Truly?

'But I knew I'd not study. You couldn't just play football from rooster to hoot owl. And I had other plans.

So I'm back in Houston. Aim to split at first slim chance. Bunked up at daddy's, he goes apeshit at me not taking those offers. So, then, to mama's.

I came home one day. A Cadillac, pink with gold trim, in the drive. Polka dot seats. Pink and black. Inside with Betty, none but Presley. Transpires they're dating. He'd swing by on tour. A girl in every holler size enough to call itself town, most like.

My mama broke out her best Irish linen. Dinner, fried chicken. About all Presley ate. Never did see the world and school up his taste buds. Yet polite to a fault. And somethin' else.

'You know,' he says, 'I don't like it when they call me the King.'

'Oh,' says mama, 'why is that, young man?'

'Well, ma'am,' he says, 'there is only one king. And that king is in heaven.'

And that boy, he meant it. So he finishes. Wants to go in the living room, play some records with Betty.

'Ma'am, that was the best chicken I ever tasted. May I be excused, please?'

'Why, certainly, Elv...'

But she was struck mute. For he took up not his napkin, but the tablecloth. Wiped his mouth good and thorough. I waited until he'd gone.

'Born in the boondocks, mama.'

She, a high-born Texan. No elaboration required.

Daddy drove me. September nineteen and fifty seven. At Hollywood and Vine, he thumbs off some bills. *Son, you won't last a week.* He'd said *very well* to my proposal. To teach me a lesson, it was clear. He couldn't see I'd got the devil back at the Hitching Post. Fame, we'd howdied but hadn't shook. But I knew where she lived.

I'd seen him on a TV show, *Sing, Boy, Sing!* Elvis had turned down this part, so Colonel sent it his way. Tommy Sands the only head I knew here in LA. Let me bunk in his garage.

'So where to next, *hermano*?'

'Two things, Jimmy. First, get schooled up.'

'The other?'

'Never sign nothin' by neon.'

Singing teacher and vocal coach. Lillian Goodman, Tommy said. Once a minor star herself. Connected. If you sparkled, she'd talk you up to folks who had swing in this burg.

'Jimmy, how much money do you have?'

I aced her audition. But just ten dollars to my name now. She's north of seventy. Client roster, all stars. No need of fresh fish. But hot for what I got.

'What does your father do?'

Out elk hunting, his secretary said. He called back. If he could Western Union me a little Lincoln and Jackson, I said,...

'Wire it?'

He knew me too well.

'I'm on the next flight over.'

'Now, Mr Smith, Jimmy needs training. And it's gonna cost money.'

He paid for three weeks' worth. Took me to the Plantation Hotel, Sunset And Vine. Paid tariff for that same duration. *See you back in Texas, son.*

'I'm soon back in Tommy's garage. A tough bunch of months, Brett. Be at Lillian's, ten in the AM. Before that, gym, she said. An hour of basketball, shootin' hoops. Sparring in the ring. Then jog from Tommy's at Santa Monica to hers in Brentwood. Five miles, uphill. At her place, breathing exercises, all that bluegrass. But quick as ducks on June bugs, I'm down to a dime again, I confide. Then I fetch up next day as another student is leaving.

'Jimmy,' she says, 'allow me to introduce Paul Newman.'

'There she is, man. Two seater '55 Thunderbird.'

A *job*. Driving King Cool, as they called him. This includes up and down Sunset, scoping for chicks. Ol' Newman, 'twixt first and second wife. Rarin' to clown.

When not bird-doggin' babes, the gym. A fitness maniac, that boy. We'd work out. Do fun things, go get a beer. My guess, the job wasn't just drive but make it look like he had a bodyguard. So. I'm walkin' with a king. Paid for it too. Hog heaven.

'Now, Jimmy. I start on a picture next week. Studio sends a driver. So...'

He smiled like Newman smiles. At my face, fallen like a hound grown old.

'Man, that is one mean mush.'

Hands me a studio pass.

'Enough for bad hat parts anyway.'

The Left Handed Gun. Newman as Billy The Kid. Me, an extra. Saloon barfly and crowd scenes. After that, more work as a statue, that's what they called it. Or as a stunt man. Westerns. B pictures. And what we appellated as *C pictures,* for drive-ins. Y'all get the *Gidget* movies down here, Brett? Sandra Dee?'

'Yeah, Proby.'

'Yeah, I was Mr Beefcake On The Beach in all those. And did some buggy movies. *Dragstrip.* Or *Ghost Of Hot Rod Hollow.'*

Yeah. Shitflicks. Where they snap-froze Elvis in the Sixties.

*

'Jimmy, I'd like you to meet someone.'

Ray Gilbert wrote *Song Of The South,* you know, *Zip A Dee Doo Dah.* Lillian had me sing. Ray took a liking. Offered to be my manager.

'Jimmy,' he said, 'what kind of songs you best at?'

'Well, Mr Gilbert, at the Academy I sang Presley at concerts and...'

'Know any rock and roll besides Elvis?'

'Know 'em? I got some I wrote myself!'

'A songwriter, huh? Good money in that.'

Sure was. For *him.*

'You know, Jimmy? What we need is an agent.'

'You scared, boy? Because if you are...'

From Ray's short dog of bourbon, I took a dram.

'Nossir. I'm from Texas. Got more guts than you can hang on a fence.'

Took another.

The agency. Gaby, Lutz, Heller and Loeb. Above the Brown Derby on Wilshire. Had 'em all. Tony Bennett, Frankie Laine, Kay Starr, Johnnie Ray, Liberace. You auditioned live. Mess up, well, nextville!

'Well, they liked it right enough,' said Ray. 'I believe they want to make you a star.'

Now, I'm not twenty-one. Can't sign contracts on my own. But daddy's a banker. Can't miss a chance to play *Let's Make A Deal*.

'Jimmy,' they said. 'You want to sign with us?'
    'Sure! How much you want?'
    Such a rube. Thought *I* had to pay *them*.
    'Jimmy.' Daddy. 'Go sit in the lobby.'

'So, Jimmy, we got you $10,000. You couldn't beat that with a stick.'
    A sum beyond imagining.
    'Now, don't you think you owe Mr. Gilbert here something for this?'
    'Well, er, what do you thin...'
    'No, Jimmy, you decide here. You make up your own mind.'
    'How about half?'
    'Ray? Sound about right to you?'
    It did.
    'Alright, then,' says daddy. 'Ray, take the ten. Keep five. The rest, open a bank account for Jimmy. One where if he wants from it, you sign for it or he doesn't get.'
    Then he said goodbye. Were some elk needed killin'.

Well, now. Went in that day with a quarter on me. Left with ten large. But they didn't know what to with me, Brett. Their stars, just that. Stars. Didn't have to *build* 'em. So Ray set up another meeting to remedy this.
    'Jimmy,' said Gaby or maybe Lutz, 'the face of an angel you have. A *shiksa* magnet. But your name, *boychik*. I'm dying here.'
    'Jim Smith is no name for a star,' said Lutz. Or maybe Heller. 'It goes. It goes today.'

*

It came to me. Jimmy Dean in *Giant*. His name in that. Jett. And Tyrone Power big then. A last name even more toothsome in the plural. *Jett Powers*. All Hollywood came to know it real soon. For all species of wrong reasons.

That week, my debut TV appearance. The sway these Hebrews had. The *Arthur Godfrey Hour*. My first whirl on a plane. New York City.

I'm on that bird with Ray and Dorothy Lamour, she also on the show. You know Dorothy, Brett? The *Road* movies, Hope and Crosby?'

'Sure do, Proby.'

'The third guest, Charlie Applewhite. Singer. Texan like me. Big then. My agents' plan, for me to follow in his wake. Great God. I'm a *star*. And I don't even got a *record* out yet. And oh, about that. Right off that Delta twin-prop, Ray rented a car. Pointed it at Boston. Our business there, to cut a single.'

'Jimmy. Those numbers you wrote. You didn't steal them any?'

'No sir. By my own hand and mind.'

Well. A swindle. The first of countless. He put them down as by 'Gilbert And Powers.' His name and one that didn't exist. Stop me if you've heard *that* one.

Two takes apiece. *Go Girl Go* and *Teenage Quarrel*. Boyleson Street studio. Band, local cats. Vince Parle and the Raunch Hands. Good place for it. Dion And The Belmonts cut *The Wanderer* and *Runaround Sue* here.

Arthur Godfrey show. Weird, Brett. Mostpart, him singing with a ukulele. Cracking wise with sidekick Jackie Gleason. We had to sit there, as his studio audience, until we did our thing near the end.

So I'm on the TV. I got a biscuit out. I'm hot as a pot of neck bones, but when they spun that 45 on the radio, the DJs made jest of it.

'J-j-j--ett P-p-p--powers! Zoom zoom *zoom*!' Or worse, 'sounds like Elvis with hiccups.'

It died in the dust.

'That dog don't hunt, son.'

No more cabbage from daddy's billfold. And I couldn't draw on that account. Ray would blow me off, small-time bucks from his pocket. I believe he stole it all. Never did see it again.

'You gotta keep up the lessons, Jimmy, or you'll get out of practice.'

Work for rookie movie extras such as I, episodic. So Lillian gave me a job. Houseboy. Wash her car, tend her garden, laundry. I didn't care for it, so betook me to the boulevards of Hollywood. Joint called the Sea Witch obliged. Slingin' hash and pearl diving. And here, my doorway to destiny. Live music. A bandstand.

'Jimmy, this is Timi Yuro.'

One of Lillian's students. Her mama had a joint down on Melrose, Mama La Rosa's. I worked there too. Dishpig and busboy. Yeah, Timi. First LA blue eyed soul singer. Signed to Liberty Records. Had a monster hit. *Hurt.*

She was the first to tell them about me. Had 'em see me sing at the Sea Witch. Boss there, Jack Brazil, had heard me sing in the kitchen. This, my first club gig in LA. Singing drummer in the house band there. Needed no agents for that.

And as for them, they wanted to make me into what they call a *TV dolly*, sing on variety shows just to fill up the timeslot. The End. They scored me some live shows, but I was just the low card in the hand. You know, *you don't get Doris or Frankie or Johnnie lest you put this kid on to open.* It was not too swift.

So without I told 'em, I sang as a solo, with in-house bands in clubs. Or filled in with groups, as drummer or singer. Or both. On the Strip. The Boulevard. Melrose. North Hollywood. Santa Monica. All over and then some.

Some of the first hombres I met in LA, Brett. Johnny Burnette and brother Dorsey.'

'The Rock'n'Roll Trio. *Lonesome Train,*' I said.

'The very same. My taste for fistfightin' I refined in their company. Both Golden Gloves champs back in Memphis. *T For Texas, T For Tennessee,* we'd sing on a party. Sideways on redeye, we'd go pick fights. Parking lot of the Palomino. Or that club that became the Whisky. Called Come To The Party then. Johnny could fight better'n me. Dorsey better'n both of us.

And so Friday or Saturday nights, I'd often as not fetch up in the Willcox Jail. *Singer Jett Powers,* there I was in the *LA Times.* Most every week. Police and courts section. I grew famous. In a repeat offender kind of way.

We weren't the only ones. These two Bluegrassers used to fight every weekend. Out back of Ben Franks, on the Strip. I met one of them right soon.

Outside the Sea Witch, I'm on a break between sets. Jack Brazil's handing a beating to some hombre tried to hand *him* one.

'Hi, man. Mah name's Ford. Jim Ford.'

Right off a Jack stomping, no mean feat, this Kentuckian staggers up. Desires we be amigos.

'Me and that man there, we just had a misunderstanding.'

Wipes blood off his lip. A friendship here forged, Brett. We tore LA three new assholes.'

Yeah, I know of Jim Ford. More don't than do. Just one album. *Harlan County.* A pearler. And Ford on a rip and tear, well. Think of a Proby and triple it.

*

'Today's the day, Proby.'

Rehearsal. We've told him that the venues are in a bidding war. *So the tour could start anytime, Jim.* This, to obviate his freakin' procrastinations. We book the band and a room, then he claims he's crook as a full graveyard. Three times now. So what he don't know won't hurt us a bit.

'How do, Clyde!'

We meet at the Hoey on the way. Proby insists. To see Clyde go on his way, so the Texan will know the band's ready to rock 'n' roll when he fronts. Or he *will not sing today*. And so Clyde can see that I've prised Proby out of his cave. *And* because Proby demands a pit stop for a frosty en route. Despite the six pack aboard the Kingswood. Don't ask.

Sound Level studios. Opposite the Wenty Park dog track. Dank rehearsal caves. No windows. White walls. Strip fluoros buzz and flicker. Feel like you could run into Eraserhead.

'Boys, meet Mr PJ Proby.'

The vibe a smidge astringent. This band, like some far out order of monks. Aloof bunch.

'Sure hope you people can read,' says Proby. 'If not, there's no place for you in this outfit.'

This to players with charts on music stands. Yeah, they don't say much. Maybe it's his manner. Or that pre-noon beer in his fist.

One big ray of the sunny stuff here. Robbie Souter's on drums. A head we know well. Dynamic Hepnotics, Happening Thang, the Mentals. Later, Slim Dusty. Does his perfect gentleman bit. Takes out his cigar to say *how would you be, fella?* And speaks rock 'n' roll. A lingo unknown to these nimrods from Planet Pit Band.

'I want it to start at the *start.*'

'We *are* starting from the start, Jim,' says Robbie, sweet as stolen apples. Proby's on the sniff for a blue. Whinges about the band. I mean, sure, apart from Robbie, who's right in the groove, no Famous Flames, this crew. Stiff as roadkill. But Proby wanted readers after all, and anyway, for day one, they're not too dusty.

'No. That has got to *improve*. That does not seem *right.*'

But only Proby's missing cues. No one else.

'Y'all show me what y'all can do. Then I decide if y'all are worthy.'

Steady on, Tex, I'm thinking. These humans are employed by *us*. He's not paying them. Now if we were dealing with a normal human being, we'd proceed minus the griping, *then* critique it post-sesh. Changes needed, make it so. But I reckon it's got legs.

'I can't do this. I'm out. So's everyone. This guy's impossible.'

On a break, the piano banger hoiks the dummy. *Oh hell.*

'Mate, it's PJ *Proby*,' I say. 'You know these prima donnas. Listen, I reckon it's chuggin' along reet petite. And today just the first of five, so...'

'You're fucking kidding, pal. I mean, if *this* is a *good* day...'.

Proby's oblivious. Becalmed on a sea of VB.

'The mail is that's it from this crew, Robbie.'

The band's bailed. He's packing up his kit.

'But we were wondering...'

We need the Souter. Gun drummer. And one of *us*.

'No biggie, fella,' he says. 'I'm still in if you want me.'

Leans in so Proby can't catch it.

'I know what he's like.' Slides his eyes at him. 'I knew before he got off the plane.'

Robbie's a tipster you can trust. In this game for yonks beyond number.

'Smaller the kingdom,' he grins, 'bigger the princess.'

Robbie's gone now. Not the only one. But the best of us.

*

Yeah. Talent herding. No task for flakes. Take Stevie Wright. I booked him into Max's a few times. Let's just say conditions applied before he'd do it. Example, he rings one day. For a gram of goey by taxi to his in Balmain. *Fix you up later.* Gear obtained, it is reported. Cabbie pre-paid. Cash. Hefty tip. Then half an hour on, Stevie strolls into the Pismo Bar. Front bar of Max's.

'Thought I'd pick up the gear myself. Can you pay the cab?'

He means the one he's just rocked up in. Out in the jungle, first cabbie finds no one home. Heads back. Seeking second fare and tip, for initiative and discretion. Fair play to him. Yeah, Stevie. Some good times, but needed a minder. You know. Like the dope who's put his hand up for Proby here.

Then there was Ian Rilen. I gave his band X Friday nights at the Leichhardt during my time driving that pub around. No two gigs the same disaster when that mob gets at a big rider and each other's throats. And I set up a live recording at the Annandale for them. Mobile studio on the back of a semi. Fair to say it crashed on takeoff. The brawls between them, fine and dandy sport if you like it slug ugly. And then there's Rilen's say no to nothin' need for self-destruction. On a range of levels.

Yet I failed to absorb the lessons. Took on Rilen's next band Hell To Pay with Spencer Jones, among other fun lovers. Scored them a deal with Redeye for their only album *Steal It* and its single *Saints And Kings,* their take on St. Kilda and the Cross. But two of 'em, Cathy Green and Rilen, in a relationship you'd best describe as abusive. A lotta stuff I can't say. So Proby, after that sideshow of coneheads, a deadset snack. This I still believed.

*

So. Week Two. Close of play. No gigs. No band. But no give-up option. Which was *what?* Stick him on a plane home? Write off outlays to date? I peer out the window of this train to fuck knows where. We're long past that station.

'You called for backup?'
Nini. Thank fuck.
He's whining for a 'nurse' again. She's down the Hoey in two shakes. 'Lady bassplayer! Like Carol Kaye!'says Proby. Yeah, she'd got around alright. Apart from the Saints and Weddings Parties, a cool hand on the beast of four in the Young Charlatans with Rowland S. Howard and Ollie Olsen. Then the all-female Kings Of The World. Guess who was foolish enough to try and manage *that* gang of rowdies. Yeah, well. Dysfunctional bands. I mean, name one that ain't.

CHAPTER TEN

'Thought you'd never ask, Proby.'

'I reckon the Dolphin,' says Clyde. 'Just a block from here. Top seafood.'

'Alright, Proby. On your feet. We'll walk down and...'

'Brett. Clyde. I do not walk. Make me *walk,* there will be no *tour.* Do you understand?'

So. We walk to the Kingswood. Takes longer than walking to the Dolphin, given where I'm parked. Then ten minutes circling the block for a new park, and as long a walk again. Waiting to hoof it across at the lights, I stopped myself from lobbing his hat into the traffic.

To see if he'd go after it.

'Ah, lemme have that T-bone steak there. Rare. And give me that half a lobster.'

Well, if you only eat once a week I guess you need to go in hard. As he chowed down, his memoir rolled on.

'In LA, I ran into a guy from military school, Jim Blumberg. I'm sweet as corn syrup on this Dottie Harmony. Showgirl. Danced in Vegas. The skinny is that she's Presley's valentine. But set to dump him. Didn't dig on his roving eye. Blumberg's heard me howlin' at the moon for this chickadee. One day he calls. Says she lives on Fountain Avenue in Hollywood. See, he'd gone to Fairfax High in LA after San Marcos. Met this girl there, Shari Sheeley. This pad on Fountain hers.

'Shari has extended invitation. 1500 hours. You hear me, soldier?'

'Blumberg. You are so full of shit.'

Went anyways. *Be other honeybuns there*, he said. Well, I'll have me a hunk of that buttercream pie anytime.

'See, Blumberg? There's no Dottie here.'

Shari Sheeley heard me.

'Oh yes there is, Jimmy. Look at the top of the stairs.'

I beheld. Oh, great God. In this red jump suit. Short pants. I was transfixed.

A great day. Shari's fiancée came by. We played guitars. I sang into Dottie's eyes, to convey my designs. Shari's betrothed, a waymore better picker than me, this Eddie Cochran. They're both signed to Liberty. She as a songwriter. Those handclaps on *Summertime Blues*. That's Shari.

'Hey, we're gonna have a party tomorrow, Jett. Why don't you come over?'

'Oh, Shari, I *think* I can make it.'

To impress Dottie, I talk like I'm beset. Movies. Speaking parts, yet. Fact of it, let go from a shoot just one week past, me and two other extras deemed the wrong fit. Yeah, Brett. Even Burt Reynolds and Clint Eastwood had days like this.

'Yeah, well,' I said next day, 'we were to shoot today but they rescheduled. Sure glad to get off that Warner's lot.'

Made sure Dottie heard every lying word. Eddie fetched up again. Ricky Nelson. And Jackie de Shannon, Shari's songwriting partner and a singer on Liberty too.

I got tight with Eddie. See, we both liked hunting and being on acres. And Shari, she'd be my champion down the line.

As for Dottie being Presley's. She learned she was but one of three. And he was no fun at any speed. Never went out. Y'all had to go to him and his crew of slobs. So I pitched my horseshoes right and Dottie became my girl. Y'all bet the farm she did.'

Proby stopped for a tick as a fresh thought percolated into his mind.

'Oh, yeah.That day, must have been my first meet with that coonass Fowley.'

'That'd be Kim Fowley?' I said. 'Put the Runaways together. Joan Jett and...'

'The same, Brett. But back then, he toiled for Mr Sex. Scotty Bowers. LA pimp to the stars. Fowley, a dick for hire. Rich old ladies. And between said exertions, Fowley used to loiter outside the coloured record companies. These vocal groups would come out, all dogfaced.

'Hey, kids? They turn you down? Well, I won't turn you down. You come along with me.'

He'd rework their songs back at Spector's Gold Star studio, claim a chunk of the action. Then he'd hire these hookers from Mr Sex. Cab them and the new 45 round LA to the DJs. If y'all ever puzzled why bullcorn gets airplay...

One time at Shari's, some kid there. Drunk as three moonshiners. Ups and says he wrote *Poor Little Fool*. A Ricky Nelson hit that *Shari* wrote. Ricky's there too, the Burnette brothers, Eddie Cochran. And Fowley. Well, we exhort this greenhorn, best saddle up and go, boy. He pulls a knife by way of reply. So we beat the juice out of him.

But then Fowley went to *Seventeen* magazine. Sold them the story. So Dottie and Shari paid *him* a call. Kicked *his* ass to jellyjam. Then drove over to *Seventeen*. Told 'em they're next if they ran any more stuff like that about Liberty artists.

'I dropped Elvis, Jett,' she said. 'Drove him to the Draft Board. His induction. That's when I told him.'

I did come abide now in Dottie's trailer out at Burbank. Our dream, a future where we'd write smash hits. And Jett Powers would sing them. My prayers to this end, answered in due course, albeit in ways I'd not featured. All I asked for. And a world of miseration I didn't.

CHAPTER ELEVEN

'I want leading man parts. Not black hats who don't say word one then get plugged in the first dadgum gunfight.'

I let Ray Gilbert go, Brett. Told my agents I wanted a meet. With Henry Willson. Represented all these stars. Rock Hudson, Troy Donahue, Tab Hunter, Ty Hardin.

'Y'all call him. I will do whatever it takes.'

'Whatever, Jett?'

'And then some.'

'I will not submit to your *predations!*'

Well. A wrangler wranglin' nothin' but fellas called Rock and Ty and Troy and Tab. I might have known. Not my brand of lunch meat. So, refused my favours, Henry took to besmirching my name. All over Hollywood. The Black Widow, he tags me. That spider. Loves up its mate then kills it.

'Stay away from that Jett Powers, big boy. He'll sting ya!'

But then one day he calls. Knows I'm a brawler, via my fame in the *LA Times*. A job on offer.

'This works out, baby doll, we'll see about a screen test.'

Henry's stars lived in peril of beatings. And the scandal sheets, *Confidential* and its like. My posse, engaged as bodyguards. Stunt men from Warners. Jim Ford. Couple others.

First client, Liberace. These necks used to wait outside his place. Target his mother. She'd arrive in his limo. They'd beat her up. Least that's how Henry sold it.

So we hide in the bushes. Limo arrives. This car roars up. Boxes 'em in. Plain as vanilla their aim. We jump out. Smack 'em up good, Brett. Then something else.'

A yarn mighty mighty colourful. But it's freakin' Hollywood. Proby's war stories, you don't rule nothing in or out.

'Henry's orders. *Arms and legs both, Jett*. Snap.'

'They get out of hospital today, Mr Willson.'

Ordered to monitor their recovery, I call him. Meantime, working bodyguard detail for Rock, Tab, Troy and Ty round Hollywood.

'In the parking lot, Jett. Break 'em again.'

'But, Henry, they've been done.'

'They need to *remember* this. Do it, big boy.'

It was done. This man might could make me a star. Course, he never did. Story of my life.

I had to shadow Rock and Tab and such. Awards nights, clubs, movie premieres. They had female escorts. Studio's orders. Newbie starlets. Anyone even inferred these fellas were what they were, that mouth and its owner to be fetched a beating savage.

Well, Willson did get me parts. Yeah. Stunt man or statue. TV Westerns. *Gunsmoke. Have Gun Will Travel*. But the only way to advance my prospects beyond such, well, now.

An unconscionable capitulation.

CHAPTER TWELVE

'Call it the Moondogs.'

Round about this time, Brett, I formed a group. Larry Taylor on the bass. Later he played with Jerry Lee, Canned Heat, John Mayall, Tom Waits. Guitars, Elliott Ingber. Went on to Zappa, Captain Beefheart. Marshall Leib, guitarslingin' in the Everlys road band then, and Spector's session crew. Drummers, a variety. Me when none other free.

We played on the Boulevard, on Highland, Sunset, Melrose. PJs on Santa Monica B. The Crossbar. The Troubador on La Cienega. The Rag Doll. Melody Room.

Cut two singles. *Moondog.* Follow-up, well, *Mooncat.* My agents knew zero of it, so never saw a nickel off these. Then again, nor did I.

'Who are these Moondogs already, Jett?'

Some snake had seen me and tattled. So my agents said time to cut a new Jett Powers single. That they'd use the heft they had to get it on the radio. I thought *this is it.*

'It's called *Loud Perfume,*' said Bumps.'Maybelle Jackson wrote it for Little Richard, but he passed on it.'

Go Girl Go hadn't charted. So my songs deemed no good. We used the Bumps Blackwell Orchestra. He'd cut *Tutti Frutti* on Little Richard, *You Send Me* on Sam Cooke. We did *Loud Perfume* at Art Rupe's Specialty Studios, 8508 Sunset.

Well, now. DJs wouldn't spin it. *Too black,* they said. In a bid to get it heard, my agents made me do this pissbody TV show. New faces thing. Make it look like I'm being 'discovered'. I lodged robust protest. Made me look like a dadgum amateur. Contractural obligations were invoked to compel me. So, then. Only themselves to blame for the outcome.

I'm nervous. So hello, two-fifths of Jim Beam. My TV pants, I pulled on backasswards. Boots, on the wrong feet. Enter Jett. Walking like a duck, zipper on his ass.

Just before me, a seal trainer. Knee-high tank, two seacats in it. I topple over it. Fall in. Floor manager hollers get off the set. *Hell, no.* I haul myself out. Have the band take it from the top. They cut to an ad. The security they sicced on me, I served them left and right hooks.

'You'll never work in TV again, boy.'

Weren't the last to say that.

No matter. My vocal stylings had not gone unremarked upon at Specialty. Art Rupe now hired me on as a demo singer. Little Richard, BB King, all them, always out on the road. So the studio would cut a demo. Saved the stars learning it from scratch when they came in to cut. Yeah. Those boys, they stole all my moves.'

Them? From *him?* I mean, sure, I'll back a long shot if it scrubs up. This horse, *yeah nah.*

'The only white boy he'd allow, Brett.'

'Truly?'

'Oh, yeah. Little Richard had me sing in his church when he heard me. Jerry Allison from The Crickets was my guitar player by then. One day, Richard came in to Specialty. Jerry, a praying boy, turns to him.

'Can I come play in your church, Richard?'

And I thought *Oh my God, Jerry, what are you...'*

'You can please the Lord in any way you want! You can please the Lord in any way you want!' says Richard. Hands in the air like the preacher man he was. Between his falls from grace.

Part of my job at Specialty was as a courier. Schlep demos to the artist, to learn it at home. I recall Richard at his door. In but a pair of white briefs. His come on in I declined. I believe he had other than worship in mind.

CHAPTER THIRTEEN

'That's PJ Proby, right? Would you introduce me?'

'Proby, this is Pat Powell. He's a singer too.'

Proby's eyes go snakey. He don't stand up. Shakes Pat's hand. Sort of.

'I love your stuff, man,' says Pat. 'One of the most amazing voices I ever heard...'

He means it. A *believer*. Then picks up on the Texan's mood. Pat's a quick study. Reads the vibe. Nods *thanks, man* at me. Moves off. Proby eyeballs me.

'I hope that boy can sing, Brett.'

Boy? I say the only thing that'll head off a spinout.

'Oh, he's not bad, Jim.'

He's fuckin' grouse, ya miserable plank.

'I only shook the hands of two black men before. Jackie Wilson and Sammy Davis Junior. Is *he* as good as *them?*'

What can you say to a dude so lost in orbit around himself?

'Probably, not, Proby.'

'Jackie Wilson sang at my wedding. In Vegas.'

'Yeah, *right*,' I said. 'Come on, Proby. *Back it up.*'

'Well, who do you *think* sings at PJ Proby's dadgum wedding?'

A sour shadow crossed his face.

'I don't *shake* black men's hands.'

Turns out he weren't chiacking about Jackie. The rest of that rantfest, well. *Only Jackie's and Sammy's.* Alls I could say next I saw Pat was he's in truly elite company.

CHAPTER FOURTEEN

'You're hired, Slim.'
The Proby has gleaned that the Bramley is a bass player.
'But, Jim,' says Clyde,' I can't read music, and you said...'
'I don't care with you. You're in.'
'I'm touring you. Can't be in the band. A bad look. Like it's a vanity project.'
'*No!* I ain't doing it if you don't. I will *not....*'
'Well,' I said, 'looks like you're playing bass, my man.'
The Bramley silent. His thoughts not hard to read.

Two days on, Clyde's gone gold. Found some venues that might be goers. Proby's only response to this rockin' good news, not so flash. *There better be a sax player in this band* or our star's a no-show, he says.

I knew who to call. Late of The Saints, like Nini. Teddy Pepper's the name. To this day, not sure he's forgiven me.

'Have you not noticed, Brett? Less than half a gallon here!'
He shakes the cask of goon.
'And but nine stubblies of beer.'
Then *this*.
'I want *malt liquor.*'
He means *Black Fist, King Cobra, Jeremiah Weed*. Not real beer. Your rummies dig it. Cheap as milk and metho. Corn, rice and sugar dumped into your malted barley. Bumps up the alcohol volume to that place where you're pickin' fights with dogs and trucks. As a taste sensation, think Bud with a splash of kero.

It was some summers on from this, en route to Guatemala, I first saw its effects. An alky psycho with a bellyful. Street preacher fresh outta

Supermax, down on the Florida keys. You don't wanna know. But never heard of it before then.

'Not known to me, Proby.'

'This beer you get me is shit. I will not drink shit beer. I want malt liquor.'

Barflies herewith were consulted, to back up my claim. Malt *what?*

'See? We don't even know what you're chuggin' on about, Proby.'

'I want malt liquor. *Colt 45* my preferred brand.'

'You can't get it in Australia, Proby.'

'Well, then. There goes your tour, Brett. See how you do without me.'

Carlsberg Elephant Lager. Highest alcohol by vol you can lay hands on. Iced the meltdowns. A six pack a day for three days. Then switched back to VB. He didn't even notice.

CHAPTER FIFTEEN

'**N**ow,' says Clyde. 'Guitar player.'
'Got one from left field,' I said. 'Don't know if you know him.'

Ged Corben. Lime Spiders. Then the Cruel Sea. I booked 'em, pre-Tex Perkins, into Max's once. Pulled three heads. Yet we had 'em back. The Dunc had spoken. Had his imprimatur.

'These cunts can't pull the skin off a rice custard, El,' he said. 'But they go off.'

El. Short for El Dorado, bestowed on me by Colin from the Psychotic Turnbuckles. Word spread of the Cruellies. You know the rest.

Ged's in, *bang.* And Clyde clues me up on a musical director he's fished up.

'He can arrange. Done it heaps before. And he's from our home planet.'

Come on down, Scotty Saunders. From Bellydance and DIG, when they were going round.

So. At last. Our Probytones. Hot as a red Monaro. Clyde sets up a couple of go-throughs. Minus Proby to start with. Get match fit before we drop in Hazmat. We need to hang on to them this time.

CHAPTER SIXTEEN

A hillside of VB empties rose against a wall. More skanky by the day in here. Proby, well, maybe he's told housekeeping to piss off. *He likes it this way.* Or they're so freaked out by this cave dweller, *they're* giving *him* a swerve. Best not even raise it.

'Eddie Cochran had this tour of England, Brett. We drove him to LAX. Shari spoke to me while he waited to check in.

'Jimmy,' she said. 'I am going to take you to Liberty. Those agents of yours, forgeddit. Jewish guys from the movie business. You need people who get what you do.'

'Who's that, Shari?'

'Jewish guys from the music business.'

'Eddie and Gene Vincent slayed 'em. The tour, extended. Shari joined 'em there.'

I knew it was coming.

'Yeah, Brett. That taxi. Gene holding Shari. Her neck broken. *Where's Eddie?* Gene lied. Said he was OK. But she knew. See, it wasn't Eddie holding her.

She wasn't expected to live. We put her ma on a plane. With Shari in the hospital, after the longest time, ma was told get some sleep. They'd wake her if need arose. Some hours later, a nurse finds Shari's bed empty. Then Shari. Out on the ward, seeking the bathroom! Well. Our prayers had cut through all that static. To the realm of divine providence.

They flew Eddie home. Shari's in a neck brace. But then she saw her picture in the LA papers. Took it off. Wouldn't wear it.

At Forest Lawn, the Burnettes and me tarried graveside. Had a six pack. Talked to Eddie. Poured beer on the grave so he had a drink too.

Life with Dottie grew stormy, Brett. She'd not respond to my needs, so...'

I wasn't game to seek further and better particulars.

'I left or she threw me out. I cannot recall. I was playing Come To The Party. As was Johnny Rivers about then. Y'all know Rivers?'

'Yeah, Proby. *Mountain Of Love, Secret Agent Man...*'

'He gave me a piece of floor in his hotel room. He's broke as I. But on with that batcrazy Audrey Williams. Widow to Hank. They're living in Nashville, but she's bankrolled Rivers so he can work in LA.'

Proby couldn't abide him. I had no clue why. Found out in due course.

'Now Ricky Nelson had a sandlot football team. Touch football. Played Elvis and his boys. I'd played gridiron in military school, the hard and mean way. So Ricky put me in.

'You know, Jim,' he said, 'it's meant to be fun, but Elvis, his boys. They try to beat us up out there.'

See, Ricky had stolen Presley's fans while he was in the army. And Elvis, he was riled about it.

'Hey, boy, how you doin' there.'

Elvis knew me, of course. And Ricky warned me. Presley a jealous fellow. Knew not of Dottie and me. *And best he didn't.*

Wasn't a formal game. No helmets, pads. Elvis brung a helmet. Studio didn't want his face banged up. We played in a park in Bel Air, or in Beverly Glen. Sworn to silence about where by Colonel. People heard tell, they could go see his boy dance without they paid cash money for it, he said.

Yeah, we played those big dogs who worked for Elvis. Red West. His cousin Sonny. Lamar Fike. Charlie Hodge. That gang of rounders.

'Heck, Ricky. A whole sack of *here they come.*'

Some secret. The Elvis cavalcade. Long black Caddies. Like a dadgum Presidential motorcade. Locals drawn in swarms. Rare we played to no spectators. Even made the papers.

Well, Elvis had his bumpkins. But we had Dan Blocker. Hoss from *Bonanza*. One big boy, Brett. Y'all get *Bonanza* down here?'

'Yeah, Jim, we got 'em all.'

'Game got rough, we'd duck behind Dan. James Burton on our team too, Ricky's guitar picker then. James Darren. Did that TV show *Time Tunnel,* the *Gidget* pictures. And Jimmy Mitchum. A spit ringer for his old man. I played barefoot. To run faster. It set Elvis to yellin' at his lardass team. *Watch the barefoot boy! Watch the barefoot boy!*

'I'm havin' a party later, boy. Why don't you come on up?'

'Well, I'm obliged, but I can't, Elvis. Got no car.'

'I'll have my guys pick you up. Where you situated?'

I was waiting for a ride home with Ricky. Say one thing for Presley. A generous host. But *boy?* Heck and tarnation. I his junior by but three years.

'Oh, my God, man! Can I come? Can I come?'

He's speaking real soft. Then I see the handbag on the sofa.

'Listen, Rivers...'

'*Sssshhh,*' he says. 'Audrey is sleeping.'

She's passed out in the bedroom. Trouble. I wave my finger, *no, no, she is not welcome.*

'She won't let me go alone if...' he whispers. My face tells him *message received.*

Gene Smith, Presley's boy, pulls up outside. Rivers in the bathroom. Quiet as I can, I tell him. But he keeps on combing his hair. Don't want to wake polecat Audrey, so we whisper loud. Hissing like a pair of Texas coral snakes.

'Rivers. What in the nation you doing?'

'Gettin' ready to meet Elvis. Gettin' ready to meet the King!'

'Don't fret 'bout your dadgum hair. He couldn't give a damn about your hair.'

And something else.

'Oh yeah. Don't call him the King. Not ever.'

'Elvis, this is Johnny Rivers.'

'Pleased to meet ya, King.'

Elvis slams him up against a wall.

'Don't ever call me that.' Voice low and mean. 'The king is in heaven.'

He points at the sky to confirm this. I wag my finger at Rivers. Make sure Elvis sees my face, made mad as a beehive at a honey-eatin' bear. It caused me a pickle down the line. Dadgum Rivers. Dashed, what might have been.

Well, I never took Rivers back, but for me, visits to Chez Presley, Hillcrest Road, Beverly Hills, became a regular thing. Now, Elvis forbade booze. Mama Gladys, ruined by it. Died young in consequence.

But hell, Brett, this was but a box of beer. That ain't *drinkin'*. Stashed in the bushes out front. I'd sneak out. Fill a glass. Passed for ginger ale. And a fist of Old Grandad, concealed about my person, consumed only in the bathroom.

Yet I grew careless. They found suds I'd clean forgot about out there. So I get a call. The Colonel. Elvis never did the dirty work.

So, then. Cast out. Same from Chez Rivers. Ol' stray cat Audrey's paying the freight and won't have me there. I am left no choice.

'Dottie.' A knee in the dust at a trailer door. 'Will you marry me?'

Shari had these films from England, and a projector. TV shows. Limey singers. Cliff Richard, Marty Wilde, Adam Faith, Billy Fury. *Weaklings,* I declared. And here, I perceived, a kingdom fit for conquest.

'He's gonna make a show in LA. A pilot. I told him about you, Jett, and...'

Among Shari's collection, *Oh Boy* and *6/5 Special*. Produced by Jack Good. But I had qualms.

'Shari, if this Billy Fury is what he's fixin' to have, I'm not interested. Is this *Jack* what he seems? How *did* those sissy boys get on the TV?'

'This time for all time!'

That voice. She'd quit Brooklyn but it never quit her. One night, in a state from tipplin', a trial to stand straight in my boots. Dottie flung me out. Then my stuff. Then her ring. I turned twenty-one in a five dollar a month hotel on Highland. A hole in a hole in the wall.

CHAPTER SEVENTEEN

'Shari, I'm still but twenty. My daddy has to sign and he will not do this.'

She'd hyped me to Si Waronker, Liberty boss. Then today, great commotion.

'C'mon, Jimmy!'

I hear Shari outside. Beeping at the wheel.

'Twenty-one today! Pull some britches on!'

Took time to process. The fuzz of last night's wine. *Hot damn! You are entirely right!* I poke my face out the window. Shari and Jackie de Shannon, in Shari's white Caddy Coupe de Ville.

'Let's go scare you up a deal!'

Me, my guitar, one song. All it took. Si sent us to Dick Glasser. A producer here. But something pecking at his skull.

'Jett,' he said, 'I'm not sure we can make you a star right off the bat.'

'Hey, c'mon, Dickie,' said Shari. 'Si said…'

'Jett is known all over LA. For the worst of reasons. Here's what we do.'

They signed me. But at first to sing only demos. And as a contract songwriter.

'We need to take it slow,' said Dick. 'You're banned from TV. And Jett rages around, they say. Busting limbs and so on.'

He serves me a *hate to break it to ya* face.

'Jett's dead, son. Shari, what can we call him?'

'Proby,' she smiled.

'Proby?' I say. 'What kind of a…'

'A boyfriend I had.'

It's not important, Jimmy, the look I get.

'Sold,' says Dick. 'First name?'

'Initials,' I say. Or sure as armadillo pancakes on Route 66, they'd pick a sissy one.

'PJ. As in PJs.'

'His favourite bar in LA,' Shari says. 'One of many.'

That day began with fifty cents in my Levis. At its end, a $500 advance. The same again as monthly paycheck. But the flipside, Brett, an all-grey rainbow, a pot of fool's gold at its end. See, back then, if you were called songwriter, people rated you no shakes as a singer. It did Willie Nelson harm for a time. Then again, his the face of a beaten heavyweight. So newborn PJ Proby doused his doubts. And lit out for glory.

Songwriting division at Liberty. Metric Music by name. A hut in the parking lot. We called it the 'Brill Shack.' Jackie de Shannon worked here. Fella called Randy Newman. Glen Campbell. David Gates. Leon Russell. Shari of course.

We worked fast. We'd write one. Track a demo on a two track mono. Cut an acetate. Run that up to one of the producers, ol' Snuffy Garrett, our A and R mugwump, in the main building.

If they heard money, they'd cut it that day. On Bobby Vee, Brook Benton, Ricky Nelson, Johnny Burnette, Del Shannon. Or Vikki Carr, Julie London, Jackie de Shannon, Darlene Love. Novelty singles too. Worse they were, more they sold. Y'all know *Alley Oop*? One of ol' Fowley's studio bands. Hollywood Argyles. I clinked those Bud bottles on that sucker.

The writers played on demos and on the real thing. Shari, Jackie and Darlene Love sang leads on demos for female artists. Did backups on the studio sessions, but not the demos. For these, we boys did 'em. Falsetto, really, really high. Like you got your balls up in your throat. They wouldn't pay the gals for a demo. Dadgum skinflints.

Glen Campbell got paid more than most of us. Hot picker. Knew it too. Often tardy. Kept his golf clubs in his Caddy. I had a bitty 250cc motorcycle.

'Jim,' they'd say,' jump on that hoglet and go get Campbell, boy.'

So to Lakeside in Burbank, or Riverside Country Club. He'd comply. With some reluctance.

Dick Glasser started talking of cutting a 45 on me. And Don Law from Columbia heard me too.

'Jim, me old cock sparrer,' he said, he a Limey, 'that baritone. Just the ticket. Some demos for one of our stars.'

For that deep and wasted sound like said star had, I'd drink hard. Get in the worst shape this side of a pine box and a hole in the ground. Make the studio in the AM. Cut it quick. See, by noon, my voice'd be up there like Wayne dadgum Newton.

And so ol' Johnny Cash, the star in question, he put what I did into his take. You're welcome, Man In Black. But I pulled down no extra pay for jobs like that. Liberty hired me out. Kept all they paid for me. My paycheck, all I got. Yeah. Never sign nothin' by neon.

'You gotta write like it's for children, Jimmy.'

Shari showed me how. Liberty sent one of mine to Elvis. He all the way planned to cut it, his next single. Then heard it was by my hand. *Forget it.* This, on that dumbdick Rivers, Brett. Calling him King in my company.'

That a fact, Proby? You rock up at his, stashing slabs in the scrub, a fifth of paint stripper in your boots. Yeah. Nothin' to do with it.

'The song, *In My Dreams.* Rick Nelson cut it for an album, *Spotlight On Rick.* But not a dime have I seen. I been played more times than a jukebox.'

Oldest story in the world. This one I didn't doubt for a second.

'Johnny Burnette a solo at Liberty now. No taste for the schmaltz they bid he cut, but did as told lest he be thrown off the train. I wrote a country song, *Clown Shoes.* Again, Elvis in mind for it. Guess how *that* went. So Burnette says *I'll have me some or all of that, Jim*. Well, that dood it, Brett. A hit.'

I'm a massive Johnny Burnette fan. I was about to ask Proby more, but now came this.

'Just three years on. Dang fool. Out fishing by moonlight. Unlit boat. Cabin cruiser happens along, at speed. So long, Johnny.'

I raised my glass. Proby, his. Both of them.

'I wrote a mess of songs, but they rejected many. So I fell to hustling sidebar action. Songs for cash. There was this duo played on the Strip. Scott Engel and John Stewart. You'd know Engel as Scott Walker.'

The Sun Ain't Gonna Shine Any More. Did I what.

'They did Pandora's, Kismet Club, Peppermint Lounge. Same joints as me. Looking to cut a record.

'Cash in the hand that wrote it, boys. And y'all don't print my right name on it.'

They went for *I Only Came To Dance With You*. Cut it in some short-order studio on the Strip. Billed themselves the Dalton Brothers. Like the outlaws.

Well, that's all fine as frog fur. But then I find those fools put my right name on the label, James M. Smith. Liberty heard tell. Took from my paycheck all I'd got for it. Then sold it on. I didn't make a cent. One version on Reprise. Sinatra's label. This gal Pat Powdrill. And the Challenge label, by Jerry Fuller.

'Read your contract, Jim,' Leon Russell said to me once. 'Part where it says *trick or treat*.'

'Jimmy,' said Shari one day, 'Dickie says it's time.'

My first single as PJ Proby. *Try To Forget Her*. Glasser wouldn't cut my songs. See, *he* had written one. So if this was a hit, he'd grift all the gravy there was to be had.

It was a steal from an Orbison ballad. Dick had me sing it like the Big O, too. And some Gene Pitney notes, he said.

'It'll get this doggie a bunch of airplay, Jim.'

But radio already had all it could eat on Orbison and Pitney. *Try To Forget Her* perished unwanted. Ol' Glasser's crystal-ballin' me a sack of whangdoodle. The song turned up on my EP *Proby Again* down the road in '67.

See, Brett, I was just Liberty's pig. And they ate everything but the oink.

CHAPTER EIGHTEEN

'Know why these old showies have backup singers, fella?'
'To beef 'em up,' I said. 'The pipes get reedy. BVs thicken it up a smidge...'
'That too. But really, it's to prompt them. They forget the words.'

Robbie suggests the mighty, mighty Christa Hughes. Top Sydney blues belter, hot and strong as you like it. See, we've dropped Proby into rehearsals now, but he's tanking. Can't recall lyrics. Misses cues. Goes flat or sharp all the time.

Clyde's all for it. Christa learns her lines. Proby's too.

'It will pay off, my man, full bonum and excelsior,' I reassure Clyde. *We're away, Brettski,* I tell myself. Well. *Drink to the fool.*

'How's it goin' over there, *Boobs?*'

The Proby knows Christa's name, been introduced, but he's calling her *boobs* or *legs,* a freakin' pig. He's perverse. And she's doing a top job, *for his benefit,* keeping him somewhere near in tune and across the words. She bailed after just one go. *Top effort, Proby.* We offered Christa the support slot. Least we could do by way of compo.

'...we'll need 'em out there, for the kangaroos and those koala bears.'

Proby bending Clyde's ear at the pub. The Bramley's eyes frozen over. And Spencer Jones, a grin wide as a cut throat as I return from the bar. *Oh fuck. What's he want now?*

'Hunting rifles too. Wild pigs out there. Big as elephants, ol' Spencer here says.'

Spare me days. He wants to go lookin' for shit to shoot out in the mulga.

'Whoa, Tex!' I say. 'The outback, the real deal, that's a three day drive, bwana.'

Just as a brainwave came.

'And all dry communities out there.'

'Like your counties in Kentucky.'

Clyde. Swift in with backup.

'They bust you with liquor,... '

'Those bush cops. Carry shotguns,' says Spencer. 'And shovels.' He's jerried the need.

'I mean, fuck, Proby. Imagine if the Kingswood broke down.'

A close one. For the great outdoors trip Proby now craves, he settles for the Royal National Park. In the fat white belly of the Sutherland Shire.

'I need a whole mess of it, boys.'

Quite a crew up for this picnic. So Proby decrees *he will cook.* Seafood, he wants. So I suggest a side trip. Pyrmont Fish Markets.

'But we're right next to the dadgum *sea!*'

He's just noticed Bondi Beach after three weeks opposite the same. So we drive, *I will not walk,* fifty freakin' metres to the Campbell Parade fish shop in Bondi.

'Let me have two dozen of those oysters on the half-shell there.'

Points with his stubby.

'Some of those shrimp. Two of those cherry red lobsters there...'

Exy as all get out. He bids Clyde, with desperado's eyes, to pay. I can't bear to look no more.

'What are you doing, Proby?'

He don't shell or shuck nothing. Chucks it into pots and pans from Bondi. Then a pile of chili. Tabasco. Method, random to say the least. Result, inedible.

'Oh, man. This cat Proby gives a whole new dimension to drinking.'

Spencer, who could grog on for Australia or his homeland New Zealand, had spent two days going one for one with him. Come this, the third, he threw up. A dude not known for lack of fortitude.

Spencer's light went out just shy of 62. Eight years ill. Packed sixty into his first thirty. Never knew a soul didn't like him.

'Running on empty, Proby,' I said. Held up an esky. Pinky hooked round the handle, to prove it. A wave of panic across his face. It worked.

'Yes. I'd like to go now.'

Swerves to Nini, my soon to be-ex Caroline, and our pal Sue Squid.

'Y'all ride with me. In the Kingsford.'

Turns to me.

'Three and me. Not my first time.'

CHAPTER NINETEEN

'I've busted near as many hearts as heads, Brett.'

Proby's wives. The tally varied from one rave to the next.

'Early in '62,' he says, 'my first. Marianne. To escape her psycho mama. Only way to have at her, wedlock. She's sixteen. I, four and twenty. That was some picnic.'

Not sure I want to know, Proby.

'She kept scramming back to the mad old vixen I helped her flee. A wildcat. I forbade her to dance with other men. Or go out with her friends. I'd not suffer a jezebel.'

Which bit of this to process first?

'Now with my paychecks, I bought a car, motorcycle, boots, liquor, cigars, firearms. Finery for the lady Marianne. Her beauty parlours, shoes. Rented a house. Crest of a ridge in Laurel Canyon.

My buddy Jim Ford can't resist. Connubials with his wife in poor health. So Ford commences to having relations with Marianne.

Now, a fella could take them to task. But Ford, quick to blade or sidearm. Best left unstirred. Meantime, Ford's wife, at home with their baby. Lonely and blue. Flirted with me at a cookout there one time. So I contrived assignations of our own.

That was what it was. But now Marianne took to every damn dick in the five counties of LA. Delivery boys. Roadworkers. Door to door salesmen. Then quit school. One time I get home from a gig, she's double-teaming two cops. LAPD.'

Like so many Proby yarns, well, who freakin' knows?

'These two just laugh. I cross 'em, it's a beating and a night in the tank. So, then. After they'd gone, time for correction. But she grabbed a knife. A sting in my back even as I took off my belt. Blood all over.

Cops came. Not the sportin' fellas from before. They'd had calls from the neighbours. Our melee, they claimed, drowning out the coyotes in the hills.

Now, a new PJ Proby single, *The Other Side Of Town*. Shari and Jackie wrote it for me. But Glasser made me sing it like Pitney. Airplay for sure, he declared. Flopville. Went noplace but wherever noplace is.

'Yes, Jim. I can accommodate you.'

By my hand, *Ain't Gonna Kiss Ya* had 'hit' all over it. Yet Liberty demurred. Ol' Fowley pestering of late. So for cash under moonless midnight, he sold my song to The Ribbons. Girl group from Specialty.

'I'll put my name on it, Jim,' he said. 'Fifty-fifty on all we make.'

And I'll be smoked ribs over post oak if it wasn't a hit on LA coloured radio, the R and B stations. Just one concern. Dadgum Fowley! The label. My *right name* there, *J M Smith*. Sleeve, too. But he said those rednecks at Liberty never listened to the black stations, so fret not.'

'Jimmy. Why?'

Liberty president, Al Bennett. Good and steamed.

'Well, Al, I gave y'all the song and y'all didn't care for it, so...'

'Got that in ink, boy? We didn't *care for it* so y'all could go pawnbrokin' our rightful?"

'No, Al, but that ain't the point...'

He re-lit his guinea stinker as he spoke on.

'Jimmy, that's exactly the point. So here's the next of it. We sue. You stand up in court. Say *they* stole it from *you.*'

'No, Al,' I said.' I had taken a drink. Thus emboldened.

'I'll not let my songs lie in the weeds as if untended tombstones. I'm gonna stand up for the little man.'

'Oh,' he said, 'you *are*, huh? Well,...'

They cut off the power in time. Landlord noised up. Unpaid rent.

'Marianne. No paychecks for now. I'm suspended.'

Car, motorcycle, repossessed. Furniture. Then the strangest intercession.

'I heard your demo, Jimmy. That Bobby Vee number.'

Ben Weisman from RCA. My phone not yet cut off, an act of providence.

'Can you come in for a meeting?'

Hired out by Liberty before I got benched, I'd cut this demo, a song Ben wrote. *The Night Has A Thousand Eyes.* A smash. I sang the gizzards out of it. Ol' Bobby Vee, he copped my stylings right off me. Now, the payoff.

'I write for a lot of singers, Jim.'

Weisman worked out of Radio Recorders on Santa Monica.

'One of them, Elvis.'

Oh. Best not mention that Presley and I were estranged.

'My goodness, Mr Weisman. That, sir, is a feather in your hat.'

'Keeps us busy. Now, Elvis makes movies all day. Not a lot of time to cut records.'

Three pictures a year. Ten songs each, he said.

'We need demos cut fast. So he can lend an ear, ace it in two takes.'

'Mr Weisman,' I said, 'let's get to it.'

First, for that boxing picture. *Kid Galahad.* Then *Follow That Dream. Girls! Girls! Girls!* Oh, and *Fun In Acapulco.* Fine as you fancy, but my end, Weisman paid me just ten dollars per song. Didn't even meet my bar tabs.

We cut daytimes but Presley never came in until six in the PM. He'd listen. Maybe take 'em home. Cut 'em next day. Only came in but the once while I was in there.

He'd had no clue it was me on these. But didn't call Colonel to fire me this time. Instead, he pulled me up. In front of the band, the engineer, the producer.

'You're workin' them songs too hard, boy. Way too hard. You got to ease it up a little.'

He just wanted to play big boss man. It was clear he liked what I did. For he stole it all, Brett. Breath for *breath.*'

I've heard those demos. *Yeah. Sort of.* I mean, both of 'em lifted heaps from Mario Lanza, Billy Eckstine, Roy Hamilton, Johnnie Ray. Best not say so, that said. Hazmat here would go into orbit.

'For all that, I thought I'd been forgiven. But one day Colonel calls Weisman. After all this time, Presley's heard about Dottie. Yeah, well. Singin' those movie songs 'bout as much fun as a bucket of warm spit, anyways. And I, Proby, now free to pursue greater and higher destiny.'

CHAPTER TWENTY

'Yeah, Brettski. Gonna be a ripper.'

Seems Spencer's yaks with Proby had a purpose. Spence has called Tex Perkins. The plan, these three write some songs, record and release them. Me, I can't hardly get Proby out of bed. Spencer's got him geed up for *this*. Hats off to the hoodoo man.

Bondi. Spencer's brought a guitar and a cassette recorder. They got some noise down but took a while. Proby droppin' all these names he's worked with. Gabbin' like a jackhammer. Just like at rehearsals. His top dog war dance.

Yet they came back. Several times. Once, Proby pulled out some lyrics he'd brought with him. Sang them. Spencer nuts out chords. They taped that. Then got sidetracked onto bourbon-stoked exits off that highway.

Another night, Tex is bangin' on about dropping his gig at the Lansdowne because it was ruining his Sundays.

'God*damnit!*' says the Proby. '*Ruining My Sundays!* That's a *hit!*'

Drops into a rave, to conjure up some rhymes. Got that down too. The last the world heard of it.

*

'So, Proby. How's about we go out, check out the competition?'

His taste, not broad. Clyde's brainwave, the Annandale Hotel. Jeff Duff Orchestra. Jeff's monster baritone. Likes what Proby does. Does what Proby likes. *Bang.*

'That pantywaist up there, Brett! Ripping me off! My whole act!'

Yeah. He cops a bit of Duffo and goes off. But came good when word spills round the 'dale who this gronk in the wrangler chute cowboy hat was.

'Call me Jim!'

He's lovin' it. Five Jack and cokes on the go, these all shouts from the mob bunched around him now. For me, a spell from Planet Proby. Much needed. I get into a rave with some other humans.

The band's on a break now. Then I see Proby's being introduced to Duffo. A worry at first. Proby's foamings on the subject and Duffo a known flamboyant. But the sitch looks well enough, and Duffo, famed as fearless and formidable should the Texan stack on a turn. Leave them to it.

'Hey, Brett.' Clyde. 'Have a go at this!'

I swing round. Proby's up on stage! Duffo gives him an intro. Crowd, loud and lusty for it. *Then he does it.* The full pipes. *Maria.* The joint silent. Spellbound. I realise I've got a grin on. First one in weeks.

'I'll take him home, Clyde. Wait for the coma to kick in. See you down there.'

The Lansdowne. Next race on the card tonight. Rob Younger's New Christs. Hmmm. Proby. Detroit Thrash Metal. *Nah.* Can't see it. What he don't know won't kill him. Or us.

'You boys are headin' out after this! And I'm comin' with ya!'

Well, we had this freakin' entourage now, milling round Proby. Odds-on, they're Landy-bound too. And he's got wind of it.

'Now, Proby,' I say. 'You won't like it, bwana. It's rowdy music...'

'I'm comin',' *compadre.* Or I will not do this *tour.* I will not...'

Righteo. I'm takin' PJ Proby to see the New Christs. *Dios ayudanos.*

*

'Oh, *Jim!*'

Two eyes full of stars. *Proby has come to see his band.* Younger's lit up like a Xmas Day bushfire. On him like a puppy. Proby don't register

Rob's even there. *Uh? Nunh?* I jump in. Wish Rob a top gig. And brace for fate to choose. Who knows? Proby's recorded with Jimmy Page and JP Jones. All of Led Zep on *Three Week Hero.* Knew Hendrix. The Who. Cream. Those Savoy tracks, his takes on the Pistols, Iggy. Maybe he gets it. Maybe this'll go good after all…

'What is this shit? Get me out of here! Don't waste my time! I'm PJ *Proby! I...'*

'I *said* you wouldn't like it, Proby. Would you just fucking calm down?'

Punters swerve eyes our way. Bouncers too.

'I'm goin' *home!* I'm not listeni…Brett, take me home *now!'*

Now a normal human being, a few frosties on board, will whistle a taxi or hop on a train *and don't need adult supervision to do it.* But Proby had told me he'd never done these things. *Ever.*

I give it one more pass.

'Proby, this guy up there loves what you do. You don't like his music, fair enough, but…'

'They're noisy, no-talent *bums!* No *idea,* all *useless...'*

The punters around us back off a bit. Sense a blue about to erupt. That's when Clyde grabs him. He's got the finger out. The chest-jabbing one. Clyde never loses it. *Never.* Son of a preacher man never. Until now.

'Listen!'

He don't shout. Ever. Points at the stage.

'This guy loves you. You don't have to like him. *We told you not to come! Piss off!'*

'Righto, Clyde!' Realise that's *me* hollering now. 'Stand down!'

Driving Proby home. A hard case from the Newtown Hotel when I booked bands there comes to mind. What he used to do when his kid played up. But the Kingswood's a wagon. Don't have a boot.

CHAPTER TWENTY-ONE

'I did *what?*'

Of last night, the Texan has no memory. Deep-fried as dim sims. I tune back in. Radio Proby. Only station on the dial.

'So I'm on suspension from Liberty. At home in the dark. Power cut off. Dinner on the floor. Tacos by candlelight. Comes a banging on the door. I assume and dread the worst.

In music back then, you upset people, no telling what might betide.

'Marianne, would you answer that?' I said as I fetched my handgun. So I brace for heck knows what – to Shari Sheeley and Jackie de Shannon!

'Well, hello, girls! What brings you up here?'

Jamming the roscoe into the back of my Levis.

'Got someone to see ya,' says Shari. A geeky hombre. Black horn rim spectacles. Without a word, he grabs my long hair. Grown to my shoulders, as I lack fifty cents for a barber. I'm all set to roundhouse this pointdexter when he speaks.

'My *God.*'

High class British voice.

'It's *real.* You're *hired,* dear boy. Be at CBS tomorrow morning. Ten o'clock.'

With that, he's gone. *Vamos,* into the still of the night.

'What the Sam Houston was that about, Shari?'

'That's Jack Good, Jimmy. I played him your 45s. He's gonna make you a star.'

'Yeah, about that, what he said just now. My car, my motorcycle...'

'I'll pick you up. Eight o'clock.'

'Marianne, take that beer from Jimmy's hand,' said Jackie. 'And put him to bed.'

'Jimmy,' said Shari,' if you are one second late, I will leave without you.'

Well, now. Over two days at CBS on Beverly Boulevard, we taped a TV pilot. *Young America Swings The World.* Me, two numbers. *Endless Sleep* and *Turn Me Loose.* Jackie de Shannon sang on this hootenanny too, plus the Chambers Brothers and Clydie King. The band, Leon Russell's at the piana. Glen Campbell and Delaney Bramlett, guitars. David Gates, Fender bass.I think it was Earl Palmer on the drums. Jack's play, to charm from the network the wampum for a series.

Jack had swing, this was plain. So I'm up for whatever.
    'Jim,' he says, 'have you any Shakespeare?'
    'Well, I've heard tell of it, Mr Good. At school. Supposed to read his plays, but...'
    'Do you know Iago? From *Othello?*'

Right there, Jack cast me in a musical he'd crafted of that very play. *Catch My Soul,* he called it. His aim, the West End, on Broadway. And a *movie.*
    'You know, Jim, for Othello himself, I want to cast Little Richard.'
    Or, he said, Muhammad Ali, still plain old Cassius Clay then. A mad design. But Jack might could do it for me, so I play along. Queer for me maybe. But at least he didn't get his ding dong out.

'Dear boy. They're going to be big.'
    At the Chateau Marmont, Jack's packing for England. Said to bring my singles. A photo of some English group on his wall.
    'Well, looking at this, Jack, I harbour doubts.'
    'Jim, I plan to play them your singles. Get you on their TV show we're making in London.'
    'Big? I think not, Jack.'
    I point at what they're doing in that picture.
    '*Pillow fights?*'

I didn't think they were worth a shit. VeeJay Records had released a 45 of theirs. It scored some airplay on LA radio. Sang harmony, but weren't good at it. Not like the Everlys or the Mills Brothers. We did favour the same hairstyle. I'd seen a busload of French students at the supermarket one day had it like that so I did the same. Way before America heard of these dadgum Beatles.

Now, a fresh *contretemps* with Marianne. Me at the wrong end of my own hunting knife.

I had to vamoose, back to the threadbare shelter of the Highland Hotel.

Fella called Don Grollman was concierge. Round Hollywood, he's always at my gigs. Now, hearing of my fix, a guardian angel. Said to schlep over to where he lived with his parents. He'd throw TV dinners down from his window upstairs. Stolen from their freezer.

He had a disablement. Misadventure. Fell down an elevator shaft, so he walked a shade like Quasimodo. Son of an LA dentist. Had these vampire fangs of porcelain. Toted bongo drums round in a bag, and books on werewolves and vampires. I dubbed him Bongo Wolf.

'Hell, Bongo. Vampires and werewolves. Sounds like the music business.'

'It didn't fly the last two times, *Dickie.*'

My suspension's lifted. Can't get rich off a dog ain't working. We cut a new PJ Proby single, *So Do I.*

'We did Orbison and Pitney and they got born dead!'

Now it's Johnny *Cash* Glasser wants. This number, by Donna Kohler. Wrote these quick buck novelty singles like *The Hula Hoop Song.* This *So Do I* is but a ghostwrit *I Walk The Line.* Same chug-a-chug guitar. That *mmmmmm* to signal key changes. Stone ripoff. Only good part, this dogface, arranger on the session. Spector's guy from Gold Star Studio. Even looked like him.'

Only one of my favourite producers ever.

'That'd be Jack Nitzsche, Proby?'

'The same, Brett. We'd meet again in time. An entirely daffy episode!'

That tale would come. And it was.

'*So Do I* went splat like bugs on a windshield. So I said, *Dickie*, let's drop this sounds like insert name here flummery. Here on in, *my* voice. *My* dadgum songs.'

Wicked Woman and *Darlin'*, I'd penned these for Ray Charles, but he'd passed. So we cut 'em on me. But now Glasser, he goes all goosey on me. *It's too black, Jim.*

'Well,' I said, recalling Fowley's ways with the coloured stations, 'let's give me a name to match.'

And we did. One that went with those songs like beans and fatback on a plate. Coloured stations heard this Orville Woods. Snatched it up as if the bread of heaven. Airplay. Chart action.

'See, Dick? Let me sing like *me,* we'll all get a new boat out of it.'

Music press got all broiled up over ol' Orville. Then *KRLA Beat* magazine divined that *he* was *me.* Ran a story. With a picture of my white ass.

Those black stations killed that record quick as a copperhead. Civil rights people called for my head on a stick. I'm all but dropped from Liberty's roster. Then the call came.

*

'You'll be splendid, dear boy.'

Jack Good on the turbid trans-Atlantic line. The Beatles TV show. PJ Proby, top of the bill!

I must contrive a passport, he a UK work visa for me, he said.

'Be packed and ready to leave at any time, my boy.'

In four spins round the sun here in LA, I'd gone from a drop of nothin' to fifty barrels of it. In my mind, I was already gone.

'Hello, Mr Proby?'

Bongo had called me to the phone at the Highland.

'Vyvienne Moynihan here from Rediffusion Television. Now, PJ, Jack tells me you're free at present apart from learning Iago for his Othello.'

Jack loved spreading stories of dubious veracity. For now, best dance to it.

'You're entirely right, ma'am.'

'Quite,' she said. 'Well, that is most convenient, because we would like you to come over to England and do our show. It's called *Around The Beatles.*'

'Ma'am, I would be flattered and delighted.'

'Smashing. There's a ticket for you at LAX. BOAC.10.30 AM tomorrow.'

Tomorrow. These Limeys did not mess around. As I came to find in a cluster of ways.

CHAPTER TWENTY-TWO

'Here, Proby. Finish your brekky in the car.'

Clyde's booked the big room at Zen Studios. Full run-through today. So I squirt the Texan a cask moselle before he's even out of bed, his heart starter. Beer Two, after his first in the shower, I stick in his mitt as I shepherd him out the door. None of this linger longer rebop today, my man.

At the Hopetoun, Clyde sees the talent is boxed and travellin'. Takes off to get the band set up. And something else. Proby sees *Clyde* take the beer and goon. *You don't go, you don't get*. We got Hazmat snookered.

So now I wait for him to sink his schooey. And then...

'I want a *real* drink.'

I'm past tryin' to jerry why he does this. But no way we sit here for an hour while he sips JD with another beer he'll demand. Nuh. I buy a half of Jack. Reel him into the car with it. It's ten freakin' thirty AM.

Every dadgum song I ever did. Making a fusski about this Harrods bag since he fell off the plane. Full of charts, he says. Clyde's chosen not to dip into it until we have a set list. Band's worked up twenty numbers. Based on raves I've had with Proby, and then passed on to Clyde what sense I could make of that.

'I must have a lounge chair. I will not sing without an...'

He's rolled up in the corner. Clumsy kiddie grip on the Jack. Baby with a bottle. Clyde sighs. Sets down his bass. Goes off in quest. Me, I try to get Proby to engage with the band. Nuh. On the sook. Denied his *orchestra*.

We hear squeaking in the corridor and now Clyde's back, pushing this grime-blacked maroon armchair on castor wheels.

'What in the nation is this, Clyde?' says Proby. 'Old Sparky?'

I grope around for a laugh but me sense of humour, long since bolted. I test his mic. *Check one two scooby dooby doo.* This dill's the freakin' singer but he don't do nothing. His stand I adjust too. So's he can sing without effort, sunk in his wino king's throne.

'Let's have a look then,' says Clyde. The Harrods bag. Scotty has a dekko at the contents. From sessions at Abbey Road, Proby says.

'Well,' Scotty says after a bit, 'these are all for *Somewhere.*'

First violins, *flick,* second violins, *flick,* cellos, *flick,* first, second trumpet, *flickflick.* He eyeballs Clyde. *What do I do with this junk?* Clyde flicks his eyes Proby's way. *Humour him.*

'Jim,' says Scotty, 'I'll take 'em with me. Work them into ours.'

Chucks Clyde a wink that Proby don't see. We did a lot of that around him. Like the jail telegraph.

We get into it. Band, mighteous. Proby, military grade passive aggression.

'This ain't my first rodeo, hoss.'

This to Scotty's query as to how he'd like to finish a number, the recorded version a fade. Some numbers get the big tick. Others, victim to his mood swings. Mid-verse.

'No. No. *No!*' Band stumbles to a stop. 'I will *not* perform this.'

He's got bushed halfway into the first verse. Lost in the scrub, he blames the band. But they're on the money. It's Proby who's missed the boat. Missed the freakin' fleet.

Robbie keeps the band geed up. *That's the way, fella. Right on the knocker.* A top hand at this team building caper.

And we've taken on board a new backing singer to keep Proby on the sunny sonic path. A young'un. Studying opera at the Con. I said I'd cut off the grog if he slings her any of that yabba like he did Christa. This one's across the lyrics better than Proby is, *without no charts.* Drops them in when he stacks it, to help him back on the bike. Which is often. And the band, the patience of the First Nations at his wobblers.

Yet Proby's freakin' snowblind to all this goodwill. A hole in his soul from a freakin' affinity bypass. I found out some years on that like Proby, Donald Trump had gone to military school. Explained a few things. More than a few.

'Well done, Clyde! Top effort.'

'Newie first. Midweek.'

I translate for Proby. Newcastle, like in England. The fabmost Cambridge Inn will play host to our Tuesday night out of town road test.

'And for the Saturday, Paddington RSL.'

'A top room, Proby,' I tell him. 'A fine big space where a thousand punters of the line may safely rock at anchor.'

Luck's in. Too right. Tales of his clubland crimes had by some miracle not reached Paddo.

We rattled cages Melbourneside now too. The Prince Of Wales in St Kilda. The Espy. The Corner in Richmond. There was interest. But no speccy guarantees on offer. And getting Proby there, shipping the band down, playing butler all day, carting him round...

And yet...if we pull off this Paddo gig, that triggers demand for more in Sydney. Off that, yeah, maybe shows down Mexico way. Listen, there's been worse organised tours by far bigger players. Truly. And Proby's in no rush to get home. Not now he don't have one.

CHAPTER TWENTY-THREE

'**B**est you not be there, Marianne.'
So now, to England. And here's me, Brett, all my clothes back whence I'd fled.
'I'll get my duds and get gone.'

Well. No jeans, jackets, shirts or tees there. Nor boots, hats, belts, even jockey shorts. She and new lover boy, bugged out overnight, rent and bills past due, with my all of it. Cleaned me out. Then I see it. Staked to the floor with my knife. These dainty blue panties and a note in her hand.

If these fit, wear THEM.

A fine imbroglio. I'm on a jet for London come the AM. So I call Rock Hudson's secretary, Nan Morris. Do anything for ya. She came right over with Tuesday Weld. Nan couldn't raise Rock, so we made for Troy Donahue's. I'd been his bodyguard and a statue in a couple his pictures. *Monster On The Campus*, all that tarradiddle.

'Well, Jim, you're tall, but I'm even taller than you.'

His pants don't fit me. His shirts do. Gave me one of those. And two velour sweaters.

'It's cold over there, Jim. Even when it's not cold it's cold.'

To Warner's at Burbank next. I swiped one of Newman's cowboy shirts from wardrobe. And Russ Tamblyn's boots from *Seven Brides For Seven Brothers*. Dancin' boots. Buckles. They'd last but a week on the street. But they'll come up jim dandy on the TV.

At the airport, they gave me twenty-five bucks. Perfect. Eight hours' worth of bourbon.

CHAPTER TWENTY-FOUR

'Jim! *Jim!* Welcome to *England,* Jim!'

I'm drunked up as who shot John. Top of the jetstair. Jack's down there. Reporters, photographers.

'Do something British!' they shout. *'Do something British!'*

First thing that came to me in my swoggled state, given the cigar between my teeth. Churchill. My fingers in a V for victory.

'No, Jim! Turn it around! Turn it *around!'* shouts Jack.

Turns out it wasn't V for victory but flippin' the bird, English style. What Jack called a *Harvey Bristol.* No harm done. Page One on Day One. These Limeys, a mess of questions. *What are your plans? What is the purpose of your visit?*

'Why, to fight all your men, fuck all your women and steal all your money. Then buy a yacht. Sail off into the wild red yonder.'

Agape, every one. Mission accomplished.

Now Jack had this burgundy Rolls Royce on the tarmac. But soon as we're out of that airport, he leans forward. Says something. Driver pulls over.

'Right, Jim. Out we get.'

'What in hell and purgatoriness, Jack? Why are we...'

See, he'd only hired that buggy for minimum distance. Told the press it was mine.

'They think you're a star in the States, dear boy. Hence rich.'

So now, a taxi flagged down, to my lodgings here. Little semblance to that Dorchester Hotel he'd told those news pugs about.

'What squalid hellcave is this, Jack?'

'A bedsit, Jim. Fret not. You won't be here a lot, so...'

Calls me a king. Gives me Earl's Court.

They're just back from their first tour Stateside. Jack had sold 'em all this baloney about me. See, they'd requested a star from America for their show and Jack's budget somewhat constrained, so...

Well, I played my part. Like I'm big as Presley and they don't mean a supper of possum and a six pack to me. George, Ringo, deferential. Paul, polite. But wary. *Suspicious*. And then...

'Here's your star, John,' says Jack.

'Fuck *you!*' says John to Jack. Then to me, 'You're no fuckin' *star!*'

'Fuck *you!*' Me. 'I can out-drink you.'

'Okay, star man,' says Lennon. 'Let's fuckin' find out.'

Me, Lennon and Karl Denver, this folk singer. A bottle on me. More in the Green Room there at Rediffusion at Wembley Park. I split when they passed out. Went lookin' for trouble.

'You're fuckin' John Barrymore come back to life, mate.'

So said John next we met. Good buddies after that.

'Well, I sure do like to think so, John,' I said. Yes, sir, Brett. A two-fisted whiskey cowboy who baulked at no man's challenge. Or hand of friendship if such served my needs.

Around The Beatles. First ever TV show went out live and global, by that Telstar satellite. We rehearsed for fifteen days. Me, three numbers. *Walkin' The Dog*. Rufus Thomas number for Stax. The Stones had just cut it but theirs wasn't out yet. *Cumberland Gap*, an Appalachian folk song. This guy Lonnie Donegan had charted high with it here so we stuck that baby in. To close, *I Believe*.

'Frankie Laine had it at Number One here for months,' said Jack. 'And his, a head like a robber's dog, dear boy. The kids will go spare.'

That Jack. A dadgum prophet.

Outfit called Sounds Incorporated backed all we songbirds on this clambake. Cilla Black, Number One on the Limey charts right then, with *You're My World*. Her manager, same as the Beatles. Brian Epstein.

Little Millie from Jamaica, her *My Boy Lollipop* Top Fivin' it at that time. Long John Baldry, a blues guy. A good boy, but liked me in that Liberace way. I shook his hand, but that was the first and last of it.

Three sweets on backup vocals. The Vernon Girls. After Vernons, the football pools company they worked at, they said.

'Well,' says I with best wink and smile, 'I bet your boy Vernon's not as big as me.'

We cut my songs for the show at this tiny studio, IBC, opposite the BBC. Couldn't sing or play live. Had to mime.

Rehearsals, first in a bare studio with a floor plan, then with the set. Three sided tiers. And scaffolding, like a construction site. Came to be much imitated. Jack filled those with selected Beatles' fans. They themselves, in this Royal box. Presiding this calamitation.

'Dear boy, that's wonderful. *Wonderful.* We'll go in tomorrow and make a recording.'

'Verily, Jack. A most exciting prospect.'

In truth, my expectation, I'd be on the redeye out of Heathrow come Monday, and not be had back ever. This day, Little Millie getting a guitar lesson off me. I'd showed her this number. Jack had said try to write a song like the Beatles. I had this old ballad by Dick Haymes, *Hold Me.* A pail of mush. But I sped it up, and sang it a twist like Lennon. Gave ol' Jack a lump in his tweeds.

At IBC, a Limey A team. Clem Cattini drums. John Paul Jones on bass. Big Jim Sullivan, first to use feedback on the lead guitar, it was said. And on the rhythm guitar, just fourteen, this peewee. Went by Jimmy Page. Jack produced, albeit he knew zip about flying soundboards. Fella that did, Charles Blackwell, played piano on it.

'What say we sprinkle some on this puppy, Jack?'

Lennon had played one on *Love Me Do* and *Please Please Me.* Helped push them well north of south in the charts. It was well that I'd brought my harmonicas.

'I said pirates and sailors, Jack! Not Peter Pan and dadgum Tinkerbell! A girl's blouse on the TV?'

'It's a blous*on*, Jim. A sailor's shirt.'

Yet this not the worst of it, Brett. The shoes...

'Silver buckles? White socks? Where I'm from, that will fetch you a two-fisted pounding.'

Now, they'd clipped on this fake ponytail at the back of my head, as per my explication of those old-timey swabbies. But...

'Bound in a velvet ribbon. In a *bow!* Jack, I fear that...'

'Dear boy! You are the only man who has dressed like this in England for two hundred years. Camp it up for all it's worth. For this will make the news.'

Well, he got that right. And then some.

*

'Give us a song, then.'

I'm at lunch with John, George and Ringo. A voice. I turn. A newspaper in a pair of hands. Paper's lowered. Paul. I'd been pallin' around with the others. Not Paul. Been keeping his distance.

'Give you a song?'

'Well, you're the *singer* for Rosie And The Originals,' he smiles. 'Give us a *song*, PJ.'

'Eat your lunch, man.'

I'm mad as Texas tree snakes in a forest fire. Rosie, one of Paul's favourites. So before I'd made landfall in England, Jack had told him *I'm* Rosie. Too bad she's a coloured chick. But Paul thinks this bait and switch is on me. Anyway, Jack had the Beatles draw names from a hat, to introduce one each of we singers. And guess what.

'And now, all the way from America, a great lad, a good friend of ours, the first time on telly in England, how about a big hand for *PJ Proby!*'

Well, now. Paul's called me their *pal!* Shocked, I froze like Alaska. Floor manager had to prod me at the cameras. So I skipped on out like

Jack had said to. Let 'em have it. Black diamond eyes and the pipes of Caruso.

'That was great. That was fab, PJ.'

Paul, shaking my hand at the apres-party.

'Call me Jim, Paul.' Lennon, even more blown away.

'All *hail*,' shouts Johnny at every warm body in the room. 'Elvis is *back!*'

'Elvis in a bottle,' says Paul.

From that day forth, it was like the good fairy, or mayhap the fun-lovin' one, came every night for a year, near about past goin', and left a million-pound banknote under my pillow. Like that Mark Twain story. Then things changed.

CHAPTER TWENTY-FIVE

'**B**rett, I need a vitamin shot.'
It bubbles up again, like a corpse in a swamp. Nini can't be found to nanny him down, so I call an ex-nurse pal. Gear acquired.

'Elvisosis,' my diagnosis to Clyde. Proby, a real down on ganja. He'd never have a spliff with us. But pharma, benzos or gakk, somebody stop him. Well, it livened him up. And fuck, did he need it.

The band and Proby run through *Hold Me, Niki Hoeky, Hurt*. Not bad. Not out of the box.

'*Maria*. I would like to do *Maria*.'

The talent takes the wheel with the goey on board. First go here at one of his biggest hits.

'Well, we've learned it,' says Clyde. 'Sort of,' he smiles. Scotty's made them all charts. So a bit of rummaging, then he hits a chord.

'There's your key, Jim.' *Pling*.

'*The most beautiful sound I have ever heard...*'

And out it comes. Finger in ear, hand to his face. Rises. Feet apart. All the hand moves. And that *voice*. Deeper than space. Wider than oceans. The last falsetto notes, loud, long and red hot blue. I look up. Every eye here, misty. *Fuck. This is why we're here*. A golden moment. These, few and precious.

'Has to have it, he says. Won't sing without it.'

Next day, new drama, fresh as country killed meat. Clyde makes for Fabulous Furniture. South Dowling Street. A closing down sale for about forty years but still charge you full tote odds. Chrome. Leather. High back. Arms. As stipulated.

'Got a problem here, Brett.'

Chair not collapsible. Won't fit in the Jag. So I drag Proby into my car. Go pick it up. Cart it around in the 'Kingsrow' for the rest of these most peculiar days in the life.

'I'll go now, Brett. Get the band ready.'

I hand Clyde the Bottlemart bag. He bails with it. Proby guzzles. I jangle me keyring, a Pavlovian bell. *Come on, Proby, let's went...*

'I want a *real* drink.'

Every freakin' time. See, you had get him early in the day. Not much chop by late arvo. And now, oh fuck. In a rave with some dork who chooses *now* to roll in to the Hoey to pay homage. All praise and glory be, this goob, so Proby's in no rush to give him the hip and shoulder. *Then the dude shouts him a Jack.* To wrench it from him unfinished, inadvisable.

So it goes. An hour late. Not that far. Seven Ks. But a cross-town deal, east to west. A lotta lights. Me being a Sydney taxi driver, a case could be mounted that not all the road rules were followed. A reasonably full tilt ride. Not full on. Just a bit on the edge.

'I'm not budging from this here Kingshead.'

'What's up your clacker now, Proby?'

'You *worried* me.'

'Whaddya mean, I worried ya?'

'You drive like a maniac.'

'No, I drive like a Sydney taxi driver. Anyway, we're here now. Come on.'

'No.'

'Whaddya mean, no?'

'I *mean* I am not going anyplace.'

Silence.

'So, what, you just gonna sit here?'

'*Yes.* I am *not* going *in.*'

He's down to two VBs. More grog can only be had *inside.* Slow as an agent's cheque.

'Oorooski, fun lovers!'

The mob's raring to go. But Clyde, stony. *He knows.*

'Whoa, yay, yeah, Brett, my man!' Pause. 'Um, where's Proby?'

'Out in the car. Not happy.'

'Fuck him.' Clyde. 'You do the rockers, Brett. I'll sing the ballads. Just guide vocals.'

I set down the Probythrone. Clyde took 'em through *Somewhere.* More talked than sang, for the band to follow. I had a bash at *Hold Me,* then *Niki Hoeky.*

Clyde's narrating *Maria* as a face peers through the control room glass, most amused. Proby circles around to us. Beelines it for the boozebag o' joy as the band collapses to a stop, one at a time.

'What y'all need *me* for, boys? Get *Clyde* to do it!'

Leers as he says it. Freakin' infantile. We did three numbers with Proby, but time was up. Still, as pile-ups go, this day didn't even run a place. That trifecta, yet to come.

CHAPTER TWENTY-SIX

'*round The Beatles*? Brett, after me, those boys were *barbecue*.'
  'No time to lose, dear boy,' said Jack. '*Hold Me* must be
released pronto. And we'll get you on *Top Of The Pops*.'
  'Is that a touring show, Jack?'
  'No, Jim. Telly.'
  'But I want to *tour*, Jack. With the Beatles.'
  'Jim. Right now we need you on the box. I want all of England
talking about that ponytail. Be of good cheer. The other will come, my
chary boy.'

'We'll start with you concealed behind this, Jim.'
  I'm set to mime *Hold Me* on TV. This thing like a drum skin, but
jumbo size. A hoop, six feet five high. White paper skin stretched across
it. On this, a profile of me in silhouette.
  'When the song starts, rip the paper apart and step through it.'
  I had a waymore better idea. Kept it to my own self. On cue, I leap
clean into it. Slice through like gunfire. Land sailin' on my belly. Come
morning, England talked of naught else.

'But, boys,' I said, 'I already have a deal.'
  Martin Davies, the manager Jack stuck me with, said the UK labels
all wanted *Hold Me*.
  'Oh,' said Jack. 'Rather a sticky wicket.'
  They took me to Decca, the highest bidder. My contract, I explained,
but a formality.
  'Liberty have no interest in me,' I told 'em. 'I just need to get a release.'
  We asked they delay on *Hold Me*, that I fly back to LA to make it
so. In truth, Brett, I had the feeling these Limeys would can the whole

thing. Bouncing around above the Atlantic, my despondency mounted as a flood. Five feet high and rising.

*

'This time for sure, dear boy.'

CBS had passed on *Young America Swings The World*. But Jack's back in LA now. Got business here same time as me. A new pilot. *Shindig*, he calls it. Country-themed. He had Johnny Cash top of the bill. Roy Clark, a hot picker, as compere. Me, I did *Cumberland Gap, Rock Island Line,* and a Buddy Knox number, *Hitchhike Down To Georgia.*

This didn't do it for CBS either. But a second one Jack made later that year full took their fancy. Yeah, Brett. *Shindig* would raise me up so high. So much further to fall.

'Jim. You sitting down, old chap?'

Murky phone line from England. At Bongo's one dim star hotel, I'm drinking up the gumption to go front Liberty.

'Hell, no, Martin.'

Bad news surely.

'Let me die on my feet. So Decca passed, I expect, and...'

'Jim,' he said, '*Hold Me* is at Number Three on the British charts.'

'Martin, do not jest with me. I said don't release it until...'

'Well, cock, they *have*. Number Three. With a red bullet.'

'Mister, you ain't in any way funny. So...'

'Jim. Is there a newsagent or a chemist or a corner shop near you?'

'A what or a what or a what?'

'Oh. Forgive me. Drugstore or grocery store. Find a *Billboard*. Chop chop. I'll hold.'

I sprinted down the hill to the corner of Highland and Hollywood. Not a nickel on me. Snuck a peek.

'My God! Martin! You're entirely right!'

'Jim, I've called Jack. He's bagged a spot on the Adam Faith telly show. Get back here, cock. Quick sticks.'

Ol' Adam. Kingsize star in England right then. Davies wired the fare. But first, Liberty could keep. Tonight, I was gonna buy Hollywood a drink.

'I'll come back with you, Jim. Be your drummer.'

It's maybe the ninth club in. Gazzarri's, 9039 Sunset, WeHo. I'm waylaid by Gary Leeds. His group the Standells on the bandstand. I'm high on Jack and glory. Amenable to any proposal.

'Listen, Ruppa Pum Pum, I don't give a Hoot Gibson what you want for Christmas. You stand your own fare, I'll see you on stage in London, England, boy.'

Thought no more on it. No musicians in LA had the bread for air travel. I ran into Fowley. Ford. Diverse others. Had fun. No fistfights. No matter. Needed my face winsome come the dawn.

'I thought you was in England, boy. So that mule didn't plough then, son...'

'Al, you've not cut on me in a long time. I'm fixin' to move on, and so...'

'Jimmy. Do I look like a fool to ya? You always think I was a fool, son?'

'No, Al. I have never been of that opinion.'

Then I saw. *Oh, great God*. On his desk. *Billboard*.

'Jimmy, you must be. For here you stand as the Lord is my shepherd, a record in high cotton over in London, England. And it don't even bear the name of my beloved company.'

His voice flat now. All music gone from its tone. I tried to speak. His hand went up. *Hush*.

'Now, you go back, Jimmy, like you say. For this will serve our common purpose,' he said as he dialed a number. 'Cy? Cy, come on over heah a minute. Got that *boy* here.'

Cy Warneke ambled in. Liberty's lawyer.

'Now, here's the bit,' said Al. 'Cy and me, we're gonna fly over there to London next week.' He raised up his chin. Smiled round the Double Corona between his teeth. 'To sue you sky-high.'

'Boy,' said Cy, 'you can't go changing labels like your socks or your cottonbottoms.'

'I'm fixin' to sue Decca,' said Al. 'And sue *you* back on to Lady Liberty.'

'Y'all will be obliged to pay all court costs.' Cy.

'From what you get off this reckid.' Al. 'Me and Cy gonna check into the Mayfair Hotel. Penthouse.'

'That's up on the roof,' says Cy. Thought me a bumpkin like Elvis.

'After that, I intend, Jimmy, to take you out for steak and lobster. Then offer you the use of my suite, room service, gratis, for a week thereafter. Due reward for your service.'

'Al,' I said, 'I don't need your suite. Or your sit-down groceries. I just want out of my deal.'

They beamed at me. Like alligators. Famished ones.

'Jimmy, I don't care what if you do or don't. My hospitality, yours to use or refuse.'

The smile left his face.

'The rest of it, well. There ain't no accommodation for your druthers.'

'What the hell you want from me?'

At LAX, I am set upon. This Gary Leeds kid.

'Jim, you said I could be your drumm…'

Oh yeah. That. Boy's got a dadgum ticket. Didn't ask how he scared up the green. I should have. Would've spared me a peck of woe down the road. We climbed above the LA smog. Made for London. There for me to hatch my own surprise.

*

'Liberty Records are coming for you.'

They were being done great service with my forewarning, I said to Dick Rowe at Decca. So as they'd let this dog outta the gate, not me, I'd now like my money – all of it – due from *Hold Me*. Leeds and I were left in the boardroom, jet-bedraggled, while they conferred elsewhere.

106

'Not a problem, old boy,' they said on return. 'If you sign an indemnity.'

'Er, what's an indemnity?'

'This. Here's a pen. At the bottom.'

He slid across a blank sheet.

'We'll fill in the blanks, old fruit. Absolves us of liability if your chums get the old red mist.'

Well, great day in the mornin', Brett. Half a mill if I Hancock this here piece of paper.'

Half a mill? Rave on, Proby. But whatever the truth of it, no doubt a good round sum.

'In other words, PJ, you didn't tell us you were signed to them when we signed you. Savvy?'

I saw no impediment to their terms. That's me, Brett. The man who shot Liberty Records.

Right there. In banking bags. On the desk, in the office of the chairman, Sir Edward Lewis. Then out in the lobby, Leeds and I toting these dadgum sacks, we see Martin Davies charge in like a roadrunner on hot blacktop. For sure after that loot for himself. So we didn't even speak, or eyes meet.

'My good man,' this to the taxi driver, 'take us to a liquor stor...I mean, an off-license.'

Thence to an estate agent. To rent a house in Knightsbridge. Shirley Bassey owned a pad there. I paid a passel up front. Not free for a week yet, so we elected to take up Al's offer. Called the Mayfair each day from my flea-bit bedsit. Check if Al and Cy were still there. Two days on, they'd retreated in ragged defeat. Their Napoleon to my Moscow.

'If you are wonderful in any way, someone will fuck with you. I am here to protect you from such. And to fuck all the dirty bitches you can supply.'

At my door, if it ain't Fowley. He's flown in off what I'd said back in LA of this London diamond mine. I hired him on right there. Publicist. To get my records on the radio, and me, front page.

'How to con, bribe, blackmail and steal,' he said. 'The earth, air, wind and fire of the music business.'

So we three get jungled up in the Mayfair's penthouse. Steak and lobster dinners, champagne and the same gals Al Bennett bought himself and his winkledick lawyer. A week on, wiped out. Couldn't do a lick of work for a month.

'Viv, meet the boys. Boys, your world just got crazier.'

Viv Prince, drummer for the Pretty Things, I met at the Flamingo Club on Wardour Street. The *Flingo*. Viv was Keith Moon even before Keith Moon was Keith Moon. At my Knightsbridge pad, Fowley and Leeds took a room apiece. Viv, a sofa. That fella drank and smoked with both hands. Fowley, never either.

'My drug is bitches,' he'd say. Get his cock out. Show it to the girls. Their numbers round our doorstep rising now as my fame spread. And my infamy.

Now Gary Leeds had no money. *And* no work visa. Dadgum limpadick hadn't wrangled one. But Fowley sells Leeds to the Limey press like ol' Gary's big as Texas. All the way from LA, a star in his own right, and they buy it. But I couldn't pay Leeds for gigs without he had that permit. We'd be deported. So for his room and board, I made him my houseboy. His performance in the role was poor.

'Mr Dumbjohn! I've seen better pressed pants down on Skid *Row!* Do it again!'

My other housemate here, one James Phelge. Pal of Mick Jagger, Brian Jones and Keith Richards. Mostly chain-smoked and coughed. Viv Prince giggled a lot. Fortunate those two creeps didn't scare the girls away.

Yeah. Beset was I, by teen sugarplums. For I knew the *Beatles*.

'They all have to fuck. The only rule. No fuckee, no entry.'

Fowley's decree. Few objections from the *birds*, as the Limeys called 'em. And not only English groups came by. Boys from the music press too.

'Private Leeds,' I'd summon Gary. 'Fetch drinks at once. Move it!'

'These news boys know the Beatles too.' Fowley to the girls. 'So come on, now. Heck, they might even write you a five star review!'

'It was a time, Brett.'

Listen to yourself, Proby. It don't bear contemplation.

'I took a fancy to London's nightlife. The Flamingo went all night. Fistfights to be had, easy as two plus nothing. Or the Speak, the Speakeasy. The Cromwellian Club. The Oxford Club. Or topless bars owned by the Kray Twins. Maurice King's Starlite Club. Ronnie and Reggie hung out there. The bordellos of Piccadilly Circus. Till dawn and further.

I had caterers deliver fine comestibles, from Harrods Food Hall. Booze in mighty quantity. My secretary Pat Hayley took care of it all until Finchley, Barry Finch, walked into the picture. In love with me, poor Pat. But no match for the feast abounding.

'I cannot imagine the why of all this ado. Why, I only took time off my schedule in the States to scoot over here and buy some antiques.'

The hooey I told those UK newsmen. They still believed I was a star in the US. So they'd print all the gab that fell from my yap. My home resembled a saloon brawl. When I boogied downstairs in the PM, bodies passed out on the floor. Few or no clothes on. Booze bottles. Upturned furniture. Broken glass. Panties and bras. Charred newspapers, lampshades, curtains. This, down to Viv Prince. A dang firebug! Flames extinguished with beer or champagne spat from his mouth. If no beverage at arm's reach, peed upon.

Everybody came to Knightsbridge. All London. Christine Keeler one night. Just out of prison. Perjury. My kind of wildcat. Her bought and paid for sex romps with politicians, Russian spooks and all had by now all but brought down the British government.

Fowley, like I say, never drank, but this day had a few beers. Soon plain why he most days refrained. He got naked. Put on this negligee. Cut a hole for his dick to dangle from. Fixin' to answer the door like this, very next knock or ring.

'Welcome!'

Yessir. Christine Keeler, bestowed a faceful of Fowley's cock. She didn't get down and party naked like we hoped. But few in Swingin' London, our patch anyway, were so shy.

CHAPTER TWENTY-SEVEN

'Clear as tequila. You were fixing to gyp me over that Decca money, boy.'

Our disputes, frequent and torrid, Brett. Dadgum Martin Davies. I'd aver he got more for shows than what he told me. *Trousered* the difference, as the Limeys say. English groups just accepted this. Jellybacks. I told 'em, refuse to play until full fee forthcoming. *I* sure did.

Swindon, McElroy's Ballroom, summer of '64. Davies cancelled a show on me. Claimed the promoter wouldn't meet my fee. Well, *bullcorn*. I declared we'd make the gig anyway, death or glory. Hell, four hundred kids had paid ten shillings each! My suspicion, Davies and the promoter aimed to split the take and pay no refunds. Claim it all got et up by expenses I inflicted on them. Yeah. Showbiz, Brett. All snakes with two dadgum heads.

We arrived late. The kids, riled. At my command, the band waited in the dressing room. I busied myself autographing PJ photos. As did my staff, well practiced at it. I kept out of sight while they handed 'em out to the kids, to win their hearts and minds. I paid the band with my own checkbook.

We left by a fire exit so nobody saw us. A riot when those kids found we'd scrammed. Davies had to refund them all. The day was mine.

Being a pal to the Beatles got me into VIP clubs like the Ad Lib, where I ran up a tab of five thousand pounds per month. To maintain the pretence that I was a star Stateside, this the line Fowley continued to feed 'em. And the casinos I favoured, the Clermont Club, Golden Horseshoe, Charlie Chester's, full of royals, these English dukes of earl, and movie stars. Did me enhancement to be seen with Princess Margaret, Lord Snowdon, Peter O'Toole, Richard Harris, Richard Burton. Brett, between us all, we drank for England.

The world.

In time, I met The Rolling Stones, Kinks, Yardbirds, Animals, Hollies. Their singer Allan Clarke, he's a good boy. Them with Van Morrison, Lulu, Dusty Springfield, Cilla Black, Petula Clark. The Pretty Things, I got tight with Viv and Phil May. Moody Blues. Screaming Lord Sutch. Everydangbody.

'I'll bet y'all – all four of y'all – that *Hold Me* will not be a hit.'

But my best buds, the Beatles. This wager, the night we got sideways at the Crazy Elephant Club in Jermyn Street.

'Twenty-five pounds each,' I declared. Nigh on millionaires, these dadgum Scousers. Yet they did not disregard collecting their winnings.

My real close buddy from that quarter was Lennon. His wife Cynthia despaired. Here was trouble. One time, we're on the town with Viv Prince and Fowley. Now I cruise on the booze, but ol' John gets wrecked on the rocks. No sack for strong drink. Cyn petitioned John to head home, but he'd not entertain it.

Eight clubs down the road, Fowley hears of a party. Some swingers in Bayswater. We roll in there to see 'em rubberneckin' on this live sex action couple. Hired monkeys for their titillation.

'How about you pay *me* to fuck *you*, thou dirty wench?'

Fowley to the hostess. Can't recall if she did. In another room, some geeks eyeballing a blue movie. Great God. Those Limeys don't call it a knees-up for nothin'.

Reefer there. A joint passed to John. Coughed like he'd caught the Great Contagion. Just made the bathroom. Threw up in the tub. This, months before that famous joint with Bob Dylan. Yeah, ol' Bob. Some singer, that one. Sounds like crows on a dadgum fence.

One night it's all around the water tank at home with Viv, Fowley, Gary Leeds, Phelge.

I had a new kitten. Gift from a fan. Andrew Loog Oldham, the Stones' manager, dropped by. Graham Nash from the Hollies and Lulu there, they a couple then. Then Brian Jones shows his creepy face. After a time, I notice two things. Kitten's gone. And Brian Jones.

'Hey!' To silence the chatter. 'He's up and stolen my itty bitty kitty!'

'Then, Jim,' says Fowley, 'we must give chase.'

We caught up down the street. Sure enough, that critter in his jacket.

'Hey, Brian,' I said, 'I concur with ya, that's a pretty kitty. But it's mine.'

'You guys are such arseholes,' says Brian. 'How could you two possibly be nice to this cat?'

'Hell, boy,' I said. 'Give me my cat back. Or Fowley and I will beat the shit out of you.'

He knew of my taste for pugilism. All London did. Spared himself a face gone all Picasso.

Lennon and I, we loved pranking ol' Brian. We'd go over to where he lived. Get in through a window, steal his clothes. Leave our dirty laundry there.

'Come on you guys, bring them back.'

He'd call every time.

'Even if I could get into your filthy clothes, they don't fit. Please.'

He'd as close as get to weeping. No fun, that short dog. And not the last Rolling Stone with whom I'd rumble.

'How about it, PJ? Would you be in it?'

Jimmy Savile compered *Top Of The Pops*. Filmed in Manchester. Savile did fundraising for Stoke Mandeville Hospital here. Recruited pop stars for same.

'The press think I'm the bee's fookin' stripes.' He winked. 'And the little tarts.'

I stayed with him when I was up that way doing *TOTP* or a live show. Glad to oblige him, I'd visit the kid's wards. They used press and TV of it for their charity drives. Yet Savile's motives gave me pause...

'Yeah, but what's it *really* for?'

Savile had this trailer, or *caravan,* as these Englishmen brand it. In the hospital parking lot.

'Oh, it's joost handy, PJ. For a bunk-up if I'm tired after me volunteer porter shift here.'

Damn, that swingin' dick could tell a lie, Brett. This germsville, up to giraffe's ears in starstruck nurses, and guess where that goes from there. Savile had secrets. Some I heard said, unspeakable. But I never eyewitnessed anything I'd rate as untoward.'

Yeah, well. Proby's idea of *untoward.* A case could be mounted it ain't exactly everyone's.

'Well, aren't you the one, Tex.'

First thing Diana Dors said to me, as she ran her finger down my nose. Now Dee, she's seven long hot summers my senior. Married too. But plain she's hot for me. We became friends for life. We have a bond, Brett, like... I have never been one of the lads.'

Yeah. This the same schmo who used to wake up in the holding cells for punching on in car parks. *Righto, Proby.*

'But the bond that men have, I had with Diana. I told her of my feelings.

'Dee, I can picnic and boogie with you all the time and it feels righteous.'

She was a fading movie star. Once a Limey Marilyn Monroe. So via Dee, I met starlets. Like luscious Hayley Mills. Just eighteen. Our courtin' was brief. But many like Hayley at arm's reach now, Brett. The best of 'em.'

It was fair doin' my head in. Proby's teenage bride in LA, his getting wisty over sweet sixteens, maybe south of that. And he goes in to bat for Jimmy freakin' *Savile.* In my temple of the gods, Proby's pedestal was crumbling.

'Diana's house, Orchard Manor, Berkshire. Like Presley's, booze *verboten.* A safe bet there's still whiskey of mine stashed in that rose garden there. She hosted soirees. Well, sex parties. Couples and more upstairs. Closed circuit TV cameras on all that steamin' teamin,' shown on a screen downstairs. Cannabis abounded.'

Proby drained his beer. Regarded me as if his valet from past and better times.

A fresh beverage and be swift about it, my good man.

'Next I know, Dee's leading *me* to the boudoir. Layin' there afterhand, her husband happens along. TV actor. I fix to defend myself. But it's like he's used to it. Diana slides out of bed. Says, you boys gotta see *Doctor Zhivago,* the year's big movie. Walks out. He's got a question.

'Jim. Mind if I join you two next time?'

CHAPTER TWENTY-EIGHT

Well, Brett, I had to be shot of Martin Davies. I needed Epstein, Mr Beatles, on my team.

'Jim. A word, if I may. A business proposal.'

Fact of it, on that Beatles TV show, he'd made overture to manage me.

'Well, Mr. Epstein, although that your offer is charming, I have to decline.'

'Jim, I could do big things for y...'

'Yes sir. But you have too many acts on your books. You'd need to devote yourself to me. Like Presley with the Colonel.'

See, he had the Beatles but also Cilla Black, Gerry And The Pacemakers, Billy J. Kramer, The Big Three, Tommy this and that. And way I hear it, they're all boiled up about it. See, he expends all his vigour on Ringo and pals. The others, just Beatles support acts. I'd be but another of *them*.

But bigmost the Beatles now about to be, Stateside, just as Jack Good had forecast. Me, a hit to my name, a top star in England, and the Fab Four US-bound again. *Get on board, Jimmy.*

'Be wary of Epstein,' said Fowley. 'He'll make you his bitch before he does a thing for ya.'

'Fowley, I made ol' Brian as a fruit from the how do. He's a good boy. His predilictions of no concern to me. Pass me that dadgum phone.'

'Well, Jim, I'd like to. But Jack and Martin, I'd have to buy them out, you see.'

Dang me. Best to be had from Eppy was, if I had a second hit, he'd stick me on a tour with Cilla Black.

Still, when Davies heard of this, he got off his ass. Eve Taylor, Adam Faith's manager, had a big live show coming up. Davies called Eve. Got me on the bill. Albert Hall. I had a vision. Ol' Adam. Face down in the street as his hat rolls away in the dust.

Independence Day, July 4th, year of '64. Me, first on of eight acts. So seven foes must die. Now on TV, it had to be white shirts, black pants and shoes. No colour then. But for the stage, I turn up the heat. Velvet shirt and britches. Shoes with buckles. All in violet. That dick shade of purple.

'What am I to do *now?*'

My shirt had not made it to the Albert Hall from the tailor's. Davies was delivered a punch in the face, but that did not make it appear. My battle plan in tatteration.

'Well, then,' came this voice,' let's try something that will drive them *crazy,* darling.' Backstage, this countess. Queen's cousin or such. Pal of Dee. This lordlady says *don't despair, darling boy,* brushing her hand over my parts.

'Take off your t-shirt.'

She split the seams open. A puffy shirt effect. And a whole lotta skin. Hell, yes.

I spoke from behind the stage curtain, into my vocal mic.

'Ladies and gentlemen, I want to apologise. My manager brought my shoes.'

I had the pants on, but the legs pulled up above my knees. Stuck a shod foot out, and naked calf. Waggled it. They went loco.

'But no pants. Nor shirt. So, but for my shoes, I'm...I'm...*nekkid.*'

Stuck the other out. All they can see is my leg, unclad. They went mad as a longhorn stampede. I signalled the band to strike up *Hold Me.* Sang the intro, still concealed.

'*When you're with me I feel so romantic...*'

As the band hit the faster body of the song, I burst on. Dropped to my knees, slid across those boards, did front rolls, like to set 'em ablaze.

Nutsville. Girls wet their smalls. Or threw them at me. I picked up some. Made like to mop my brow. Brett, this was a *show*. Thirteen musicians, hired at my insistence and to Davies' alarm. The PJ Proby Orchestra. Now I'm shakin' it like jello on a plate, so the seams on that ripped-up t-shirt start to pop. I yank it off. They go berserk. *He's topless.*

Oh, and the pants hadn't been finished. No zipper. I had to hold 'em up with one hand. So here I be. Nude save these and look like about to drop *them.*

They rushed the stage like Pickett's Charge at Gettysburg. The boys, loco on jumping beans, pills. The girls, for a piece of me. The lads, to fistfight this fop stealing their poontang. Or each other, they weren't particular. I encouraged the latter practice. That's what rock 'n' roll is all about, sure as angels lay eggs.

Anyways, the police wrench me off the stage by my legs, back down a ramp, girls grabbing. My fake ponytail, torn clean off my head.

A cop threw me into this corrugated tin toilet. Stood sentry outside. Then his arm comes round the door, ponytail in his fist, to return it to me. Blood dripping off it. Before the show, Jack had weaved it into my real hair so it wouldn't come off.

Those teenies loved me more than candied catfish eyeballs. And, up to my ears in Seagram's, I felt no pain.

Bedlam. So Adam Faith, an hour late onstage. Most fans gone by then, so dull the acts after me, but that's his red wagon. I split for the Flamingo, there to get on the razzle with Georgie Fame and Chris Farlowe at one of the Flingo's all night longs.

Still out come sunup, I grabbed the morning papers. *Proby Blows Them Out At Albert Hall.* Not one drop of ink on Mr Faith. Yeah, Brett. A fightin' rooster found there a flake with white feathers jammed in his ass.

'Put me in, coach! I played against Elvis!'

Van Morrison and Them had a team. Soccer, of which I knew zero. Did more grief than good for Van's boys versus the Dave Clark Five, Herman's Hermits, the Hollies. Sent off by the ref. A *red card,* they call it. They don't brook no spear tacklin'.

'Dat dere dat Special Brew you fancy, Jum.'

Van brought it so I'd stay on the bench. Weren't nothin' to me. Meant first crack at the suds. And the birds gathered hereabouts.

'But leave some of dat dere for the rest of us, fella,' Van said.

'Leave some of which?'

'It didn't knock me out,' I said of one. 'Doesn't deserve to be a hit,' of another. A *Melody Maker* column, *Blind Date*. Pop stars reviewed new singles. Not told who they were. Play nice, the golden rule. Well, my mission was *me*, not *them*. So I poured it on 'em. None made the charts. Complaints aplenty. The artists. Record companies.

'Deadbeats.' My response. 'I've heard better singing from buzzards.'

'They go on with the show or the show don't go on. You hear me, Davies?'

He's howling, Brett. The cost of my team on the road. My orchestra. Barry Finch, my personal assistant. Spider, my hairdresser. This Manc skullbuster Terry, my bodyguard. A prizefighter. Jimmy Henny, road manager. Pat Hayley, secretary. All army, all the time.

'I need my own, Davies. These Limey comperes, take their pulse, they're all dead-thirty.'

So I deputised Fowley to stoke the kids up. We'd have the English emcee announce thus;

'Ladies and gentlemen, there is a young man from America now who wants to speak to you.'

The kids scream like mass murder at midnight. They think he means *me*. But then Fowley comes on. Fistfuls of items. Holds 'em up, one at a time.

'Who belongs to *this?*'

Waves a jockstrap in the air.

'PJ Proby, that's who!'

Then my boxer shorts. Same riff. A shoe, ditto.

'Right now PJ is backstage. And as you can *see,'* Fowley hollers, 'he's completely *naked!'*

He'd toss that stuff at 'em. They went cooglebrain and we grew prosperous.

Now, Brett, we advertised a ninety minute show. But our aim, back in London before last call at the pubs. So we whipped up frenzies. Played two numbers at best before the kids stormed the stage and the stage manager dropped the fire curtain on us. Just like we planned. Barry Finch, Finchley, in duplicate outfit to mine, plus clip-on ponytail, served as a decoy. They'd all giddyup after him down the street outside the theatre, as I slipped away unseen. Easiest money I ever squandered.

Decca wanted a new single. At sabres drawn with Liberty now, who couldn't prove in court that I'd okayed release of *Hold Me* - because I hadn't. And they couldn't sue Decca, as I'd signed that indemnity.

So Decca gave me *Together,* by three of their inhouse writers. We cut at IBC. Big Jim Sullivan, Jimmy Page, John Paul Jones. Ginger Baker played drums and drank all my Chivas. Made Number Eight in the UK. Top Ten. Beatle Country. That same week, those four dadgum bowlcuts had the *top five singles*. I had to get Epstein drivin' my train.

'Good lord! Well, just how much *do* they have, Jim?'

Decca panicked that Liberty might put out PJ Proby records when I told 'em. All those old Jett Powers cuts in their strongbox. So we got busy on a long player. IBC again. Same band, but for Bobby Graham, finest first call sessioneer in London, on the drums mostpart.

'Fellas, let's make their hair turn white.'

Time to wake up the world. A number wholesome, now seasoned up like to make the devil dance to it. *Que Sera Sera* by Doris Day, fetched the feel of *Twist And Shout*. Did *Rockin' Pneumonia And The Boogie Woogie Flu*, Huey Smith And The Clowns. *I'll Go Crazy* by James Brown. For *The Glory Of Love,* the Velvetones, the doo wop take. And that Jimmy Dorsey weepie, *The Masquerade Is Over*. We stuck horns and a tail on that one too.

'They've *what?*'

Liberty had some judge injunct my new LP, *I Am PJ Proby*. Decca couldn't put it out. And they rush-released their *own* dadgum PJ Proby single, *Try To Forget Her,* a Jett Powers number, cut back in '61. It killed *Together* in the US, dead as a hill of bones.

Then this Limey beak rules that we must surrender *I Am PJ Proby* to Liberty. Made me sign a new deal with them, in cahoots with EMI. Decca, cut loose. But I, now slave and prisoner.

'You're all gurgle and no guts, boy. You're *through.*'

See, Jack Good was back in the US now with his new show, *Shindig.* No Jack around, with all the swing he had, so Martin Davies of no use to me. A thief with it.

Diana Dors put me in a room with one John Heyman of International Artists. Big time operator. Could swing me one night stands at the best joints, top star on theatre tours. Break me in Europe. And get me into movies. See, he was also a film producer. Screen stars on his books. Peter O'Toole, Liz Taylor, Richard Burton, Oliver Reed. Right where this Texas ranger longed to be. Bunny Lewis from Heyman's outfit handled my bookings. Started out great.

We all did *Juke Box Jury* on the BBC. Me, October of '64. Panel show. The mission, lend an ear to new releases. Predict if they'd be hits.

'Well, Jim, they said we must listen blind, so...'

The comedian Peter Cook and I drank that Green Room dry. The other two panellists this day, Julie Rogers had a hit right then with *The Wedding.* Judith Chalmers, from this fuddy-dudd BBC show *Come Dancing.* They played nice, but ol' Cooky, well,...

'Well, it sounds rather trite. Dreary. Lifeless. I can only draw one conclusion.'

'What's that, Peter?' asked compere David Jacobs.

'It will be a massive hit.'

Other selections fared little better.

'What we're listening to here is a crime.'

'What crime would that be, Peter?'

'Murder.'

Heyman and Lewis set me up headliners. Hammersmith Palais. London Palladium.

The A League ballrooms. Odeons, ABC theatres, Top Rank. Ritz Cinemas. Owned by the Grades and the Delfonts. Biggest shakers in the game. The bill, me and five no-count supports.

And they scored me Prince Charles' sixteenth birthday party at Buckingham Palace that November. Sounds Incorporated opened. Then Peter And Gordon. They had a monster hit UK and Stateside right then. *World Without Love.* Beatles wrote it for 'em. I took to thinkin' my *hermano* John might oblige me likewise.

Had to line up at the end so these royals could glide by. Prince Phillip said I sounded like a *jungle bunny.*

'Why, thank you, Your Highness.'

My response, as instructed.

'I was worried you might spear us and cook us in a pot. Carry on.'

New Years' Eve nineteen and sixty four, I headlined on this BBC2 pop show, *Beat Room.* Graham Bond Organisation backed me. Jack Bruce, bass. Ginger Baker, drums. Three saxes. The same in trumpets and trombones. All England looked upon it and called it fab. Happy New Year. And it was. For a brief piece of time.

CHAPTER TWENTY-NINE

It woke me. Downstairs. Gary Leeds. Cryin' on the phone that he wanted to go home. That he had no money and I'd not stand his fare. Hell, Brett, *he'd* imposed himself upon *me*.

And no good on the drums. I'd had to get in one of EMI's first call guys, Clem Cattini, for gigs. Stuck ol' Gary on the tambourine. Yet I'd kept him on. That piddlee'o never thanked me for it. And now *this*.

'Mother,' I hear from my hidden vantage at the top of the stairs. 'Proby is a debauched *pervert. Sex maniac*. Depraved *orgies* every *night*.'

He paints this motion picture starring Fowley and me, but not *him*. To his parents in Hollywood. Now they'll go tell all LA like it's Bible-sworn true.'

Yeah, OK, Proby. No shock that the Texan has his own wonky take on the truth.

'Fowley and Leeds did the tomcattin', Brett. I was out with Lennon or Diana Dors or Princess Margaret, the quality. I come home, find some English group in one corner down and dirty with some birds, Fowley getting his rocks off in another. Leeds, what he could salvage around the perimeter.'

Yeah, sure. But grounds to be snitchy, it became clear.

'I waited for him on the staircase. Near soiled his jammies when he encountered me there.

'Gary,' I said, 'I don't want to punch you out. Just tell me. Why'd you say all that?'

'W-well, I had to, J-jim. Or they w-won't send the money.'

'OK. I can understand that,' I said. 'OK, chickenshit.'

Well. He was gone two days on. You don't want to know what he did, Brett.'

'I'm game, Proby. Rave on, my man.'

'An act of treason. I retired that night. But *he* stayed up all the way to grey dawn. Rifled my contact book. Wrote it all down. Names, phone numbers. The big agents. TV producers. Managers. And he'd kept all these clippings. Stories on me, pictures, with him in them. Back in LA, he told his stepdaddy he was a star in England. Showed him those, to make it look true. See, Brett, ol' *step*daddy is Rockefeller-rich.

Now Scott and John, the Walker Brothers, they're still just playing clubs on the Strip then. So Gary says he'll ship 'em over to England, on his dime – if they fire their drummer, Tiny, so *he* can join. And ol' stepdaddy calls up Gary's contacts. *My* contacts. Guarantees that if the Walkers lose money on a show, he'll reimburse it in full.'

Yeah, well. Granted, a low act. Not that ethics ever troubled no-one in this game. And Proby fair came across as a mug in a lot of his dealings. In this case, he reckoned Gary Leeds had planned it from the off, back in LA. A Trojan Horse move. I dunno. I'd say he just saw an easy in and went for it. Not many as wouldn't. Sad but true.

'So next I know, Brett, the Walkers hit Limeytown. Get big, fast. Their show, identical to *mine*. This could not stand. I'd have them see that they monkeyed with Proby at their peril.'

'Well, ain't no party where I hail from if no damage is sustained,' I said when the press pulled me up. Shirley Bassey's pad, trashed to smash. We, betrayed by neighbours.

'I plan to buy a houseboat. Big as that Queen Mary ocean liner. Line it with mattresses,' my line when the press wrote up the eviction. 'Y'all see where I'm *goin'* here?'

I found me a place in Chelsea. Now Finchley, my gofer and stand-in, was a trained chef. So now I make him my cook. Bedrooms all taken, so I had the coal cellar cleared and cleaned for his quarters. I was heading out on tour the day he moved in. Just finished my customary evening meal. Steak with eggs and potatoes.

'Finchley,' I said, 'feed this same to my dogs while I'm away. And to me on my return.'

There were press and TV stories about the Chelsea place. My new daisy Sarah Leyton by my side for a photo shoot. Nursing an antique musket I'd bought on the Portobello Road. A symbol of true manhood. Even more so when she held it like another kind of gun.

'We need fear no intruder with you on deck. Welcome, trooper.'

Made flesh, my pledge to Bongo Wolf. To show him the world, for his kindnesses to me. Flown in, my privilege to pay. And about this time I met Donovan, that singer from Scotland. Busted flat, so I let him lodge with us. Some nights, ol' Bongo slumbered on a pallet at the foot of my bed. A shogun's loyal retainer.

Open house was Chelsea, Brett. Ample free booze. Party ice in buckets silver and gold. They all came. Dave Davies of the Kinks. Lennon, Ringo, The Searchers, Yardbirds. Dusty, Cilla. Eric Burdon, the Animals. Wayne Fontana and the Mindbenders. Wayne and I, we got tight. Stayed so for many years. Screaming Lord Sutch. That madass Keith Moon. Wall to wall dolly birds. Models. The Shrimpton sisters, Jean and Chrissie. Patti Boyd. Twiggy, Penelope Tree. Short skirts. High hair. And I, Proby, their host and king.

We were all hot for Marianne Faithfull. One night she swishes into the Ad Lib. Proposes marriage to Fowley. In front of me, Lord Snowdon, Ringo and Bongo. She'd been steppin' out with Pitney. But Gene, in town playin' the Finsbury Park Astoria, told me she was a needy pain in the ass. A fraction unkind. Heck, there were claims that Marianne had evaluated ol' Pitney the best lay she'd ever had.

'Never seen a thing that wild in my life, and I come from Hollywood.'

Fowley's take on Anna the Potato Girl. Maurice King managed Van Morrison, Shirley Bassey, those dadgum Walker Brothers. His chauffeur brought this Anna to Chelsea. Next anyone knows, Fowley's in the kitchen boiling up spuds.

'Come on, cocks and bitches! Gather round!'

She gets naked, lies on the rug. He packs taters into her ladyhood. She gets louder the more he loads. Then has this climax. They start to pop out. Everybody screaming. Fowley catches one in his mouth. She came back, time and again, to do her thing.

Now ol' Finchley, he'd rolled into London from Canada, ragged, not a penny. Learned to hustle, fast. I'd noted his after midnight skills. I took to out louding it that I fancied this or that. Found that it would be there at Chelsea next morning.

'Will that be all, sir?'

It got so that after he'd cleared my dinner, we'd take spins round town in my Rolls Royce. I'd spy things in store windows or clubs or on people. Make known my desires. Jewellery, moose heads for mounting. No prize, it seemed, beyond his acumen.

'I behold there, Finchley, an ideal Christmas gift for all my pals.'

On the Kings Road, this tiger's eye ring on some stud's pinky. 'Tween midnight and dawn, two dozen found their way to me. One artful dodger.

'You are exonerated, Finchley. I'd have done no other.'

His only mission failure.

'You see, Jim,' he said, 'I had these polar bear skins. I'm leaving the premises when this truck comes along. Headlights about to swing my way. So I stash them in a dumpster, conceal myself. Thing is, it's a garbage truck.'

He shook his head in self-admonition.

'The dumpster's contents, loaded aboard. One of those trucks that grinds it all up.'

Finchley did it all. Taxis home for guests. Kept an appointments book for all at Chelsea. Gave us reminders each day. Of course, he reaped the benefits of association with me. He's up close and personal with all those groups and singers, managers. So he prospered when he set up his business, The Fool. First call guy for record cover design, poster art, stage threads. Even to psychedelic paint jobs for the Beatles, on their dadgum cars.'

'We come for debutantes to fuck and free food!'

Fowley announcing us. He, I, Bongo and Viv Prince, he not welcome albeit it was his bandmate's shindig, hit the engagement party for Phil May of the Pretty Things.

Oh good God, I said. For here before me, Judy Garland. Can't stay on her feet. So *tiny.* People laughing. Cruel jibes.

'Whoa!' I said. 'Next one disrespects this woman will answer to me. *Outside.* Why, she is an American icon, you Limey simpletons!'

I stooped down. Offered Judy my arm.

'Kim Fowley and I will now escort you, ma'am,' I said, 'to wherever you want to go.'

'I want a fuckin' *drink!'* says Judy. 'I want the *Ad Lib!'*

A most enchanted evening.

CHAPTER THIRTY

'Like the Beatles, Jim. Each new single differs in some way.'

Heyman had a point. *Hold Me* and *Together* both all cherry red thunder. But his pitch now, a gag, surely.

'Forget it, John. Johnny Mathis, Matt Monroe, Streisand, all took a pass at it. They had to call for screens and the shotgun.'

'Yes, Jim. They sang it too straight. Too much reverence.'

'Needs the Proby treatment, old son,' said Bunny.

I had my road manager Jimmy Henny go buy those very records. Then I holed up in a hotel room for a week. The Dorchester, to evade the distractions of Chelsea. Played them over and over on a portable player. In time, it came to me. These warblers are singing *Somewhere* all wrong. This, a song of the Upper West Side. Blue collar hard. Yet they sound like they're yukkin' it up in the dadgum Polo Lounge with Zsa Zsa Gabor.

'No way we can cram all that noise into that bitty basement.'

I meant Studio A at Abbey Road. EMI owned the English portion of my hide and my soul now, so I must record there. For *Somewhere,* a full orchestra. And choir. So, then. The big room. Upstairs. Studio B. Where the Beatles did their thing.

This, just as Jack Good and compere Jimmy O'Neill hit London to pre-tape a 'British Invasion' ep of *Shindig.* Jimmy, Shari Sheeley's husband three years now, since 'bout a year after Eddie went. Shari, a producer on *Shindig* now. All in the family, Brett. Including Cousin Proby. For a stretch, leastways.

'This will break ya Stateside, Jimmy,' said Shari.

For *Shindig*, fine company. Top of the show bill, The Beatles, with *Kansas City, I'm A Loser* and *Boys*, from their new long player, *Beatles For Sale*. I did *Hold Me* and *You'll Never Walk Alone*. Jack and Shari sold me on *Shindig* as Buddy One to the Fab Four and *the* US counter attack to this consarned British Invasion.

Sandie Shaw on this as well. A Number One smash in England then. *Always Something There To Remind Me.* Her gimmick, she sang barefoot. The rest, Adam Faith, Karl Denver and that chump Tommy Quickly. Ol' Tommy, managed by Epstein. Only reason that yapdog made the cut. *His* gimmick, a toy dog he talked to between songs. Gone as the gold rush a year on.

I whupped 'em all. Yet they chose *Adam Faith* for the next *Shindig* shoot back in LA.

'My God, my God, Jack. Why has thou forsaken me?'

'Adam is British, dear boy,' he said. 'Catch the wave of the British invasion, say the wonderful people at ABC Television. And if we do, the wonderful people at ABC Television will give me more money for more *Shindigs*. Your turn will come. Keep calm and carry on.'

Well, the others served up sunshine and lollipops. Me, a fireball storm. I gave the Beatles the news after the taping. *You're through*. Smiled as I said it. That *Shindig* ep screened in October. Jack called from LA. I'd turned heads, coast to coast. We fell to plotting. *Conquest*.

We put *Somewhere* out in December. Radio played it clean through to the B side. My stylings here, from Della Reese. You ain't heard Della, Brett, you ain't heard singing.'

A rare admission from the Proby. Minutes later he's rippin' into insert name here, take your pick, for stealing *his* act. So passed my days in *las cantinas* of Surry Hills and Redfern.

*

132

'I was asked by Robert Stigwood to headline a tour.'

'Oh, yeah,' I said. 'Managed Cream, the Bee Gees and whatnot.'

'The very same, Brett. Main support on this carnival train, the Pretty Things. Twenty-four dates. Now I had to sign the contract at ol' Stiggy's suite at the Mayfair. Yeah, *adelante,* said the spider to the fly. He's a chickenhawk if you take my meaning.

I'm out on the town all night, so I head there directly from shootin' out the lights. They find me face down in the lobby bathroom, adjourned therewith for restorative repose.

So Stigwood, denied his boymeat, tells the press I'd overdosed on drugs. A foul calumny, to get a story up the front end of the papers, of Chuck Berry, now booked in my place. But then he tried some carny move over Chuck's money. A grave mistake. Ol' Stiggy had to cancel the whole swing. Never got to steal from me. Nor shoot his gravy.

Now *Somewhere* shifted 250,000 copies in but nine days. Number Six on the British charts. Then those dang Beatles put out *I Feel Fine.* My quest again rendered elusive dream.

CHAPTER THIRTY-ONE

'I own a house in Sydney, Brett.'

I didn't have the heart to break it to him. On one of his tours, he reckons. Told he'd earned too much. That he'd have to pay it all in tax. Unless...*this old showie saw Proby coming a week before he got here.*

'We'll buy you a piece of property, he told me, boys.'

'Hang on, Proby.' Clyde. 'What, *you* own a house? *Where?'*

'Not far over the Harbour Bridge, I recall.'

Oh fuck. We chuck names at him. *Milson's Point? North Sydney? Crow's Nes...*

'Crow's Nest. That's *it!'*

'What, he showed it to you, did he?'

Ice hangs off Clyde's every word.

'Proby,' I jump in, 'a lot's changed since you were last here, my ma...'

'Drive me over that bridge,' he says. 'I will find that house.'

'Hey, Proby,' says Clyde. 'Want to buy the bridge while we're at it?'

Four lanes rise up on the Coathanger.

'Which exit, Proby?'

'Oh, it's round here someplace. Yep.' Sips a stubby. 'This is the right bridge.'

So. Up the Pacific Highway to Crow's Nest. Drive around. Let him cop a butcher's at all these joints that no-one bought for no-one. Took him a while.

'It's all changed.'

'Yeah. Thought that might be the case, Proby.'

I turned the Kingswood around.

'I own it! The guy brought me here! Told me, *it's yours!'*

'Jim,' I said, 'we could try the Land and Titles Office. But...what name would it be in, you reckon? *Smith?*'

'Well,' he says, *fuck, he's diggin' in,* 'I'd know it if I saw it.'

'Jim,' says Clyde. 'It could've had five owners since then.'

Proby ponders this for a flicker.

'Can you get me on *Neighbours?*'

*

He was up from Melbourne. As ever, best not ask. Fronted in his maroon Buick at the Hoey. A serious American car freak. CV can't be beat. Band of Light, Blackfeather, Rose Tattoo, X, Hell To Pay, Sardine V. On guitar, bass, or munted front and centre, Ian Rilen.

'Buicks are the black man's Cadillac, mate.'

Meant as a compliment, as in more funk and groove than a Caddy. A somewhat more respectful version of Proby's take on the make. It was Buicks got 'em talking.

My guess, Rilo's here about *Bad Boy For Love.* Wrote the Tatts' breakout single back in '78. A top lurk. On hits and memories radio for eternity. So record companies forever offering Rilo new publishing deals. *Write more like that and make us rich.* When one ran out, he'd hit another mob. Jawbone himself a new advance. Now, after a time, even these numbskulls notice the total lack of new songs, and all bets are off. A scam with limited repeat plays, but he got more out of them than they did him. In this biz, an all too rare result. Rilen and Proby got on like a canefield on fire.

'Oh yeah', says Rilo.' I know some of your stuff.' Close as he gets to a compliment. They got into it deep and wide. Grifts they'd pulled. Mayhem wreaked. *And Brett the minder here off the hook. First time in weeks.*

'A breather, eh, Clyde? Just let 'em go, eh?'

Sometime later, Rilen comes shuffling over from Proby's table.

'I'm here for a few days, mate,' he says.' Jim's not doin' nothin' tomorrow. You get him to yours, I'll pick him up from there.'

Rilen and Proby. Unsupervised. Code Red.

'What's the plan, Rilo?'

'Oh, well. Turns out he loves golf,' he says. 'And I love golf too.'

I just burst out laughing.

'Listen, bwana,' I said. 'Proby won't walk to the *Dolphin* from *here*. Feet are shot ducks. How's he gonna go on a golf cours...'

'Oh, nah, different, mate. Different. He'll play golf. It'll be tops.'

A day off for Brettski. Go on. You know you want to...

'Well, alright, Rilo,' says Clyde. 'Line it up.'

'Here's your six pack for the drive, Jim,' as a horn toots in the street.

'Oh,' says Rilen. 'Travellers. Most impressive. Jump in the Buick, Mr Proby.'

Around noon, Clyde suggests a feed up the Dolphin. No Proby. Grouse.

'What happened to golf?'

Rilen and Proby. Clyde had ponied up for 'green fees' or some line Rilen had sold him. And here they be. Yakkin' fit to bust over the surf 'n' turf and copious beers. Rilen shrugs.

'Had to drive him here.' Points his fork at him and cackles. 'He don't like to walk.'

CHAPTER THIRTY-TWO

'Come the first moons of '65, EMI released *I Am PJ Proby*. But Liberty, they put out a whole other LP, *Somewhere*. With the EMI singles *Hold Me* and *Together* plus some cuts from *I Am* and a few old Jett Powers tracks. A junkyard dog's breakfast, I declare. See, Liberty kept back a chunk of *I Am* for future singles, EPs, albums of their own design. Those carpetbaggers released every track three ways, three times. But artists were only paid the once, if that. Dadgum cribbers. Now I contend that *I Am PJ Proby* is a fine piece of work, Brett,...'

'As do I, Proby,' I said. And meant it. Even after weeks as dogsbody to this mutt.

'...but EMI did scant promo for it. Put it out in *January*, dagnab it. TV shows in recess. Their intent, clear. Fetching me a whippin' for what Decca done did. Liberty, likewise.

Live shows that January helped sales some. I headlined over The Who. The New Theatre in Oxford. Those birdbrains mashed up their guitar, kicked over the drums. But I came out in front. See, they weren't stars yet, Brett. No singles out. And ugly. But that Keith Moon. All the way cattywampus, that boy. And a thirst for that red popskull abreast of my own.

'Well, I have just the remedy,' I said to Heyman and Lewis.

The American press had grown unkind. Called me traitor, based as I be in England. And said I dressed like a dandy out of Dickens. Implying all that goes with that. So we planted stories of our own with Reuters, AAP, UPI. Went a little like this.

'*Somewhere* is PJ Proby's swan song to the UK. In talks with Hollywood now, he assures his many fans Stateside he is a loyal citizen of the US and sorely misses his homeland.'

No such talks, nor US fans in such multitude. But this would *create* both.

'Hell, John,' to Heyman, 'this'll fool Warners or Fox or Paramount that one of them's wavin' a deal my way. They'll come running with contract and fountain pen.'

And in fact, Heyman had made noise to this end with his contacts there.

'We gotta lay it on thick as a tomahawk steak,' I said. 'Kill this talk of high treason and tutti frutti tendency.'

'When not out entertaining folks,' went my dictation to Pat Hawley, 'you'll find Proby at home, with Marmaduke his cat, Genius, his dog – and a blonde.'

And then this, Brett.

'My last UK tour is upon me. I'm comin' home, America. This is England's last chance ever to see me.'

Not exactly the whole and nothin' but of it. But *England's last chance* got 'em good. Such sport to watch those Limey promoters rassle over me.

Well, now. Best offer in that regard, Epstein called. The deal, co-billing top star with Cilla Black. Twenty-two cities. February '65. Supports, Eppy's loser acts. The Fourmost, Tommy Quickly. And ol' Tommy Roe from Atlanta, Georgia. Cilla headlining. My slot, close the first half. Well, Cilla. I'd have our positions reversed were it mine to make it so. So war it must be.

'You heard me. Twelve suits of it.'

'Velvet you want.'

This tailor, Brett. Gives me a face like I'd asked for marital aids.

'Yes. From these bolts here. All the shades of the rainbow. Plus this hot pink.'

In Paris to play the Olympia Theatre, I'd bought this special velour Jimmy Henny had told me about. I also ordered buckled shoes. Twelve pair. Each a colour to match a suit. To top it all, a cape. Made from a Lone Star flag of Texas. Cilla was a goner.

Mine, a high energy show. Knee slides, high kicks, backflips. First gig, Friday twenty-nine January, I still recall. Castle Hall Theatre, Croydon. How it got started, my pants ripped a little. Just across the knees. Then I danced it up some more. Crowd, gone in delirium at what came now, rippity doodah, inside leg, from thigh to crotch. Tatters. Poor tailoring, Brett. Delicate material.'

Oh, break it down, Proby. Still, a canny move. Headlines guaranteed.

'Whatever it takes, my man,' I said. 'I get it. It's just showbiz.'

'It was an accident, damn it,' he says. Tetchy. Best let it go. *Yeah. Accident my arse.*

'So I'm Page One with photo. On my back, singin' up a tempest, britches in shreds. Tour sells out off it. But now the thunder. Mary Whitehouse and her Morals Committee call me 'insane moral degenerate' in the *Daily Mirror*. For this too sold papers. Yeah, Brett. Fleet Street! I sold so many for 'em, they should've cut me in on the action.'

'So what then?'

'Show must go on, my friend. Next night, Walthamstow Granada theatre. And I'll be. Two songs in. Pink velvet pants fall down. Button on the zipper popped. Happenstance.'

Yeah, sure. I mean, I get why he did it. But maddies like Whitehouse don't go into a blue to lose it, and the press always back a play like hers. Still, I don't say nothing. Proby's not a big listener.

'Fowley ran on. Wrapped my cape round me, just like Danny Ray, James Brown's emcee. To cover the torn-up britches. Yeah, Brett. That's the part the papers never told.'

A revelation to me. But I know what came next. The fire this time.

'Soiled their bloomers at first crack of musket,' says Proby. 'These wimpass theatre owners go the Watusi on me. And Heyman wants a public display, chastisement from him, contrition from me. So I stroll in there, shot of Chivas in my hand, bottle in the crook of my arm.

'Lunch is on me, John.'

Well, he declined my invitation to a sippin'. Served me a shot of rebuke, but I knew he was right pleased deep down. See, he'd booked my own tour to follow this here Cilla swing. The *PJ Proby Motor Show*. This too, had sold out now. So I gave the press my pledge.

'It won't occur again,' I told 'em. 'I will inform my pants of this in no uncertain manner.'

Next show, Wolverhampton. Police, press, in swarms. My baby blue velvet pants elected to stay together that night. They were thanked onstage for this.

Then at the Ritz Cinema in Luton, well, Brett, I guess red velvet must be a less robust fabric than the blue. Ripville, ass to ankles. Fowley sprints on with my cape. They dropped the stage curtain. Hauled me off. Midst backstage bedlam, the police arrested me. The charge, indecency. But couldn't make it stick. Had to cut me loose. Then came a message from the stage manager, hollered in my ear. Just four words I can't ever forget. These I met with rapid fire response.

'They're coming to see me, not Cilla!'

Reporters here had overheard it. *You're off the tour.* So I swerved their way. Set to kickin' up the sand, down to the dinosaur bones.

'They hold up big home-made posters of me, my name on and blood red hearts, while the other acts are on! Toss their elastics at me. Puddle in their *seats!*'

Then Epstein's assistant Alistair Taylor said Brian wanted to see me.

*

'Mr Epstein. In no way was there deliberation prior to...'

We're in his Rolls Royce. Out back of the theatre.

'Jim, I'm afraid it's out of my hands. The theatre owners have banned you.'

'Say *what?*

How could they already know what had just now gone down? Foul play afoot, sure as heck and damn.

'Well, you best fix that, Brian. Because I want to tour with the Beatles.'

'Well, given the state of play...perhaps some bright day to come. But right now...'

As he spoke, he placed his hand on my naked thigh, exposed by the rippin'. *Whoa.* A good swing behind my punch. Left him there, out cold. Had some drinkin' to do.

Like the man sang, the news was out all over town. Lead story. Radio, TV news, Fleet Street. My bein' bounced off the Cilla show, that is, not the state of Epstein's face. He'd not want *that* public. What he did, illegal back then. He'd pull hard time. Anyway, all this noise fuelled fevered demand from the TV pop shows. PJ Ratings, that's me.

So I'm about to go on *TOTP*. In the Green Room, in walks some old fussock. Shabby overcoat and pants. Dirty tennis shoes. Cussin' and rausing me. All manner of epithets. Well, he stopped soon enough. As well he might, he now smacked to the dirt. I necked my drink. Went on and mimed to *Somewhere*.

'Jim. Jim. What have you done, you daft bugger?'

'Why, Bunny, I have no idea.'

'Jim, you knocked out Billy *Cotton*.'

'That croaksack in the Green Room? Ain't he the janitor? Looked that way, goin' by his wardrobe.'

'Jim. The *Billy Cotton Band Show* is part of the BBC furniture. Since 1949.'

Something gripped my guts but I stood my ground.

'Well, he's long about dead going by looks. So what does it matt...'

'Billy Cotton Junior might disagree.'

'Who?'

'His son. The director of BBC Light Entertainment.'

'*Oh*. Well, so fix it, Bunny. How do we fix it?'

'Bit late for that, Jim.'

He pushed the telegram across to me.

'Banned from the Beeb, sunshine.'

'Oh, Bunny. They do that all the time in the States. How long for?'

'In Junior's own words?'

'Why, yes, so's we can plan ahead to…'

'Eternity.'

Well, Brett. By nightfall, I'm banned from every damn thing. The big theatre chains, TV shows, radio airplay. Politicians join this hangin' posse, to get their bulldog yaps on the news. Heck, a goodly sum of them, child molesters and partial to sex fetish games, I'd aver. And Whitehouse had dirt on 'em all. She'd let it loose if they didn't back her play. Also, the target, me, American. Way ol' Mary Witches' Britches styled it, I'm filching work from wholesome British entertainers. And the squares bought it.

*

'Jim, best do nothing at all.'

He had his reasons. Heyman had other clients, his Limey movie stars. And Whitehouse and her broom-riders had stuff on *them* as well. But that was *their* oil rig afire.

'The hell with that!'

My staff were put to work. Terry, Finchley, Spider, Jimmy, Sarah, Pat, Bongo. I had 'em write the papers. Fake names. Pleading my vindication.

'Then call the radio shows and do likewise!'

These, moves that politicians pulled every dadgum day. Some lord or viscount or something told me about it at the Ad Lib one time. Next, I called some heavy friends.

'This Proby business is terrible.'

John Lennon railed at the press.

'TV shouldn't have the power to rule a bloke like that. It's up to the public. And I don't believe they want him banned.'

And Dusty Springfield said what I did was not beyond any bounds of decency. She was castigated for it. Lennon, too. Once the killin' starts... But here's the thing of it. Wasn't my britches got me put off that tour, Brett.'

'How's that, Proby?'

'It was that ghost-faced bat, Tom Jones.'

'Eh? What about him?'

'His new single came out just before this. On *Decca*. *My* old label.'

'*It's Not Unusual.*'

'The very same. Now ol' Tom's in a fix. Got no big live shows to shake his ass and sell some records. Then Decca and Tom's manager Gordon Mills see Whitehouse foaming and bubbling about me. Thirty pieces of silver later, ol' Tom's in my spot.'

A *buy-on*. Classic rort. Proby not first or last to be bumped from a bill for a fistful of shrapnel slung to the promoters. But try telling *him* that.

'Only one thing for it, my friend.'

'Tom Jones is an impostor and a thief of ideas!'

Next stop on that tour, Bristol. First night with ol' Tom in my place. Out front of the theatre, up on the roof of my Rolls Royce, I testify. Set the kids a-hollerin'.

'*PJ! PJ! PJ!*'

We're going good. Cops arrive. Then my chauffeur James goes all flopdick on me.

'I want nothing to do with this,' he says. 'I'm leaving this minute for London.'

Me in harm's way. And this meatball vamoosed! I hotfoot it. Chased by girls, by the press. Didn't faze me a hair. The face on Page One next day sure ain't Tom Jones.

'Fuck! Know what this means, Jim?'

Bunny served me a whomping. Consequent to theatre bans, the only gigs we can get now are these workingmen's clubs. They feature liquor and one-armed bandits, gaming tables. So the kids, teens, *no pasaran*. These joints off limits to my whole dang fan base.

'What that means, Bunny, is we got to make a *noise.*'

'Jim, please. No more of this cobblers if you...'

I know not what he said next. For I hung up on him.

*

'Get to it, y'all.'

I ordered a thousand poster size photos of me. Had my staff sign every one, *PJ Proby*. At Cilla shows, as I hot-gospelled it out front, they gave 'em out. Inside, just as we told 'em to, the kids all held 'em up when Tom Jones came on. All he could see, these bigass PJ Probys. My fans, bless 'em every one, all screamin' *PJ! PJ! PJ!* All through his half-dead act.'

'Outlaw status duly conferred, my man,' I said when Proby stopped long enough for me to respond. But there's no tellin' him that on the losing end of biff like this, a smarty plays possum. It's a filthy game. Crook as the dishlickers. If you've got it up here, you make with the *mea culpa*, don't matter how unfair, then drop your brainbox out of sniper range till the goblin swarm simmers down, gets bored and peels off to find some other butterflies to burn. But Proby, well... the war rolled on.

'I still had friends in high places. I let Fleet Street know all about it. Just after I was run off that tour, the Beatles had me to their show at Hammersmith O. This night, I near started a riot myself. I'm spotted by fans. They mobbed my car. *PJ! PJ!* My driver somehow got us out of there.'

Yeah, well. Accidentally on purpose, says the inside running, but I kept my beer hole shut. For a quiet life.

'The walkin' wet bar is here!'

Four crates of beer I brung, Brett. Girls backstage, selected by Beatles road managers Neil and Mal. Supports this night, the Yardbirds, Sounds

Incorporated. Compere, Jimmy Savile. Hell, that dog liked 'em young. Befriended the Fabs for just such purpose. '

I don't want to hear it, Proby, I almost but didn't quite say.

'We made for Chelsea, with any girls who had the sand to tag along. After that, The Speak, the Flingo, the Ad Lib. Club crawl.

The Ad Lib was owned by Alma Cogan's boyfriend. But he's not her one and only. Alma's a singing star from the nineteen and fifties. Got eight years on Lennon. And he's married.

I warned him of trouble ahead. For Marianne, my lost bride, had filed for divorce, bein't I'm rich like J Paul Getty now, or so she surmised. I had to lawyer up to set her hat on straight about that...'

'Well, maybe you saw her first, Jim, but I fucked her first.'

He just had to whoop about it. My beloved, Sarah. Of this pond not his to fish, Fowley broadcast loud and wide.

'What you gonna do about it, Tex?'

He used to blow it out his hole how he'd been a street dog in a gang back in downtown LA, but he didn't go so good as a single. I sat him on his ass first punch and all that followed it. Duly fustigated, he amscrayed back to the USA.

Now, Sarah was a model. John Leyton's sister. He, a pop singer. We'd met on *Ready Steady Go*. I had her do pics for the papers with me all the time. Help her along. If that didn't snag her a mess of catwalk jobs, I'll eat my boots.

I go for drinks. Proby babbling at Clyde the whole time I'm gone.

'...so we just never stopped, Clyde,'as I returned, 'with these press releases. One week, of my doctors. Concerns I'd never sing again. Hinted at cancer. Or news of my new car or boat or hound. It *sells*. And on that subject, I forget who dreamed up PJ Proby Poppers. Why, they weren't but skipping rope handles. Tassels on 'em. Gold *PJP* monogram on the handles. Kids held 'em in their hands, shook 'em as they danced. The boodle we made off of those gizmos.

'I drive all those British pounds of yours to the bank every day in my Rolls Royce,' I told the press. 'This keeps up, I'll need two more of those flying lady buggies to fit it all.'

CHAPTER THIRTY-THREE

'Well, the Delfonts and Grades own all *their* venues, Jim. But not these.'

Promoters Joe Collins and Mervyn Conn had this brainwave. The *PJ Proby Motor Show* tour had its ass canned by the theatres ban. To thwart that, Brett, these fellas lined up a passel of town halls. Called it *The PJ Show.*'

But this tour don't go so good, Proby reveals now. The press orders punters to boycott. Parents won't let kids go. Proby chucks a wobbly at the promoters like that's *their* doing. Washup, this pair of chancers declare they'll never work with him again. *And now I know why.*

'Now, says Bunny, some charity gigs I must do, Brett. To show I'm not the depraved scapegrace they claim. Empire Pool Wembley, March, for disabled kids. With Adam Faith, Them, Pretty Things, Lulu. Headliners, Billy J Kramer and the Dakotas. I said *I* should be. Hell, it's all me in the news, not Billy J Nobody. But Epstein managed them and they're big at that time. For three New York minutes.

Meanwhile, in matters of *el corazon*, it's gone from hot as *habanero* chilis to cold as a blue northern. Sarah fled Chelsea after we quarrelled. But now she sails back on a river of tears. Fool that I am, Brett, I welcomed this prodigal. But I grew to suspect ulterior motive.'

This Proby. He don't have a clue that he don't have a clue.

'So I said, marriage, a no go. Lest she get to gold-diggin' like Wife One, the part I left unspoke. In response, she railed at my frisky ways, so I told her to take it on down the road this time, unto the Day of Judgment. So, then. This was the genesis of my Nymphet Clubs.'

'Nymphet *what?*'

'Young girls used to camp outside my home. No-one tried to stop 'em, nor moved them on. So I said, hey, kids. Skip on in out of that weather. I schooled 'em. Etiquette, deportment, discipline. As I'd been taught at the military academy. Their parents knew and approved.'

I didn't know which end to start from here. Maybe he's ridgey-didge. Or he's spun it this way so many times, he's come to believe it. Or he's just bignoting, none of it ever happened at all, these kids never existed outside the theatre of his freakin' mind. We'll never know.

'Course, it wasn't all drill. We'd go on field trips after class, Brett. Climb the flagpole outside the London Hilton. Nude, that is. Or steal horses from Hyde Park stables at three in the AM. Went riding on that bridle path, Rotten Row. Mighty purty. A barenaked doxy astride her mount, bathed in moonglow. Or three or four.'

Belted me flat, what he told me. It don't do to dwell on what he didn't.

'I spent high and wide on Chelsea. Some four-poster beds. *PJP* monograms in gold, on everything, all over. On the shelves, miniatures. Civil War cannon. Little lead soldiers in dress blues. Antique weapons, mounted or hung. Prow of an old sailing ship affixed to one wall. Portrait of me on another, as bold buccaneer. The helm of a cutter mounted elsewhere. Sinbad the sailor, that's me, Brett. Sin *real* bad.

To Carnaby Street and Savile Row, I gave ample custom. They'd open, just for me, round midnight. Lunch o'clock in my world. *Vogue* magazine proposed a fashion shoot. As did a footwear outfit, to market PJ Proby buckled shoes. Then Fleet Street stomped on 'em. Both withdrew their offers.

But no nation of storekeeps could stop me having a time of it. Hell, Brett, Lennon once blew off a Beatles studio date to make one of my parties. He'd come to Chelsea, get pied on my liquor, pass out in a chair. Of course, Cynthia grew full umbrageous now. So as a sop to her disquiet, John took to having me up to their spread at Weybridge. She'd cook Southern fried chicken. I'd allowed that I'd been pining for Texas. A sweet gal.

'Have a look at this lot, Jim.'

Lennon's attic. All matte red and black. A model racing car track here. We'd play for hours. And in his music room, he'd play bass or electric piano. I, guitar. We'd sing. Cowboy songs. Elvis. Sun Sessions. *Good Rockin' Tonight, That's Alright Mama.* He didn't much care for post-Army Presley.

One day we bought this string of cans, coloured lights in them. Party lights. Set them up round his fireplace. As it happened, George Harrison stopped by.

'What's all this then, Johnny?'

'Oh, that. It's my new security system.'

'Fab! How does it...'

'I can tell what's going on anywhere on this property, George. Can't I, Jim?'

'Yessir, John. That is a true fact. NASA worked on this baby!'

'I knew when you came on the property, George. It's fuckin' gear.'

'I've got to get one of these!' says ol' Georgie. 'Where can I ...'

'Call me later,' says John. Rolls his eyes my way, *not in front of Proby, eh?* How we two kept straight-faced I cannot imagine.

'No more juice for me, Jim.'

John one day, to my offer of red liquor.

'I'm on the peace weed now.'

But he rolled it up too loose. When he sparked up, dang thing burst into flames. Near burned his face off. Now, I've no truck with maryjane. I'm asthmatic. But I had the savvy on how to roll 'em easy. All Texas boys do. So I skun him one, good as store-bought. The payoff, I get to drink all the bourbon I brought for me. And all I brung for him.

Yeah, the weed, sad luck and trouble, way I saw it. And that LSD. Heap bad medicine, Brett. One time, I'm back from a Euro tour. Two blonde Helgas I've shipped in on my Lear jet from Stockholm. Ol' Donovan Leitch starts dancing with 'em. But he's dropped that dang acid. You can't do thing one on that stuff, let alone the dance of love. He slid by my bedroom next morning. Still flashing. And me, still enwrapped in those vixens. It's no drug for a stud.

Yeah, none matched me for wild. Mayhap save one. Jet Harris, the bass player, he quit the Shadows. Had two solo hits. But he's in and out of police lock-ups. Fistfghtin' and such.

'Nary a night goes by,' he told me. 'The coppers lock me up for my own safety, Jim.'

'A man after my own heart and soul, Brett.'

Yeah. You could say that.

'Albeit not quite my equal. At my parties, I'd break out my handguns. My .45 and all. Take shots at my mounted wildebeest heads, antelope heads, *zing* just over the heads of my guests. They so gone on hooch, scooby doo and trips that it amused more than provoked perturbation.'

Yeah, well played, Proby. Roomful of ripped humans and a shickered nutcase discharging live rounds in their direction. It don't bear thinking about.

'Bongo Wolf, he and Donovan ran a safe trippin' room on the second level of the Chelsea place. But Bongo also had a bowie knife, 'bout as big as he was. So he'd tote that around. And stick in his porcelain vampire teeth. Bare them at folks he didn't care for when they had dropped some LSD.

One night, people up in that room, tripping. But they went a-wandering. Found my bedroom, strictly off limits. Decorated with Gonks, these little Scandi dolls. Vikings and wizards. Fans there gave me these. So ol' Bongo wades in. Commences to stabbing at these Gonks. I fancy those people are still running, Brett.'

Yep. A headful of acid and a fistful of knife. *Some kinda fun.*

'That's a valiant flea that dare eat his breakfast on the lip of a lion.'

His first words to me, from Shakespeare. A nod to my courage. I met Burton and hellcat wife Liz Taylor one day at Heyman's office.

'Astounding, Jim. You can match me Bloody Mary for Bloody Mary,' said Richard at the pub where we adjourned. And the martinis after that for lunch.

Dick and Liz, a ding dong domestic one time. He needed a buddy. Everyone else off making pictures, he said when he called.

He flew me London to Zurich. Then, a chopper to his chalet at St Moritz. He's exiled from the main house, to the servants' quarters. Three days we drank. Then Liz appears on the balcony. In a black negligee.

'O Richard!' she called. 'You can come home now!'

'Jim,' he said. 'I must, 'pon my soul, excuse myself, to what yon mistress commands.'

Craziest three days of my life, Brett. That week, any rate.

ABOVE: The Proby decorated his homes back in his better days with mounted heads of elk, wildebeest and so on, so we figured this might appeal to his inner Hemingway. This tiger a real one is the story, that some drongo somewhere had gunned down.

LEFT: The locale for the shoot was a deconsecrated church in Newtown that this local filmmaker lived in. My housemate Sally Geschmay's brainwave and she set it up. Proby used to get that look on when hanging a spray on me for slackness in matters of his grog supply chain.

The Legendary
P.J. PROBY

APPEARING:
PADDINGTON RSL
SAT 24 FEB 7.30-11.30
W 50 MILLION BEERS AND
CHRISTA HUGHES

ABOVE: Myself (left) and Clyde (right) jumped in for this one, just for the historical record. This was likely towards the end of the shoot. The talent a bit shagged out and weary by mid-arvo most days. Me too as the weeks ground by.

LEFT: The tour poster, featuring one of the best gets from the shoot. Sadly, didn't get as much use as it might have. There was also a tour T shirt featuring a head shot of Proby and his autograph in red. Like whisky. Or blood.

Jim Proby was brought up a Southern Baptist, so he knew all the hellfire preacher moves. The stained glass windows and the wooden pulpit still onsite handy and dandy. There was also a baptismal font still in situ, but we couldn't think of how to deploy it in a pic.

Jim Proby brought what looked like his wardrobe entire with him to Oz, including his cowboy hats. Not sure what the finger in the mouth was in aid of. He insisted on doing all kinds of poses and moves that day. Some of them worked fine and well. Others,...

CHAPTER THIRTY-FOUR

'So, Brett, apart from those no kids allowed clubs, we could only play town halls too small to hold all the teens who tried to cram in there. Or too big when parents forbade 'em.

But elsewhere lay vistas not so censorious. I stormed Europe. Paris. Stockholm. Amsterdam, Hamburg, Copenhagen. These Continentals, they gave not one damn about split pants. Loved me for who I was.

For touring, I leased a Learjet 23. Passenger aircraft designed like a fighter. My kind of bird. At the shows here, no ban on teens. Had me a ball. In a number of ways.

Yet my britches stayed unsplit. Netherlands press called me 'Mr PJ Probity.' I had my staff buy a mess of copies, clip the stories, mail them to the British press.

In Denmark, girls invaded the stage. And boys. Not to fight but to shake my hand. At first, I figured them for hostiles. So I set to punching them out! Oh, my goodness. To get to me, they made their whole body rigid. The crowd would propel 'em at me, above their heads, with their hands. Kids were doing crowd surfs at my gigs before it was even dreamed up.

As to Scary Mary Whitehouse, branding me *unclean* and *impure*, I devised a new routine. I'd stroke my body. Pelvic thrusts while I'm at it. Call on the girls in the crowd.

'Am I Clean? Am I pure? Don't you want to touch me?'

'Yes, PJ! You are clean!'

Took it round the world. For that world begged to be taken.

My full retinue on the road in England. Orchestra. Secretary, road manager, stylists, bodyguard. Bongo Wolf, my new fetchit. And when

I let him, bongo player. For a time now, as intimate companion, a coloured chick, Lesley. Dressing rooms required for all. This meant commandeering the domicile of the town hall's caretaker. The whole home, that is. He no vacate, we no show. Booze ban at these venues, so woe upon Bongo if he didn't have my sour mash mixed into bottles of Coca Cola as bespoke. He's uneasy about all the tasks I set him, but I said, in my outfit, soldier, you don't work, you don't eat.

A typical date. California Ballroom, Dunstable. Packed. Thank you, Mary Whitehouse. Three supports. Once they're done, my orchestra. Instrumentals, like the blues and country acts do. Then, *me* time. Mopped my face with *PJP* monogrammed handkerchiefs all through the show. Threw them into the crowd. Catfights broke out over 'em. Curtain falls. Back to the caretaker's home. Thirty minute nap. Then, for their own good, I raused out my staff.

'A disaster!' This to Henny. 'That security, front of stage! Those girls should have access should they jump up and...you let those goons stand to and hamper their passage!'
    'It was venue management, Jim. I tri...'
    I had already swerved to Pat.
    'I told Bunny I won't play these small sorryass ballrooms. Big rooms only! You should have warned me! And *you! Bongo Wolf!* Can't mix a drink for shit! Why am I beset by imbeciles and goldbrickers?'
    I had no choice, Brett. For I am a star and I cannot abide...'
    I tuned out for a bit. Had to. Lest I snot him.

'My show got wilder. When the *PJP* hankies ran out, I'd yell I needed new ones. Came there fusillades of girls' knickers. They did this to Tom Jones too, but I'd take wager they were *paid* to squeal and toss 'em at that Welsh gooney bird. In fact, I put this to the press. To get a feud started. I said stuff all the time. You know, 'Tom Jones never did have a good voice. Just a loud one.'
    The press knew I sold papers, so now, *I* used *them*. I'd have 'em to Chelsea for a good drink. Then I'd drop the hammer.

'Tom Jones is just a wholesale copy of my act.' Or 'that's not him singin' on the records. It's some guy they pay to keep it secret. Onstage, he just mimes to that.'

Those press varmints chomped that hook every time. As did Tom. Fact, he wrote an open letter to the papers.

'Dear Jim,' it went, 'as far as copying goes, I've just heard that James Brown has started to imitate your act.' And for a PS, 'I can recommend a good tailor.' This, in regard to my busted pants. I replied with reference to my trademark pout. Said I'd copied it from Chrissie Shrimpton, sister to fashion model Jean, and Jagger's girl.

'Tom stole that from me too. But when *he* does it, he looks like my beagle Mr President.' Surely one day we'd come to blows. I couldn't wait.

'So I offer this heapin' helpin' of public remorse to England. And we score a Number One hit off it.'

That was my pitch, Brett. Cut a Billy Eckstine song, *I Apologise.* But Billy's take, all silk and warm air. Mine, those VU meters redlined all the way. One for the ages.

But the press took a dump on it. Cast doubts as to my sincerity. Only made number Eleven. And the Stones released *The Last Time* right then. Decca, to knock me off the charts, turned on a PR rainstorm for their boys like to choke the frogs. So, then. Hot war it must be. I am a soldier. I can do no other.

CHAPTER THIRTY-FIVE

'We need to make this look more like a tour.'
Correct weight, Clyde. Proby's lobbed here, no merch, no product. No PR photos, videos, *nada*. And a head like a dropped pie. But luck's a fortune. Here in Sydney, a dude who can render the roughest of mugs as gods. For pix and merch. T-shirts, posters. Whole showbag.

'Job for you, Tone,' says Clyde on the phone. Glances at Proby. 'A big one.'

'Where is my *hairdresser?* There will be no *shoot* until my hair is in an acceptable *state.*'

Thank fuck Nini's had the smarts to tote along a bag of brushes, combs, clips. A towel to drape round his shoulders. Proby snake-eyes Tony Mott, gun rock 'n' roll photographer.

'Is *this* the only mirror you *have?*'

'Come on, Jim.' Nini, all husk and come hither. 'Here's your beer, darling. Let's get you smartened up.'

'Why is there no *makeup* person? Must I do this *myself?*'

Nini reefs out a makeup kit. Gets to work on him. Proby turns to Tony again.

'Well, shooter, it is of no matter. You see, I come from a theatrical background. Movies too. I can do my own if need be. But this lady bass player will suffice today.'

'Oh, that's very big of you, Jim,' says Nini, painting him a face to hide a thousand sins.

'Are these the only cameras you *have?*'

There were days he just wanted to start a blue.

'Why, no, Jim,' says the Mott. 'In fact,..'

'Fetch the rest.'

Behind Proby, I give Tony a face. *He's nuts, my man. Just play along.*

'And these lights. Place them so half my face is in shadow. Not *this* half. The *other* half.'

He don't say which half he means.

'Airbrush out this turkey neck here. Or there'll be no question of payment.'

The Bramley says not a word. Just a look Proby can't see. Think *The Hills Have Eyes.*

'Say, shooter. You ever work in TV?'

'Yeah, well, I have, Jim,' says Tony. 'I...'

'Can you get me on *Neighbours?*'

CHAPTER THIRTY-SIX

'You boys have skimmed that which is Her Majesty's. Kept it for your own selves.'

Another day of Proby won't rehearse, won't do promo, nothin'. Pubside, the blur went on...

'I needed money now, Brett. Lots of it. Inland Revenue now hellhounds on my trail. Taxes unpaid. No returns lodged by my managers.'

'Jim, we're not your accountants, old son,' said Heyman when I braced him about all those missing frogskins.

'We've paid you all of your end. That includes any tax liability.'

But they must meet this debt, I said, or I'd dismiss 'em from my employ. *Read your contract*, their rejoinder. They could sue any other I assigned their remit. Me with it. Or any venue, should I book direct.

To the record company, I advanced the same claim. Their response, ditto Heyman's. An approach to Her Majesty for clemency I considered upon, but I was in no fit state. Awash in red whiskey below decks and no repose across days of revelry now my custom.

'A sure-fire hit, Jim,' he said. 'It's *gear*.'

Chris Curtis, drummer from The Searchers, played me a Ben E King number, *Let The Water Run Down*, by Bert Berns. Wrote *Twist And Shout, Here Comes The Night, Hang On Sloopy* and waymore.

My producer on this at EMI, Johnny Scott, had worked with the Beatles some. That's his flute on *You've Got To Hide Your Love Away*. July '65, they cut *Water* on me. Jimmy Page, JP Jones. Bobby Graham, drums. Vernons Girls, backups. The sound of the jungle in flames.

Yet it rose no higher than Top Twenty. Lasted there but a week. Only one thing to do.

'Whaddyasay, Johnny?'

They wrote three for Cilla. *I Wanna Be Your Man* for the Stones. *World Without Love* for Peter And Gordon. The Fabs had their own table at the Ad Lib. Truth of it, I'm liquored up, half-assed kidding. And distracted. Some fashion model dolly birds do I spy with the Pretty Things, so I mosey on over there. *Why, how do!*

'Hey, Jim! Don't you want your song?'

Two nights on. Lennon, calling from their table.

'What song?' I don't recall our parley.

'The one I fookin' wrote for ya! That you asked me for!'

'Oh, that.'

Came to mind now.

'Hell, John, it was just a jest. You didn't have to go and...'

'Well, here it is!' Hands me a white label pressing. 'Give it all you got, Tex.'

'All four Beatles on this cut, Brett. Just for me.'

Yeah, well, up to a point, my man. The quick of it, they're tracking demos for the *Help!* album and this one don't make the grade. They don't tell Proby that. Fuck, I wouldn't either.

*

'So. Can you get George Martin to produce it?'

My aim, Brett, as ever, Number One. More Beatles links couldn't hurt any.

'Fuck, man,' said Lennon down the phone. 'You never fuckin' stop, do ya?'

Ron Richards produced. But George Martin arranged and conducted. So his name's on the label. This biscuit, all Beatles, bar the Beatles themselves on it.

Well, now. Week one, *That Means A Lot* made twenty-four. And that's all she wrote. Lennon was an asshole, Brett. Gave me his crummiest songs...'

Proby not overmuch given to gratitude. A fresh rave now. The crimes of Beatle John. No wonder he wound up light on for mates when his persecutors went the full get square. I thought, best ignore it. Made for the bar before he noticed his bevvies at ebb tide. Back with a new shout, away he goes again.

'It's nearly ten PM, Jim. Pubs close at half-past. Chop chop.'

The Ron Richards method of making records, Brett.

'Get this Remy Martin inside you, Jim. Makes you nice and loose.'

We got along fine and well. To work now on my second long player, *PJ Proby,* through March and April of '65. We wove dazzle from Doris Day's *Secret Love,* the Ink Spots' *My Prayer,* Hoagy Carmichael's *The Nearness Of You,* Nat King Cole's *When I Fall In Love.*

'And some others we rock up a tickle,' I said. That Donnie Brooks take on *Mission Bell. Lonely Teardrops,* to hand ol' Jackie Wilson pause. Del Shannon made 'em weep with *She Cried* but my take would trigger tears of blood. The Charlie Rich number *Lonely Weekends,* a whole lotta Proby goin' on.

'Ron. Make it sound like Spector,' I said. 'Every song a single.'

Mission Bell was not released as a 45 by EMI in the UK, despite it was a sure hit. Liberty did in the US but didn't promote it. Didn't own it. Let it die. No action in it for them. But Australia, New Zealand, they put it out as such. Went like guided missiles to Number One. *Somebody down there likes me,* I told the press.

*

What a bowl of sugar. Chrissie Shrimpton. At the Scotch of St James, we just this night met, I didn't say much. Just smiled her way and plenty of it. Her boyfriend Jagger, he'd send a taxi to take her home at three in the AM, even when he was out on the road. Then call her apartment an hour later, check on her. Girl's way past disconsolate. So I took to sending her flowers and rhyming telegrams. I still recall one. *Sittin' here, Drinkin' beer, Wishin' that ol' Mick were queer, If he was I wouldn't fret, 'Cause he might forget you yet.'*

And then I bought her a diamond ring.'

That's all it took, said his upturned brows.

'The press at my door come sunrise. Someone's gone and dogged on us. *Do you have anything to say?*

'Yeah!' I hollered. 'My cock's bigger than Mick Jagger's!'

Now, Brett, Mick sent her a gift. New Mini Minor. Delivered to her place, tied in a red ribbon. He called her, time and again, from Birmingham, Alabama or someplace. No answer. The why of it, she's with me. So he figured the what if not the who of it. Told her flatmate that Chrissie's in deep ructions. But Chrissie didn't dig on Mick's pouty ways. Me, I made her laugh. And he, at the wrong end of the ocean sea to do shit about it. She came home with me again. Twice.

*

'Mick wants you, Chrissie.'

Jolted awake by my front door getting kicked in. Then two *geezers,* the Limeys call 'em. Kray Twins kind of guys. Standing over Chrissie, me and my circular bed. My Colt .45 not within reach, nor Waffen-SS issue Luger, so best let it go. Yet I was fetched no beating. Guess Mick didn't want me in the papers, my head like a wrecker's yard, his name in connection. Poor Chrissie. Stuck on a plane to Ireland, where Mick awaited.

Didn't have the nutsack to front me himself. That ring next fetched up on Mick's finger in the Scotch one night. My first impulse, take it off him. His finger too. But I let it be, lest I sully my career prospects. I was waiting on a call in that respect.

'Jim, this will break you in America.'

Jack Good on that Transatlantic line.

'I'm about to leave *Shindig*, dear boy. Spot of bother with the network. My last three shows. I want you for all of them.'

Hell was raised Stateside, Brett. Let me tell ya 'bout it.

*

'We'll get massive press off this, my boy.'

Jack's producing this charity event, to hype the *Shindig* shows. Freedom From Hunger the cause worthy. Shrine Auditorium, Jefferson Boulevard, South Central LA. Me, top of the bill.

'What's with the derby, Jack?'

'This, Jim, is a *bowler*, dear boy.'

Jack went on camera on *Shindig* with that hat and a brolly. Savvy. Americans love that England swings like a pendulum do hokum.

Some bill. Johnny Cash, The Byrds, Sonny and Cher, Everlys. Crowd, seven thousand. And I, much cause for consternation.

'Well, *how do! How do!*'

Brimful of red hooch when I ran on, Brett. Reason to be skittish. See, Jack made me wear my bright blue velvet ensemble. I feared this would stoke botheration from the US press, me in that getup, ponytail in a ribbon. Doubt cast upon my manliness.

'*Without a warnin', you broke my heart...*'

I tore into *Turn On Your Lovelight*. The Shindogs, house band from *Shindig*, rippin' it up. Backstage, it had come to me. *Give 'em a whole 'nother story.* I swept on in my flag of Texas cape. As I sang, undid the clasp. Shrugged it off slow like the strippers at the Largo on Sunset. Swung it around. Tossed it away. My hips, hula moves now. Messin' with the blue blouson. Real slow. Wagglin' my eyebrows. Nodding my head, posing the question. *You want I go further? And getting back affirmatory.*

Peeled the blouson off each shoulder. Shook 'em like Marilyn M. Threw it off as we tipped on in to *Can Your Monkey Do The Dog?*

I'd split one knee of my pants backstage. A mishap, Brett.'

Yeah, righto, Proby.

'Now it ripped further as I danced, all the way up to the sports section. Girls barrelled for the stage. Ten of 'em made it. My thumbs I now jammed into these pants. *Like I aimed to step out of 'em.* That's when they dropped the curtain.

Backstage, they rained imprecations on me. Of no matter. The city mine, its lostest angel.

*

'*Lewd. Obscene.* Jim, have you seen the papers?'

'Why, there is no need, Jack, as you have just now read them to me.'

Jack, the true of it, giddy with glee. See, this same news told all America that ol' PJ was on three comin' right up eps of *Shindig*.

'I am the new god of pop.'

I thus advised next day's press conference Jack called in LA. They branded me 'weird' and fell to confusement. Greatest of all time or depraved sex monster? I saw no cause to dissuade 'em of either notion.

Caught up with a mess of pals from the Brill Shack, the Palomino, Gazzarri's. From Come To The Party, now called the Whisky A Go Go. Went on a crawl. LA, cookin' with gas. The Galaxy, the London Fog, Pandora's Box, the Prelude. Clubs that shook and wailed. And that weren't all.

'If you must get into trouble, go to the Chateau Marmont.'

So said Mr Casting Couch himself. Ol' Harry Cohn, Mr Columbia Pictures. The Chat my choice of LA bunkhouse now but zero slumber going on. I aver the bar ran out of booze down to my carousing there that week.

Yet, albeit I'm back home, it felt like out of my element. See, I'd never made it here. All those naysayers. I must prove 'em wrong and prevail.

CHAPTER THIRTY-SEVEN

At the *Shindig* rehearsal, the Shindogs hot as Death Valley. James Burton on one guitar, Delaney Bramlett the other. Glen D Hardin piana, before he went with Elvis like Burton did. Larry Knechtel, a first-call LA session guy, anything made a noise. Hammond organ, sax, guitar, harmonica. Fender bass, Joe Osborn. Chuck Blackwell, drums. Champeens all.

One hot bill. Billy Preston, Everlys, Gary Lewis And The Playboys. Limeys too. Gerry And The Pacemakers, Petula Clark. My first of three slots, as per Jack's promise, I went on after Billy P with his *Little Sally Walker.* The *Shindig* dancers formed two lines, facing each other. They had these long prop bugles. Aimed skyward. All the singers on the show chanted '*Peeeeee, Jaaaaaaaay, Prooooobyyyyy!*'

The gals mimed blowing a flourish played by the Shindogs horns as I made my progress through the dancers' guard of honour, to the mic. Piano struck a chord. My key.

'When you're near me I feel so romantic...'

Kids in the audience already wigging out, but now went snake church nuts. The *Shindig* dancers shakin' it all round me, I sang for my life.

Next, *Let The Water Run Down.* After the Everlys did *Cathy's Clown.* But they're 'bout as coloured as North Pole ice. No white boys but me doin' the do in '65. I blew ol' Don and Phil all the ways back to their childhood in Knoxville, Tennessee.

Jack gave me the finale too. On air, he told America I'd be back next week. Cut to compere Jimmy O'Neill, to introduce me:

'No matter what anyone says- *rock on!*'

A song about animals now. Band plays a few bars of *Old Macdonald* to cue me in.

'*Can your monkey do the dog!*'

Pure madness. Dancers flailing. The other artists flooded on, groovin' in sync to my footwork. I'm handed Jack's hat. I clowned as I sang, flipping it up and down on the back of my head, waving it to and fro aft of my ass. *So hot I gotta fan me down!* The band rocked back and forth as they churned. Bassman played it behind his head. Floor crew signalling, *keep it going*. Then Jack jumped in front of me. Calling time, I thought. Handed him the mic, made my exit. But he calls me out on it.

'*Come back, Jim, come back!*'

Held out his hat in salute. Thrust the mic at me. *Take it home.*

Now the second show, Brett, well...

'I get *one song*, Jack? Merely the *one?*'

He dick-fingered with his dadgum hat. I near snatched it and stomped on it.

'In the *middle* of the show? The *graveyard* slot?'

'Now, Jim, we have many artists to consider. All stars in their own right, so....'

'Not my concern, Jack.'

'Dear boy. I had to move mountains, nay planets from their orbits, to squeeze you in at *all*.'

'A problem not mine, *dear boy*. I, too, am a star. Fix it.'

My eyes fell on the running sheet. The Byrds. *Three numbers!*

'The *Byrds?* Still life with rigor mortis!' I said. 'Shari! Every warm body on the show, all got two or three songs! All but *one!*'

'Jimmy, compose yourself. Scoot off to makeup now.'

Well, I tried, but Shari's on Jack's team now, Brett. Owed him her fealty, not me. I sought refuge and counsel in JD Black Label. Refreshed, I proposed at taping that one act be bumped from one of their numbers, and I do two. *I'm a more than reasonable fellow, Jack*, I said.

'Sorry, Jim. The subject is closed.'

172

'Well,' I said,' if it ain't reopened here and now, *I quit.* Your move, Limey.'

And with that, the Proby goes off at me and Clyde. If not for Jack Good, he reckons, he'd have been the *greatest star America ever saw.* Yeah, well, never pick a blue with a showie would be my big tip. Jack did what any smartie would. Nothin'. So now Proby don't have no show at all.

He goes the full troppo. To the LA press, a rave that Jack had promised star billing on three shows. He hadn't. Never did. Not for any mug, all the way up to the Beatles.

And then there's that strip show Proby pulled at the Shrine. A show for a charity. A *faith-based* one. So he's on the turn with humans who matter in LA. The press go to town on *him.* Jack leaves it a day or so. Then puts the word out. Proby's been speared from *Shindig.*

He don't hold back.

'Lies, lies, lies. He's unmanageable. Won't listen to reason.'

Straight, no chaser. *Bang.* Jack saves face, the news stories pull more heads for *Shindig* and Proby's numbat of the week. Game over.

Something Proby didn't mention to me and Clyde. This singer, Ruben Guevara, worked on *Shindig.* Vocal backups. When Proby went the flounce, Jack called Ruben in. Changed his name to JP Moby. Dresses him up just like PJ. Ponytail, full bit, to do Proby's slots. Figured the punters wouldn't spot the diff. But then canned the move. Or maybe Shari Sheeley did. Proby just cattle to Jack. All of them, come to that.

'Hell with 'em,' says Proby now to Clyde and me. 'I had a plane to catch. For Heyman had lined up *Ready Steady Go* and *Top Of The Pops.*

'It seems,' said Heyman, 'you are forgiven, cock. The TV ban lifted.'

With reason. My one *Shindig* show had pulled record ratings when it was broadcast in England. So eat that, Jack Good.

*

Time was tight, Brett. We went direct from Heathrow to *RSG's* Rediffusion studio. That week, Donovan, the Hollies, the Animals. Then straight on to *Top Of The Pops* at the BBC, with the Searchers, Dusty Springfield, and the Yardbirds.

'Fear not, Jim. I'm agent to a lot of Brits in Tinseltown. Know people who can put you on the movie map, cock.'

'Well, John. So advance my prospects therewith. I'm done with music and...'

'In time, Jim, yes. For now, we've got more TV over in LA, despite the carry-on with Jack. Or perhaps because of it.'

No time to even unpack.

*

No room at the Chat, so to the Tropicana Motel. On the road, I hid my cash in a Bible mama gave me. No thief pays mind to a Good Book. Now Ford hears I'm here. Heads on down. At the Trop, libation is proposed. I go down the corner to get. No Ford upon my return. *And lo.* A hole in the bedside drawer. Where that Bible used to be.

Ford not hard to find. First bar on the Strip nearby. I offer to beat him to blood and bone. He makes with a fess.

'Yeah, I took it. C'mon, man. You don't need that money. You're a star now, so...'

'Where's that Good Book, Ford?'

'Oh. I threw it out of the car. Into Laurel Canyon.'

'My *mother* gave me that Bible.'

'Awwww.' He smiles like skulls do. 'You'll get over it.'

What remained of my greenbacks, I retrieved. Took Ford out on a crawl. The man had displayed courage under fire. I could do no other.

'I was in the Ad Lib with Jim when the Beatles gave him this. Here he is now to sing it for ya, Peeeee, Jaaaaaay, *Proby!*'

Sam Riddle, bullshit king. I told him how I got that song and that's what he did with it. See, any mutt claimed they knew the Beatles, fact or no, it got 'em laid.

Sam, a hot DJ on KHJ-AM. Compered this new TV show *Hollywood A Go Go*. The theme, a manic surf instrumental. And they had the Gazzari Club Dancers. Wildest shakers in all LA. Well, bar the Pink Pussy Cat on Santa Monica.

We laid *That Means A Lot* and *Mission Bell* on 'em. Next day, to ABC for their other show, *Shivaree*. But for all that, I wasn't selling Stateside like I should. Liberty called a pow-wow.

'Jimmy, let's cut a session on ya. We got fine songwriters right here.'

'Well, Al, I have the Beatles to write hits for me. So another time perhaps.'

See, Brett, I got royalties if I did songs by outside writers. But at Liberty, by that contract my foolish hand had signed, bupkiss for me if I cut *theirs*. Yet my sass would call down grave peril.

Midsummer LA. Thirty clubs on the Strip between Crescent Heights and Doheny. Wild as they looked. Like Pandora's Box, painted gold and purple. The Beach Boys, the Byrds, Sonny And Cher used to shake their thing there.

Johnny Rivers, against all odds and justice, was playing the Whisky. Elmer Valentine, the owner, had friends in Chicago if you take my meaning. The Whisky had go go dancers in cages, short white skirts. Or you could see real singers, Nina Simone and Anita O'Day, at the Crescendo. Now all as gone as the Gardens of Allah and the Trocadero.

'Jim, they'll be cancelled by next year, but my show goes on forever.'

I ran into Dick Clark while taping *Shivaree*. Host Gene Weed, another DJ, introduced us. Dick, presenter of *American Bandstand* since long about 1958. Still highest-rating of 'em all. He had a question for me.

'Dick,' I said,' I thought you'd never ask.'

My answer, *Great God yes, I would.* So back again to ABC Television Center's Stage 54. They'd shoot three eps of *American B* every Sunday there. I did *That Means A Lot* and *Water.* Between them, an on-air interview with Big Dick.

'May I ask, when you went to England from Texas, did you wear your hair that way?'

He asked of the rumpus there. And what came to pass 'to cause all this turmoil.'

'A lotta trouble,' my reply, coy as a kitty. He enquired if I was a troublemaker. Was fetched a smile sweet as cherry pie.

'Oh, well, I have been known to be one.' But went on to say 'I stand up for my rights.'

You see, Brett, Americans don't like being put upon by Limeys. Not since 1776. I sold me like cotton candy. From sea to shining sea.

And I did live shows too. At the Red Velvet Club on the Strip, Liberty set up a showcase gig. I'd just slayed 'em flat with *Somewhere* when a note was passed up to me.

I love the way you do 'Somewhere.' Can you do it again just for me? Elvis.

I look out into this all-red joint. *Oh my God.* A table near ringside. Elvis and his Memphis boys. I'm overcome. Had to sit down on the stage.

'Ladies and gentlemen. I've just received the biggest honour I could ever hope for – a personal request from Mr Elvis Presley.'

They go shriekville. We re-did *Somewhere* right there. At the end, Elvis is gone. Last time I ever saw him. Why he came, I know not. Perchance sizing me up, he who had come for his crown.

CHAPTER THIRTY-EIGHT

'I am back to reclaim my first dominion.'

This to the press at Heathrow.

'PJ Proby has been in Hollywood,' I said.'Talkin' a picture deal. Columbia.'

And no reason to stop there.

'My first, next summer. A biopic. The life of Errol Flynn.'

Well, this some might call canard, but not all the way so. In LA, I'd run into Steve Rowland. We'd worked together as statues and stunt men and both sung at the Sea Witch. Steve's daddy Roy, a producer. Had a screenplay, *The Sea Pirate*. He thought I'd go good as leading man. As did I.

'Yeah, this I did alone, Heyman. So what have *you* done lately in that regard, pray tell?'

'Jim, that balls about Columbia won't look so flash when it comes to light that there's no truth in it.'

Seems he shared not my jubilation.

'Look,' he said. 'I've talked to casting agents. But nothing's advanced as yet. And won't if you keep this up.'

'Dadgum it, John. You call me in here today to talk of tours for Europe, Australia, New Zealand. Hong *Kong*. And *I* got *you* a front *page* says I'm a *movie star*. So call these promoters! Raise my asking price!'

Bunny sighed like the mouse he was.

'Jim,' he said. 'These tours. No more striptease. I implore you. No more splitteroonie.'

'Bunny,' I said, 'you have my solemn vow.'

I held up two fingers crossed in affirmation. And entwined two more behind my back.

Of the *Sea Pirate*, well, it went ahead. Minus me. The co-producers refused to meet my price. They shot in Italy. Used Italian cast and crew. More fools them. It sank on release. With the loss of all hands.

'I told the press you're coming. So y'all can get your picture took, get on the TV.'

Every pop star in England I told, of the launch of *PJ Proby*, my new LP. Its debut week in the stores, a tally stout and fine on the album charts. Yeah. At first. Then the *Help* record album and the movie of that same came out. I held fast. Blinked away that Beatles dust.

Got my dander up, Brett. All these PJ Proby *imitators* now. Not just Tom Jones. That dadgum Engelbert Humperdinck. Nothing but a pit band sax player, that boy. Lips like a damn sea bass. And this gimcrack stylin' himself as Beau Brummell. *Beau Brummell.* This one, from South Africa. Even had a ponytail, this damn jaapie. On top of all these, those shitbirds the Walker Brothers. None near good as me, and failin' to *be* me.

Greedcrazed, the Limeys took to shippin' in any American they could find, to jump my claim. Oldham, the Stones' manager, brought over Bobby Jameson from LA.

'You can stay here, boy. Be my butler.'

Oldham hadn't even found Bobby a bedsit. So I put him up at Chelsea. The Stones started calling him 'PJ's valet.' He'd earn his keep, I declared. My purple PJP gold-monogrammed slippers, matching smoking jacket, laid out ready each day. Drinks mixed and fetched. Shirts pressed with steam iron. My newspapers too, I decreed, like Limey butlers did.

'I'm the only honch round here doing thing one to help you, boy,' my retort when he whined. 'You get to meet all the who's who of all's what under my roof. Y'all swim back to LA if it don't take your fancy.'

Decca signed him. See, Brett, Oldham told 'em, they still hot for payback on me, that he sang just like me. And as Lennon had written for me, Keith Richards did for Bobby J. For *All I Want Is My Baby*, Keith also produced. Jagger on backup vocals. Jimmy Page played a solo identical to Big Jim Sullivan on my singles. B side, a Jagger-Richards number, *Each And Every Day*. A feel just like *Somewhere*. That cookpot shy just one herb. Talent.

'Hell, Jameson! That record of yours.'

I turned to my guests. *Watch this!* Twirled my *pistola*, a Curly Bill spin. Aimed it just over his head.

'Ain't nothin' but grand theft *Proby!*'

Crack!

He did *Ready Steady Go*. His gimmick, one gloved hand. That sad sack even stole that, from Jack Palance in *Shane*. Then his pals got bored. Next single, no Stones on it. A bad end for that buck. And fast.

'That boy, wild as a dust devil. I'll be in anything he is.'

DJ Simon Dee, partial to the booze and the ladies, ballin' the jack till his head caved in. On Radio Caroline, the pirate station, he grew so loved by listeners that their arch-foe, the BBC, had given him a job.

'It's a pilot for a TV show, Jim. You, the main guest.'

Simon as compere. The *Discotec* people came to Chelsea. Interviewed me. Used this as a voice-over for film of me in my garden, studying on my touring schedule. Inside, gets of my vintage weapons, my mounted critter heads. And a photo of Tommy Sands, to remind me who got me started. The *Sea Pirate* script too. A prop I pressed into service.

'One of many sent by Hollywood,' I said. 'They just won't let me be.'

My beagle Mr President made a cameo. And my cats. The little girls love them so. *Discotec* showed my Mark Cross luggage lined up in the hall, road-ready. And the split velvet pants hung on the wall, I made damn sure they got *them* in.

We shot two singin' videos. *Water*, at Chelsea, and at a nearby ruin, bombed by the Luftwaffe. The BBC studios for *Hold On To What*

You've Got from *Somewhere*, my new release EP. Me in silhouette, and at a lectern with a Bible. A hellfire preacher. Showcased my thespian skills. My own dadgum TV special. Felt too fine to be true.

'*Why was I not told?*'

Treachery was afoot. The *Discotec* people, without they told *me*, had filmed a second act for this pilot. And their selection, that plague of pestilence The *Walker Brothers*. Even worse, an interview with Gary Leeds. Cold lies of his time with me, what pals we were. I laid it out plain. These goofs off my show, or it must not go to air.

'Oh, that,' I said. Simon called. He'd submitted *Discotec* to the BBC. And that's how Billy Cotton Junior came to hear of it.

'Fuck, Jim!'

Discotec was axed. That pilot, never broadcast. Still, a morsel of cold comfort. Yeah. I'm lookin' at you, Walker Brothers.

*

Bunny booked a tour, *I Shall Be There- With My Orchestra!* By the Delfonts and Grades, still banned, so we went with our only option, these smaller independent auditoriums. Alhambra Theatre, Morecambe, Whitehall Ballroom, East Grinstead, others of that stripe. And I tried out a new bit for my act.

'Well, Bunny, you said these dates ain't but half sold, so...'

He's in a state. Today's news stories. I'd split the pants a little, at the first show at the Alhambra. Made great show of *Oops! Oh my*. Dashed off. Returned, feigning shame, clad in pure white overalls. Crowd went loco.

Those Fleet Street simps. I hauled 'em right in, dumb as crawfish. Off the back of all his ooby dooby, ol 'Bunny had to book a second show at the Alhambra, such was the demand. Same for the town of Nelson, at the Imperial Ballroom. Ditto four more on that swing. But then Bunny gets windy again.

'What? We pack houses where'er we roam.'

'Jim, we're losing money hand over fist.'

'Why, Bunny, how can this be?'

'Your orchestra for a kickoff. Fifteen pieces! And your staff of, what? Seven?'

Impasse. He'd book no more gigs if I'd not make cuts. And I'd not play without 'em. But I only hit him the once.

'Gunshots. Rowdy hooligans. Girls milling about. Barking dogs. The interior befouled. That's why,' said the estate agent.

So, to a bedsit back in Earl's Court. My collectibles, in storage. A Euro tour now, booked before that scrimmage with Bunny. Eviction, in such context, well, I didn't give a pin. Hell, Brett. What need of a home has a roving seadog?

Bunny wouldn't pay for my orchestra on Euro swings. He arranged pickup bands in each city. Sent 'em charts. Heyman got me on the Euro TV shows. *Beat Club* out of Bremen in West Germany. So organised you could invade Poland with it. *Baton Rouge* in France. One on Stockholm TV. *TopPop* in Amsterdam. Brett, we came to play. And, by glory, we got what we came for.

CHAPTER THIRTY-NINE

'Then, Brett, Australia. First time. A stone blitzkrieg.'

Too right it was. The hype started early. In the Sydney arvo papers, a month before freakin' showtime.

You'll have strife getting within coo-ee of PJ Proby when he flies in, the guts of it. *Police and barricades out in force.*

'August nineteen and sixty-five, I believe it was. To spook the press, before the plane landed, I'd change into freaky threads. Velvet cap. Bright red and blue pants and shirt, like to make their eyeballs explode. No parade, no circus.

As ever, it worked like catnip. Sydney press said I looked like a pirate. Girls busted through police lines. Flattened the cyclone fence. Mobbed me on the tarmac. Then taunts at the press conference that I'm but a poor man's Elvis.

'Whoever said that needs their head read,' I said. 'I don't even sound like him. I used to, but only 'cause I did demo records for him. He stole *his* style off *those*. Elvis *Presley* is a poor man's PJ *Proby.*'

I told 'em work on my first film would begin soon.

'When I become a movie star, I will quit singing.'

'Will you split your pants in Australia?'

'You'll have to ask my pants that.'

I showed 'em now. A small split at the seam. I made a squeaky voice, like it was my britches talkin'.

'Oh, my! Looky here! Splitsville!'

I covered it, all coy, *oh my goodness.* Then this from among their number.

'Why don't you wear ribbons with your ponytail anymore?'

'Girls run up. Steal them off of me. And oftimes, I get something in return.'

They asked where I lived now, bein't my eviction had been news here. Why, back in a bedsit, I said. Future plans, a houseboat on the Thames. As other stars did.

Some tour. Bobby and Laurie, a duo much like the Everlys, opened. Then the Easybeats. Dinah Lee next, they as her backing band. The bill said my own twelve-piece orchestra from England. Truth of it, local players who rehearsed up my set before I blew in.

They painted me *degenerate, immoral*. Newspaper columns by frosty men of the cloth. The more they wrote, more seats we sold.

After Sydney, to New Zealand. Auckland, Wellington. Brett, those Kiwis. Off the charts. Riots. Tour manager Barry Langford had to jump onstage, prise the girls off of me. We'd met when Barry was a producer on *Juke Box Jury* and *Beat Room* in England. And now he's in Australia, working in TV there.

So then Adelaide, the Palais Royal. Next, Melbourne, Festival Hall, a boxing and wrestling stadium. After that, Brisbane. Their own Festival Hall. A house of blood sport, like its Melbourne namesake and Sydney Stadium. This nation seemed to harbour a taste for it, Brett. My kind of people. Then back to Sydney, again at the 'Tin Shed,' as the locals had it.'

Yeah. Fair dinkum weird, Australia then. Apart from footy and blood sports, half dead and dug it that way. Then this tornado drops in. Ponytail, pink velvet, white socks. Pink *shoes*. I mean, Proby would've been stomped flat by bodgies, rockers and sharpies if he'd showed his moosh on the streets in that. But it was the squareheads he had really rattled. The Rev Roger Bush wrote in Sydney's *Sunday Mirror, Go Home Mr Proby: The Merchant Of Obscenity*. The Rev's panicked. These pop stars. Swipin' his crowd! The carnival is over, my man. He called the Texan's act *cheap, tawdry sexuality*. A bit counter-productive. I mean, if *that* don't pull heads for the Proby...

'I won over the hostiles, Brett. First Sydney show, the reviews said that stories of my vulgar act were just that. Stories. Onstage, I promenaded in all mauve. They called me a little effeminate. But who I really was, borne out in a forest of yearning nymphet arms. I sweated. Got on my knees. Some stripper's tassels I happened upon backstage, I stuck on my chest, swung 'em around. But no split pants. Pointed at 'em to prove it. Commenced to stroking myself.

'Am I clean? Am I pure?' I hollered.

'You're clean, PJ! You're pure!'

So much for Mary Whitehouse, her hexes and curses.

'Don't even think about it, Jim. Down here they deport people for less.'

No split pants, warned Barry. But then promoter James Haddleton reported some gigs as less than sellouts. No problemo, *impresario.* That night's show, I split the britches. Feign horror, make swift exit, then skip back on in the white overalls with great show of shame. The press made commotion. We sold out every seat, ringside to nosebleed.

*

'We met sat Vidal Sassoon's, Brett.'

His eyes go dewy at the memory.

'Beverley Adams. Actress from LA. Did a couple Dean Martin movies, and others like *How To Stuff A Wild Bikini.* TV shows like *Dr Kildare.* Sassoon's, a place to be seen. Show your face at this hairkeep's, get in the society pages.

I swooned for her. And she, me. She was making *Torture Garden,* a Hammer Horror picture, in London. Americans in it, to sell it back home. She and Jack Palance, Burgess Meredith. And those Limey horror movie lifers. Peter Cushing, Christopher Lee.

I hit that set. Worked it like a man on fire, to get my movie career rolling. Our love, a thing of rapture. Then Beverley heard tell of the Nymphet Club. Made all the wrong assumptions and fled from my embrace. But she'd be back.

'I'm pullin' crowds, Bunny. *Multitudes*. These paltry sums make no sense.'

Yeah, he tried it on again, Brett. *The tours lose money*, down to my expenses. But he was embezzling me. No question. And the record co, the same fables about sales.

'A single penned by the *Beatles*,' I said. 'Yet born stiff and cold, you contend.'

They tried a line of talk. A *turntable hit*, they said. Lot of radio airplay, spins in discotheques, yet sold little in stores. *Uh huh*. I felt the sting and went numb. So go rides across rivers on backs of scorpions.

After all that heat and dust with the BBC, who knows who Heyman had stroked. Any which way, I'm back on *TOTP* to give *That Means A Lot* another dance. And on the road again. Workingmen's clubs, it pains to say. I'd not had a Top Ten hit for a time. No promoter would gamble on theatre tours now.

Manchester, Liverpool, Newcastle, Birmingham. These clubs had comperes. But I needed my own emcee, like with Fowley. Pep up these near dead patrons. Get 'em away from those five card bandits and gaming tables. Just who for this post, well, no contest.

'Just do what Fowley did, Bongo,' I said. 'Sling 'em some boxer shorts, a jockstrap. Tell 'em I'm backstage naked.'

That bawdy humour those Limeys do love so.

*

'What do you mean?'

'Check your contract, Jim. We have no obligation to pay Bongo.'

'No show if not. Cash. By sundown.'

They refused. And anyway, I did no more gigs on that swing. Reason the most, I was fired. Poor ticket sales and the state of me onstage, all the talk of ol' clubsville. Then a whole new black cat crossed my path.

'What? *Undesirable alien?*'

We're flying back in from dates in Stockholm, Copenhagen. Bongo, hauled out of the line. Visa's expired. The UK not partial to renewing it. On account of *he's with me.*

I had to stick him on a plane back to Copenhagen. Directed to stand fast while I went to arms for him.

'Bongo needs a visa. It's on you to set it right.'

But Heyman and Lewis, not persuaded. Railed at me like I'm some chained-up killer on the courthouse steps. See, they'd booked me for *Ready Steady Go,* but I said I'd not do it. Last time, I'd been last act on. And they'd *rolled the end credits over me before my song was done.*

I importuned that the show's producer, Elkan Allan, must make public apology. None forthcame. So I told my managers I'd not do any TV till they used their swing to get Bongo back. Told the press, no visa, I'd quit England. Go live in a house I owned in Sweden.

Heyman said I was bluffing, that he knew I was busted flat as a tyre full of nails. My reckless improvidence, he said. Boats, cars, jets and their like.

'I can afford to wait, Jim. You,' he said, 'do not have that luxury, cock.'

'Not even the pluck to say it to my face! Yellowbellies and deserters!'

That's how the cream of UK pop heard it from me at the Scotch. Heyman quit. Bunny, too. And Barry Langford when I told *him* I'd not do his dadgum cabaret season at Mr Smith's in Hanley, Stoke-On-Trent. And now, UK Immigration set to brass banding it about *my* visa. Its renewal in jeopardy, they're squawkin', after all the twisters I'd set to spinning round this English no fun fair.

Two weeks Bongo languished in Denmark. We applied for a new visa, and I wrote an open letter to Her Majesty pleading his case. Only the music press ran it. I never knew if she saw it. No reply.

The decision, when it came, rendered us as the glorious dead of the Alamo. I had to wire Bongo the bread for his wings back to LA.

And my own visa almost done. Overhead, the roll and rumble of clouds and faint thunder.

Yet I failed to foretell the flood to come.

'Well, they've called it, Jim. Not ours to quibble, matey.'

EMI wanted a new single. To wit, something from *West Side Story*. You see, Brett, *Somewhere* had made Number Six. They didn't want another *Hold Me*. Might evoke spectre of evil PJ, doodah bobbin' like a robin through a hole in his pants. The choice, glaring at us like a gator in a swamp. They filled Abbey Road with minstrels till it could hold no more, and here was born *Maria*.

*

'Ron,' I said, 'I am destined for Hollywood. So that is the album we make here.'

'Jim, Liberty won't like it, old fruit. They want songs by their writers. And my brief is to get the sound of PJ, pop star.'

'Your brief, Ron,' I said, 'is to make records a proposition sweet to the whole round world, that all on its face storm the stores, and every moving pictures nabob in LA beats blazing trail to my door.'

A mess of standards, Brett. *Some Enchanted Evening* from *South Pacific*. *People*, from *Funny Girl*. *We Kiss In A Shadow* from *The King And I*. *If I Could Write A Book* from *Pal Joey*. I went off that reservation here and there too.

'I say we rock up this daisy. Like we did *Que Sera Sera*.'

Johnny Scott worked up a wildass arrangement of *It Ain't Necessarily So* from *Porgy And Bess,* with assist from JP Jones and Jimmy Page.'

Yeah, well, no arg from Brettski here. Not much of Proby's that don't shake my tree. This one a brain melter.

'We also cut numbers from West End musicals. *What Kind Of Fool Am I*, from *Stop The World- I Want to Get Off*, and *If I Ruled The World* from *Pickwick*. To apprise these Brits of my regard for their stars too.

188

And Liberty sent a demo by one of their writers, Van McCoy. *You've Come Back.* This, the single we must cut, they said, after *Maria*. I knuckled to. It quelled the bark and howl from that quarter. For a stretch.

A new look now, to dispel memory of wicked velvet. Bespoke three-piece.

'I rock these threads waymore better than ol' Tom Jones,' I told the press. 'No socks or carrots down my britches neither.'

For the album cover for *PJ Proby In Town*, me in this cavalier's raiment. At a table at Annabels, this toney club on Berkeley Square. A perfect match.

It was just as we made ready to release *Maria*. Press broke a story about the Nymphets Club. Their lurid and defamacious version, that is. *News Of The World, Daily Express, Daily Mirror, The Sun* went squealsville. Claims of girls as young as ten.

'*They* came to *me*. Said their parents knew. No complaints from *them*,' I said, but, well, *that* don't sell no late extra edition.

'I churched 'em up. Discipline. Hygiene. How to recognise and avoid the worst designs of men. Brett, that's the *verdad* on it, on a hillside of hotel room Gideons.'

What can you say? Sure, invoke the nostrums of beyond reasonable doubt, presumption of innocence, all that. Flip it over and, well, he's said things across the years that fair drop him in it. These, just jokes, he'd say. In the end, I couldn't call it either way. Photo finish.

'A pickle and no mistake. EMI held back *Maria*, lest radio ban it. In its place, for the *TOTP* spot for its premiere, *Somewhere*.'

*

'There is no way Theseus will be punished,' went my press release. 'I love my dogs too much for that.'

Wayne Fontana saw it happen, Brett. My St Bernard bit me. Mauled my arm. Bandages up to my elbow. So I went on the TV like that.'

A hard ask to credit that Proby's mutt would take a chunk out of him for no reason. But a wily move. Get a nation of dog lovers onside, and *bang!* All's well. But the Nymphets bizzo wasn't goin' away. Whatever the truth of it, the dude had set fire to the circus. And couldn't find his way out of the tent.

'Now, talk of a TV show, *The World Of PJ Proby*. A sitdown with a production company, via Heyman. Yeah, sweet on me again, now there's a sniff of treasure in it for him. We put that out there, to sell *Maria*. Then the dadgum producers pulled out.'

If they ever existed, eh. Yeah, well, colour me skeptical, but...

'Well, it fussed me not, Brett. But then came pale riders. A new hell rolling in their wake.'

CHAPTER FORTY

'It's all you can do, Jim. And it may not go your way.'

He had inside information. The Limeys of no mind to renew my visa.

'Unacceptable, Heyman. Why don't you tell that Queen of yours...'

'That Queen of mine is not inclined to be linked to the likes of you, chum. So. Apply for a new one. And an extension on your existing document. That'll buy you some time.'

'So what are my chances?'

'You need me to tell you that?'

Meanwhile, EMI hit on a new way to sell biscuits on me. The San Remo Music Festival in Italy. These teams of two compete. Do two numbers, an Italian singer as partner. They had me cut two songs. *Quando Tornera* and *Per Questo Voglio Te*. The writer, Mansuelo de Ponte, made the scene in London. Helped out with my Italiano. My rendition so blew him clean away, he flung his arms around me when it was done.

'Signore Proby,' he said,' 'ow do you do it?'

'Maestro, I don't *do,*' I said.

'I *am.*'

An operatic tenor, Guiseppe di Stefano, my team partner for this singfight. Partner to Maria Callas for some years. I told Ron Richards, he an opera buff.

'Oh, Jim, you can't lose,' said Ron. 'Um, if he turns up.'

Oh. Loco as me, then. I couldn't wait to get on a party.

'Look at that biscuit go, boy. Like a turkey through the corn.'

EMI released *Maria* now, for Christmas. Number Eight, first week. But then becalmed. New Nymphet Club stories in the press. Dadgum it, those Limey groups got up to well worse than ol' PJ. But they were home team. I on the gallows, a Texan trespasser.

*

They told the press before even me, Brett. Hell, that's how *I* found out. No new work visa. Nor extension. Those Fleet Street red top rags bid me begone at once. I did something else.

'I proclaim this day that I am quitting the music business. For good.'

See, Brett, when singers die, the rubes rush out, buy their records. You know, Buddy Holly, Jim Reeves, Patsy Cline, Hank Williams. So I seized the day. *No more PJ, not ever, kids.*

'My plan now, Pan Am it back to LA,' I told reporters. 'There to study on drama at UCLA, to prepare for my movie debut.'

This move, I figured, would sell records, in such volume that the Limeys would see all the money I made for 'em. They'd fold like they're holdin' seven-deuce. Make with that new visa, that I might remit that tax debt.

Well, I figured wrong. And that same day, that fuckneck Vidal Sassoon stole Beverley Adams from me. On all flanks now be I bested. And cast out from this miserablest of feifdoms.

CHAPTER FORTY-ONE

'We're going somewhere else today, Proby.'
I couldn't take no more sitting in pubs all day. The Texan's miffed but I make it crystal. *Not up for debate, Proby.* It's a public holiday. Australia Day. The nation hits the piss to toast armed incursion by foreign power two hundred years back. Our destination, The Domain. Free rock show. Half the town headed that way. Yet against all odds we found a park close by, near St Marys Cathedral. A good day to get a bet on.

'Righto, Proby. Just a short walk. Five minutes tops.'
'Brett. I told you. I do *not walk*. I am an...'
I kept on goin'. And I had the six pack.

'She's still got it, eh, Jim?'
Onstage, the mighty, mighty Dinah Lee.
'Hey, Proby,' I said. 'I know the mob running this gig.'
I'd called them about doing this.
'How about we go backstage, meet Dinah? First time since '66. Press there, TV news. Big story, *bang*. Pull more humans to the gigs...'
'Brett, she's not my cut of brisket.'
Oh, for fuck's sake.
'But say,' he said, grinning, 'does she have any daughters?'
Straight outta *Lolita*. Maybe winding us up. But with Hazmat, you never knew. Best get him outta there. Goodnight, Australia.

*

'I can sing it better than that guy.'

His first and unhelpful response. Clyde's proposed some recording. The Hoodoo Gurus' *My Girl,* and *Mars Needs Guitars.* New Proby product. Merch for our tour. Airplay on JJJ. Straight out or each way, a top punt.

'Proby, it's a new direction for you, bwana,' I said, even as I saw the game was lost.

See, he didn't know who the Gurus were. And so didn't rate them. Then this.

'I need a full orchestra. And a choir. I'll be having a choir...'

Ixnay. The moon in his eyes warned of trouble in mind.

'G'day, Dave. Meet PJ Proby.'

A cosmic coincidence. We run into Dave Faulkner from the Gurus very next day, outside the Bondi coma pit. Looks Proby up and down. Shakes his head. Swerves to Clyde.

'Why aren't you guys *filming* this?'

'Proby, this is my sister Nina.'

Then it happens again! I've just trundled Proby out of his tomb two days on. She beholds, at nine of a morning, her sibling. With this derro who's guzzling a stubby on the street.

'How do! Call me Jim!'

Then to me, not to Nina.

'What does she do?'

'She's a lawyer, Proby.'

'Oh, yeah. Lawyers. I needed one when I shot my wife in the ass.'

Eh?

'Heck, sister woman. No harm occasioned. It was like a pillow fight.'

She looked at me. At him.

'What have you *done,* Brett?'

Shot your wife, I'm thinkin.' *Just the one?* The full story came stumbling out of him later. And another that involved an axe.

*

The daily raves continued. Me as magic booze machine with a pair of ears.

'Let me see now. San Remo. Crazyass bill. The Hollies, Pitney, Yardbirds, Bobby Vinton, Pat Boone. All partnered with Italian singers. Me, with the wildest of all.

'Why, sure. Lead on, maestro.'

Guiseppe di Stefano, the Italians called *Pippo*. A stone gambler. We two just met, we make for San Remo's casino at his behest. He's well-known here. High roller. Drinks comped.

'Oh, my goodness,' I said when we left. A lotta loot lighter. Long past sunup.

Friday night. Round One. We did not make Round Three on the Sunday night. Reason-in-chief, we did not make Round Two. Trounced 'em all that Friday but Guiseppe, a bad boy rep hereabouts. And mine had followed me here faithful as Fido.

No cause to tarry, so *si* to Pippo's offer. To Monte Carlo, in his ride, a chauffeured Rolls Royce. Lost a whole other fortune at the tables there, Brett. Troubled me not. The troublin' I left to those Limey taxmen, thus denied this hunk of my liquid assets.

Back in England, I'm advanced a short grace period, to get my affairs in order. Word being I'm quitting the business, EMI now released a bunch of biscuits on me, to cash in. The Italian single, *Per Questo Voglio Te*. Then *You've Come Back,* the one Liberty made me cut. On its still cooling heels, *PJ Proby In Town,* my third LP. My last cattle drive. Me the beef.

It's February '66. Three weeks to deportee day. Taxman noised up fresh. A threat to freeze my bank accounts. So I bought a place in Wembley. They couldn't take that off me so easy. *You've Come Back* made just Number 25 then breathed its final gasp. The hell with 'em.

'Sure, why not, hoss?'

Barry Langford, despite our falling out, offered me a farewell tour with impresario Tito Burns. My pals The Searchers as support. Six dates. Two shows nightly. Birmingham Town Hall, Bristol Colston Hall, Newcastle City Hall, Sheffield, Leicester. Last of it, Liverpool, Empire Theatre. No more bets, all in all done by end of March.

Packed, every show. Gator-brained riots. Now, my last cards I played. First, appeal to the High Court, the Limey take on the US Supreme Court. No sale. Privy Council, arbiter of final resort, the same. They said the UK was finished with PJ Proby.

'But they are mistaken,' came this rebel's retort. 'For I am finished with *them*.'

'**M**y new home, up in the Hollywood Hills. Neighbours, Katherine Hepburn, Bobby Darin, Johnnie Ray.'

That joint. I'd read about it somewhere. Black plastic bags chockers with trash, piled up against windows. Proby squatting in squalor. And now, more I didn't want to hear about.

'I started to meet local mothers at the supermarket. Said I was back in LA to make movies. This led to a new Nymphet Club. These foxy mamas keen for their bambinas to study on etiquette, deportment. Only thing drill instructor Proby never did was touch 'em.'

Whatever you say. Rave on, raver.

'At my pad, fine times, Brett. A swimming pool. Adult fun. Had pals from the music world over, movie people. Airline stewardesses, fashion models, go go dancers. Any of open mind. On occasion, guests compelled to check in their clothes, all their clothes, at the door and put on these loincloths. The men, given a hunting knife and headband. A feather in it, like Injun braves. Girls, just a loincloth. A real small one. Object of the game, the girls had to persuade the feathers off the boys. *Any which way they could.* My part, tote a rifle. Oversee the action. For provender, pigs on spits, avocadoes, grapefruits. Like a Roman orgy at Caesar's dadgum palace. And then there was Judy.

In this ermine coat. Nothing on under it. My first sight of heiress Judy Howard. Her granddaddy founded the Buick Motor Company. Owned Seabiscuit and other champion thoroughbreds with Bing Crosby. And half the real estate in Palm Springs. Serious West Coast money. She dug me on sight. In my loincloth and out of it.

Judy hostessed some swingin' rip-it-ups herself. The first I went along to, this pro football player there. Giving some girls a hard time. So I threw him through a plate glass door. Despite my valour, Judy was riled and I, banished.

But I knew she was fervid for me. So I asked for a date. I go round to pick her up, she's buck naked. Writing a check for $250,000 for something. Yessir. I'd come to the right place.

We became a celebrity couple. Invites to opening nights, bein't she's loaded and Hollywood always out to duchess investors. Red carpet walks. Premieres, Graumann's Chinese Theater. So close to these motion pictures rainmakers, I could hear their hearts a-beatin'. Feel 'em through my feet.

Judy gave me ideas too, to serve my Hollywood objectives, Brett. Saw a story in the *LA Times*. The stars on the sidewalk outside the old Moulin Rouge on Sunset were being demolished. Gary Cooper's, Garland's, Chaplin's. They're remaking it into a rock club, Hullabaloo's. To replace the movie stars, they plan to line the walls of this new joint with plaques of rock stars. They asked Sonny And Cher, the Turtles, Bo Diddley, Ike and Tina Turner, Little Richard, others. They all said yes. *Not me. Nossir.*

'I refuse to lend my name to the trashing of those screen legends,' I said. See, if I'd agreed, I'd have got no press. This way, I get my picture took and a story all about me, nothing but.

'I'll never replace Gary Cooper,' I told the *Times*.

'But he did his bit. Now I'm doing mine. I proved myself as a singer. Now I've got to prove myself in Hollywood.'

I went on to imply that I had a deal with a studio.

'Not at liberty to say which one.'

Hell, it works in the music business.

*

'It's on them to come get.'

Pat Hayley had relocated to LA with me. A letter from England spoke of my tax debt. In Uncle Sam dollars, assayed at one hundred and seventy-five thousand. Judy said what to do.

'Tell 'em, Pat,' I directed her, 'that they bounced me off their island. Forced me to abide in a jurisdiction beyond it. So how they aim to collect, not my trammel and entirely theirs.'

'Well, the sad but true of it, Jimmy, is the reverse of what you contend.'

I made the scene at Liberty for royalties I deemed due.

'Them Abbey Road sessions,' said Al Bennett. 'Orchest'as, choirs, and all such getalong.'

Snuffy Garrett served me a faceful of stogie smoke.

'Extravagance not mitigated by sales. Cast your lamps across your contract, son.'

He cold-eyed the Wild Turkey in my fist.

'The right way up this time.'

'Oh, man. You don't really think it was *Spector* who did all that, do ya?'

I owed 'em some new records, the front page of it. The good news, my new producer.

We cut at United on Sunset. Jack Nitzsche, flying the desk here, brought in the First Call Gang, later on called the Wrecking Crew. Leon Russell, piana. Tommy Tedesco on guitar, or James Burton or Glen Campbell, now a star in his own right. Jim Gordon, drums, or Hal Blaine. Carol Kaye or Joe Osborn, bass. Larry Knechtel, any dang thing that toots or twangs or booms or plings. A fine and funky company.

'It's ruining your vocal, Jim.'

Of my next single, *I Can't Make It Alone,* Jack had parlayed it from Carole King and Gerry Goffin when the Righteous Brothers said nix. Now Jack never got mad. Just cold. Soft voice. Like the worst of evildoers.

'Hell it is, Jack. Ron Richards used to give me Remy Martin. Result, outstanding.'

He said nothing. For some seconds.

'No more liquor in the studio, Jim. Your voice sounds like it crawled in here from Skid Row downtown. So tomorro...'

'As you please, Jack. There'll be no booze here. Because there'll be no PJ *Proby either!*'

Well, I'll be damned. Jack swung by next morning to pick me up. Stood there like a fence post while I sassed him, and was not dissuaded.

'If relaxin's your thing, Jim, try a little of *this* do drop in.'

'I got no truck with that peace weed, Jack. Anyway, I have asthma, so...'

'Jim. Al Bennett has my back on this.'

Well, Brett, he had me at *Al Bennett.* That Arkansas hardass would bury me still pickin' and kickin' if I riled him. So I shared that scooby doo. Another as we drove. A third at the studio. Jack had quite the appetite for it.

'Whoa, Jack,' I said. 'Stop the room, I wanna get *off!*'

Giggling like a loon. And the band's sound. Like I don't believe I ever heard before.

'Do that more what you just did before, minstrels. Hey, Jack. Ain't they somethin'?'

We achieved a mess of zero. Jack next day was reminded it was *he* got *me* zonked. So today my bourbon came along. Objection overruled.

Our truce bore fruit. Three superfine tracks, *I Can't Make It Alone, Sweet Summer Wine* for a B side, and *You Make Me Feel Like Someone.* But of the third, he made me do take after take, even after my pipes were shot. This could not stand.

'Well,' said Judy that night, naked in the pool, 'here's what you do, lover man.'

I waited till we made the studio to drop it on him. There'd be no singing today. My voice in no shape. Left him gogglin' on the other side of that glass like a goldfish in a shark tank. Made for Pandora's. Or the Whisky.

Or the Galaxy, the Unicorn, the London Fog. Well, maybe all of the above.

'What the hell you *doin'?*'

This big drink of water snatched it right out of my hand. Poured it out the window as he drove. Jack's twenty-three skidooed and they set *this* yard boss on me.

'You been a shade free with Liberty's time and bread, brother. So now we do it my way.'

He wouldn't let me get beer. Nor permit others to fetch it. When I declared I'd sing no more, this Calvin Carter locked me in the booth till we were done, in measure to his satisfying.

My displeasure I made known to Al Bennett. He said he'd sue me to Mars and back if I made any more such chat.

'Well,' said Judy. 'I'd pay heed. If we're to be wed,' and I had this day proposed thus, 'I could be liable should a lawsuit proceed.'

My position much clarified.

Cal Carter, quite the pedigree. Cut records on Jimmy Reed, Elmore James, John Lee Hooker. The *Shoop Shoop Song* for Betty Everett. Broke Frankie Valli and The Four Seasons, Bacharach. Wrote hits. *I Like It Like That* and such. First to sign the Beatles in the US on VeeJay. But his ways vexed me. We were headed for a reckoning.

*

The Strip, jumpin' in '66. New clubs. The Haunted House, the Double H we called it. Horror movie decor. Skeletons. Bats. Stage roof, a papier-mache monster head. Nostrils blew smoke. Snake eyes that lit up in the dark. Groups played in its mouth, this lined with fangs. Pat and Lolly Vegas, the house band here. I sang this night. Joint went wild. Ford fetched up too. One of us got both of us thrown out.

Few days on, Pat and Lolly and later Ford swung by for a swim in my pool. Four beers in, out came guitars and a bass. We sang up every doo wop, blues, country song you ever knew and a mess you didn't. Then Pat Vegas slides into this cajun rap.

Gonna dig ya on the scooby doo, gonna dig ya on the scoobydie, booga boo, get hip to the consultation of the bulawee, all this patois of the weed. Then Ford jumps in. *Everything's copacetic now, gitcha tootsie.*

A song born right before my ears. I called Cal Carter.

'We have a hit!'

*

Pat and Lolly, guitar and bass. Ford, rhythm guitar. Leon Russell's piano, if memory serves, Hal Blaine drums. Darlene Love and pals for backups. Some horns.

'No side comments, boys,' said Cal to the stringbusters. No licks or frills, he meant.

'Leave that to the brass.'

Wise counsel. How hits come to be.

Niki Hoeky in the can, we cut more that might could be singles. Like *Out Of Time,* the Stones number. Chris Farlowe had Number Oned that sucker Englandside. That humpty didn't just steal my style. Brett. He sucked the marrow from its bones. And *Reach Out I'll Be There,* the Four Tops, I took to where even their main man Levi Stubbs couldn't.

But I didn't care for Mr CC swingin' by in the AM, me and Judy still snoozin' off our starlit fun. So next day I just didn't get up, no matter how long he idled out there honking his horn. He needed to learn who was callin' this square dance.

*

'Hey, Calvin, this ain't the way to my place.'

'Jim, we got a session, dog. Hence where this Buick Wildcat be bound. Don't get uptight.'

See, he'd just sprung me from the holding cells. I had no selection in it. On the Strip the night before, I'd been busted. Drunk and disorderly.

Now, I'm penned in that vocal booth all day. Cut loose only when he says we're done.

Well. Turns out ol' Carter's ex-Marines. In consequence, knew a bunch of old Semper Fi buddies now in the LAPD. I'd been played like a rube at the carny.

And it didn't end there. He dragged me back there again. Made me cut some R'n'B classics, *for B sides and such*, he said. Record companies often do this. To release it on you should they not renew your deal and then down the line, hanker for yet more bacon off your rump without they pay you for it.

'Asking for me? Him personally?'

'He sure has, Jim.' Snuffy Garrett calling. 'Don't let us down, now.'

An invite. Sing the theme for his new movie, *The Chase*. Marlon Brando, no less. This number composed by John Barry, who wrote the *James Bond Theme*. So we go in and cut it. Next I hear, Barry likes me for the theme to the next Bond movie, *You Only Live Twice*.

'Well, they asked Scott Walker first,' Snuffy told me. 'But he's turned 'em down.'

Oh, joy.

Then I find this boat is but a bucket with a hole in it. Cubby Broccoli, the producer, wants Sinatra to sing it. You know, *family* connections. Frank says no. But bestows it upon his daughter Nancy as if his gift to give. Then Brando drops my song from *The Chase*. Yeah. Opportunity knocked. And gave me a faceful of fist.

'I hear you, boys. But it will go good for that said reason.'

Liberty fussing, of *Niki Hoeky* being about the weed.

'Kids will buy it 'cause they're in on a little secret with ol' PJ. Radio won't make up or down of this cajun wordsoup. Tell 'em I was possessed by the spirit and regaling in tongues.'

Calling from England now, Barry Langford. To talk of touring Europe and Down Under. And of The Easybeats relocating, Sydney to London. His notion, that they flop at my pad there. Pay rent on it.'

Now the sun set on Proby's eyes.

'Say, Brett. You don't happen to be acquainted with those fellas, do you? Wrecked my home. And stiffed me. Owe me a sum considerable. I'd sure like to...'

'Nah, Jim. Sorry.'

'Well, that is a dadgum shame. Why, I...'

I let him rant. And blew out my planned support here for Proby's gigs. Prudent, I concluded, to drop a big dollop of space between this punchy Texan and my man Stevie Wright.

CHAPTER FORTY-THREE

D espite the Night Of The Lansdowne, we took Proby out again. Show punters he's still among us, gigs imminent. We brace for a spazz at the Annandale when he gets twitchy about the Bam Balams. Then I'll be buggered if they don't rip into *Niki Hoeky*. He lights up like Vegas at nightfall. Can't wait to meet the band, reveal himself to them. A good yak. Real drinks all round. Happy ending. Rare as.

Back on minder patrol, the rave trundled on.

'We called it the *Electrifying Unpredictable PJ Proby Show*. Langford back in Australia now, making a TV show, *Dig We Must*, with those boys Bobby and Laurie. So he set this up.

We took some English boys. Like Wayne Fontana. You know, *Game Of Love, Groovy Kind Of Love*. And Eden Kane, Peter Sarstedt's brother. That guy, *Where Do You Go To My Lovely*. Local supports, Dinah Lee again, and this group Marty Rhone and the Soul Agents. And to open the show, these kids. Teeth like dadgum horses. The Bee Gees. Yeah, Brett. I knew them when.

There was a clothier, His Lordship, a Kiwi. Barry cut a deal. If His Lordship dressed me, I'd plug his stores on radio, TV, onstage. And he did and we did.

I'd grown a beard at Judy's behest. Steppin' fine in His Lordship's threads. Black frock coat. Cravats or ties. Waistcoat. A gentleman gunfighter, or riverboat gambler. The Australian press, set to galumph on me for duds pink or purple, ribbons and buckles and bows. Their crestfallen faces I still recall. I foxed 'em good.

'There'll be no show if you don't.'

That dadgum Sydney Stadium stage. You could only get to it by wading through the auditorium, like the fighters did to get to the ring.

'That's no style of entrance, Barry. Fix it.'

Well, he had six kinds of seizure, but they made a microphone cord. Hundred feet long, Brett. Thus did I descend, from top row of the bleachers, singing *Maria* as I made for the stage. Six bouncers flanked me. The godking of pop takes his passage among his subjects.'

Not wrong. Sensational, that tour. I saw it on Channel Nine as a kid. The Melbourne show, filmed and screened on Brian Henderson's *Bandstand*. Hendo also interviewed him, about his tax problems. The Proby, pretty much as you'd expect.

'I don't got to do a dadgum thing, and there's no debtor's prison any more, so...'

And a plug for His Lordship. Then Proby lays a yarn on me that fair pins me ears back.

'Now, Jim, there's a problem but we think you can help.'

Barry and the promoter, Jimmy Huddleston, came to my hotel room in Auckland.

'How might I be of assist, *hermanos?*'

'Jim, the second Sydney show's not selling so well. So...'

POP STARS TO WED!

Stage One was Page One. We told the press Dinah Lee and I were engaged. But we forgot to inform her. First she knew, she saw it in the paper. Anyway, on to Stage Two.

'Jim, in Sydney, press and TV will be there. Dinah will run into your arms,' said Barry. Well, jackpot. We sold out Sydney overnight. Flapdoodle abounded. We'd be married on TV, live on *Bandstand*. Or at a show, onstage. *It could be any which one, kids!* Then, the tour still in Auckland, I get a call from LA.

'Whaddya mean, she wants to surprise me?'

'Judy's in Sydney, Jim. Said to keep it secret. But I had to call you, pet. There's a story in the *LA Times*. You and that singer, Dinah. Is this tru...?'

206

'No, Pat, it isn't. But I know one thing.'

'What's that?'

'She never travels without packin' heat.'

'How do, angel mine?'

She's zonked from the flight. Plain she's not seen the story, as she's not here in NZ, blowing holes in me.

'Now, honey, I'll be in Sydney come morning.'

'Jim, this was meant to be a surprise!'

'Yeah, and I love you for it, baby. But there's something you need to know.'

'What the *fuck?*'

'Don't fret now. It's just to promote the show. So nothing you hear is true. Alright?'

'What the fuck does that mean?'

'I can't say more than that. Don't concern yourself. I'll see you tomorrow.'

Yeah. She always flew first class. Security, not as it is now. Rich ladies from the front end, waved right on through. With or without they had shooters.

'Big bad Bo!'

On the flight to Sydney, Mr Diddley. On tour in NZ, same as me. We had a good drink. Rolled off that jet, gabbin' of this and that.

'Hey PJ! *PJ!* Aren't you *forgetting* something?'

I about face it. The press. In their midst, Dinah. *Ooooh yeeeahh.* I run to her. But they see through it, clear as clean air. *Uh huh. Suuuuure.* Then I recall *Judy is here.* Time to get there. Talk my way out from a brunch of six hot slugs.

'She said she's gone to church, PJ.'

Up in our suite, Judy's ordered flowers wall to wall. And here's the front desk, tellin' me she's a praying woman. First I heard tell. Judy's 'bout as churchy as that fella trades in souls at the crossroads come midnight.

'You'll look foolish trying to sing with no fuckin' *head*.'

Her voice cold on the phone. She's still here. Different suite.

'I won't stay in that room with you, Jim. Tell that tramp it's off. Or I'll make it happen my own way.'

No-one would come near me backstage. Word was out, it seemed. When I called to ask Judy to the show, she'd had good shuteye off her medications. Simmered down some. So she came. But still wouldn't talk to me. She'd worked out I was truthin'. But I must pay for my thoughtlessness.

'Well, why don't you two join us?'

Things thawed some. Wayne Fontana and bride Suzanne Davies had yes I do'd it in Manchester just before this tour. Now, they're Hawaii-bound for their honeymoon, so we took 'em up on it.

Later that night, she's sawin' logs off her pills. I found that rod about the fifth suitcase in. Took out the shells. Ditched 'em. She never said another word about it.

*

'Bright Light City it is, my turtle dove.'

Things grew more better. November, my birthday, we lit out for Vegas. Judy's whim. I not inclined to contest it. For she said she'd fund my movie career. Jackie Wilson playing here, so I made representation and he sang at our wedding reception that day.

'Jimmy,' she'd said, 'let's honeymoon in Hawaii.' Well, we did just that. Even planned a dream home there. But now Brett, a mess of ruckus, via Judy's fondness for pills. Old Yellers. Blue Vallies. Her moods all riptides and dangerous curves.

'*Do it or I will kill myself!*'

Cut off my ponytail, she meant. Never said why. And she dug not the upshot. Railed of that and other conjecture.

'*Leech! Parasite!*'

Yet I harboured no such aim. In fact, I went to work on her ranch in Malibu County. She raised quarter horses there, like my daddy had in Huntsville.

Well, as abrupt as her flash of madness, her recovery. Hosted a party. Hawaiian theme. Grass skirts for the gals, no tops. A lei round their necks. Wine and rum punch in coconut shells. No need for a map in the dust with a stick of where it went from there.

But she was not of her right mind. Phone rang all the live long. Judy's assignations. One day I roll home, she's doing the dance of Eros with this grocery clerk on the sofa.

She laughs at me. Kid skedaddles. Me, I spy the glass coffee table before me. Hoist it aloft. Render it to shards. Like Moses. Those tablets of stone.

Behind me. *Click.*

'Is that what I think it is?'

A Winchester. She's drawin' a bead on my skull. Ran me off her ranch. I double-timed it back to the Hills. Slid a gat under my pillow. Never went back and she didn't come lookin'.

*

'You need to get over here, chum. Show your face.'

Tito Burns calls. My manager now, did for The Searchers and Dusty Springfield. The Limey press have coloured me coward, fled to avoid my taxes.

'Hell, Tito! They flung me sprawling outta there!'

He'd tried for a work visa, but the UK government, they're scared of how the press might serve them. My new UK single, *I Can't Make It Alone,* about to come out. Only road out, tourist visa and do unpaid press, TV spots. Tito said it would show I'm willing to seek terms.

I fancied it otherwise. In my screenplay, I'm calling 'em out for a drawdown.

CHAPTER FORTY-FOUR

So, Brett, I threw those Easybeats out. Reclaimed my home. To let those Limeys know I'm back, I hit the clubs. The Bag O' Nails. Or La Chasse, Wardour Street, Soho, up from the Marquee. Fit thirty max. You had to be a face to get in. And the 100 Club in Oxford Street. Rod Stewart used to sing there. Looked like a rooster. Sang like one too.

'In my home, you dress like a man, not some chorus girl!'

I took to hosting parties again. One night, this coloured fellow trucks in. Wardrobe, all the hues of a candy store. My take, drug fiend, an undesirable, come to steal my baubles. I flung him down the steps. Later I'm talking to Chas Chandler from The Animals.

'Just now bounced this coloured, Chas. Gussied up like an LA pimp...'

'Oh, fuck, Jim. I've just brought him over from the States. To break him here, like Jack did with you...'

'Oh.'

'You said it was open house.'

So *perdoname* to Chas and ain't I'm a dog if the fella under discussion didn't return in a well-cut suit and tie.

'I'm real sorry, Jimi,' I said. 'Come on in.'

But it left me worried. This noise the kids wanted now. Where was a place for I in all this bedlam?

'Get it waived. You're lookin' at a victim of circumstance.'

Lawyer and accountant I engaged and instructed them thus.

'My managers stole it,' my plea. But that horse wouldn't run. Served with a fresh demand for those taxes, I saw now why they'd let me back in. An ambush. Sixty thousand pounds, plus penalties for tardy payment.

'They'll seize all you have if they can serve a writ on you,' said my solicitor. So I laid low. Ignored doorknocks daytimes. Left only after dark, when the process servers had quit for the day. Outlaw now. Like ol' Wes Hardin.

Tito got me onto a BBC show, *Pop Inn*, to sing *Niki Hoeky* and a chat with the other guest, Gene Pitney, touring the UK. A duet while we're at it. Then out on the town. I came to in a stranger's bed. Money all gone and one boot shy. A rockin' good time.

Tito persuaded *Top Of The Pops* to have me on, *Niki* rising up the British charts like the Great Flood. Swung a temporary work visa, proviso that earnings be set aside for that tax mess. Good for a week at some Newcastle club. Cabaret. Meantime, Liberty, all holler and shout. Owed new product. Skitch back to LA, they said.

*

In, oh, March of '67, *Niki* Number 23 on *Billboard,* I did Dick Clark's *American Bandstand,* his other show *Where The Action Is,* NBC's *Hullabaloo* and *Hollywood A Go Go.* And a neutron bomb for the US press.

'This singin' dog's done.'

Yessir. Same ploy as the UK. Off this go tell it on the mountain, sales of my new LP *Enigma,* those sessions with Jack Nitzsche and Calvin Carter, took off. And *Niki* went gold. So I went on a drunk for a week. Mayhap two.

*

'The fans have spoken. Not my place to choose.'

Three weeks on, I rethunk my exit stage left and did so make public. Liberty's attorneys had proved persuasive.

They again set me to work with Cal Carter. Randy Newman at the Brill Shack wrote hits for Dusty, Pitney, Cilla. Had this number, *Mama Told Me Not To Come.* Others had cut it, like that bigmouth Eric Burdon, but had no hit with it.

So they cut it on me. Fact is, I co-wrote it with Randy. Yet received no credit. I lost a big jumble of money when Three Dog Night made it a hit. Brett, I am owed millions, for work stolen without attribution.'

Truly? Yeah, well, in the scammers' picnic of showbiz, its desperates, dodgers and fly by nighters, Proby likely as not had a case. He and eight million others.

'*Just Holding On*, my next single. Larry Weiss wrote it. Did *Rhinestone Cowboy* for Glen Campbell. But it was too much like *Gimme Some Lovin'* by the Spencer Davis Group. I predicted even as we tracked it that the fans wouldn't buy it. And such was its fate.

'Well, I believe I'll call you Bear.'

A big boy. All face fur. Said name I gave Bob Hite when we met at El Dorado studio, corner Hollywood and Vine. His group, Canned Heat, cuttin' their first long player here.

'*Bar?*' he said.

'No, son, that's my Texan enunciation. The critters. Polar, panda. Your case, grizzly.'

The Heat's bass player Larry Taylor, we went way back, to my group the Moondogs. I had a meet with their management, Skip Taylor and John Hartmann. Knew right well who I was. Bustin' to take me on.

I played the Circle Star Theater in San Mateo just south of San Fran, joints like that. Supports, these psychedelic groups. A sound like a dadgum sawmill. Sometimes, gigs with the Heat, in LA, nearby counties. One, the Carousel Theater in West Covina, just east of LA and El Monte. A bunch of theatres like this. Old playhouses, now remade as hippie ballrooms. Kids all stoned on Ripple wine and the weed. Or flashing on Owsley acid.

Did five nights that April at the Hullabaloo, the new joint on Sunset. But opening night, same as the Teenage Fair, a big annual event, a battle of the bands affair, across the street. So that's where everybody went. You only had to be fifteen to get into Hulla's, it being unlicensed. Whole point of me there was to pull these kids. But the few there didn't give a teardrop in hell. No singer ever so ignored.

'Why don't y'all go back to the Fair? I'll even give you the money!'

Fistfuls of Washingtons I slung at 'em. That got 'em chatterboxin'. Second night and third, pulled waymore and their full attention. *Who is this off the wall Texan?*

They put on the Heat and I as a double more often as the year rambled by. San Diego, San Fran. In LA, the Continental Auditorium downtown, near Chinatown. Me and these day-glo hippie groups. A dadgum plague.

'He can drink even more than you can, Jim.'

So claimed the Bear. This group played at the London Fog. Fella in question, Jim Morrison. His band, the Doors. Me and them, we'd have dealings down the line.

Groups at the Whisky these days left me cold as a hangman's eyes. Like the Mothers Of Invention, Frank Zappa's outfit. Ugliest group ever, Brett. How they ever got laid, a puzzlement. And I can't even talk about that Captain Beefheart.

Back with pipe-puffin' Mr Carter, we cut *She's Lookin' Good,* a Wilson Pickett number. Pat and Lolly Vegas, bass and guitar, brung it to the boil. Jim Gordon played drums. Tall dude. Worked with the Everlys, Beach Boys, Joe Cocker, Clapton. Some years on, murdered his mama. Detained at the criminally insane asylum. A wonder we ain't all.

'Like an outtasight purple striped polka dotted ten mile high butterfly.'

I pointed at the lyric sheet. Addressed its composer.

'Listen, Ford. I sound like I just et all of Owsley's LSD and Owsley with it.'

Jim Ford wrote this *Butterfly High* thing and played on the session.

'Not if I get to him first, Baba Louie,' he said.

We cut more Ford songs, as his *Niki Hoeky* had fared so well. These, set to Stax and Motown beats. A marriage encouraged by Cal Carter. The arranger, Arthur Wright, played a funky guitar on 'em to boot. He worked a good deal on all those coloured labels.

That said, Mr Carter grew burdensome to me, body and soul. So one day, this here object of his monsterations upped and walked.

'Well, just seven tracks in the can, dig. Brought it on your own bad self. '

Last words with Carter. None of the advance I sought to secure my return. Instead, Liberty dug out those R'n'B standards we'd one-taked at the *Enigma* sessions. So *that's* why he made me do that. These, to make the weight on my new album, *Phenomenon*. They'd shorn the golden fleece off this here sheep. Now, drew their daggers for the meat.

You Can't Come Home Again was the new single. But the coloured labels out of Memphis, Philly, Detroit, Chicago, put out so much like it that year that my new 45 was engulfed.

A cult hit in the clubs of northern England where they loved me half to deceasement. But such be slim solace, Brett. Ol' PJ never coined a penny off it.

Phenomenon was released September of nineteen and sixty-seven. *You Can't Come Home Again* did fine in England, so EMI put on a launch for the LP. And Tito lined up a live show at Epstein's Saville Theatre on Shaftesbury Avenue. Horse-whispered Eppy of gold for all. Just one stone in my boot.

'Tito, I need a work visa for that.'

'Leave it to Tito, chum. One will see if one can't do a spot of Queen-wrangling.'

CHAPTER FORTY-FIVE

'**W**ell, all those pills will do it sooner or later.'
My response to reporters at LAX. I made Heathrow just as the Beatles returned from Wales, their confab there with that hustler Maharishi. Weren't going to Epstein's funeral. Family wanted a private synagogue service. Instead, India, to hang ten with their holy man. Yeah, Brett. Nineteen and sixty-seven. Everyone's gone to the moon.

'Well, out of respect to Mr. Epstein, one expects, Jim.'
Tito's take on the poor turnout for my LP launch. Reviews diverged. Some called *Phenomenon* below average. Others, my best yet. Well, of that latter postulation, ain't they all?

'Jim, I'd grab it with all the hands you have, old boy.'
Tito wrangled this weirdo work permit. Just one show I'm granted. And Eppy's people at his Saville Theatre said awreet awrite.
'Despite Mr Epstein's *unavailability*,' was how they put it. I do love those Limeys so.

'Consequent to this, Jim, a less than full house.'
Fleet Street incited people to boycott my show. Or go along and serve me admonition. They did both in equal measure. At the show, railed at me, *Yankee go home!* Well, if they're gonna write you up anyway, I say go big.
'America saved your sorry ass from Hitler, Limey. Lookin' at you, I don't know why we took the trouble!'

It did not go down well. And other woes cursed us. Like no access to the theatre for sound and lighting check before the show. So that night, both went from hell to Dogpatch.

'On the cards, old chum,' said Tito. Epstein, he said, had always supervised the Saville shows personally, to forestall just such. Yet at my post I did remain, jousting with malcontents. The endsville. England swings like a sledgehammer do.

CHAPTER FORTY-SIX

E ars of tin and rust, those Limeys, Brett. Acclaim for *Phenomenon* back in LA. So I had to get on TV to hype it. The sheen of my lucky stars fell on me now. My new manager, Bob Marcucci, just what I needed. Said he'd get me into movies was what clinched it. A producer himself and a song plugger, he'd known Dick Clark from back when ol' Bob had sold him Frankie Avalon and Fabian. This ol' slick's been pimping singers and beefcake since the dadgum Iron Age.

'Dicky baby, PJ's bad boy rep will reap a ratings bonanza!'

Dick had this new show, *Where The Action Is*. Co-hosts, Paul Revere And The Raiders, who Bob also handled. So via these auspices, I did both.

'Your uncle Roberto has a big surprise, *bambino!*'

Marcucci at my door. Late night. He did this instead of call. Suspect he's queer for me. That, or mobbed up. Timid of phone taps.

'You're going on the road, *mi dolce ragazzo*. America is ours!'

Where The Action Is put on a tour every summer. Bob scored me the headline slot. Went all over, near about all mainland States. The bill, sissies mostpart. Keith Allison a regular on *Action*, off his resemblance to Paul McCartney. A picker. Played on Monkees records. My God, the Monkees, Brett. Entirely unlistenable. One of their songwriters, Neil Diamond, was also on this bill. Along with Billy Joe Royal. Had a hit off that Joe South number, *Down In The Boondocks*. And Tommy Roe. My kind of supports. None but I playin' A League.

'I don't know, Jim. *That's* gonna play in these towns? We're talking Baptists and such.'

The tour band, a helping of concern over *Niki Hoeky*, what I had planned.

'Boys, it's clear there's only one hero in this outfit,' I said. 'Just keep on playin' when I go into the routine. Head back to the verse only when I signal thus. As you were, chickenshits.'

'OK, then, children!'

The band comping on *Niki* behind me, it begins. I toke on an imaginary joint. Then hand it to a kid down front of stage.

'One for you.' Then took it back. 'And one for PJ.'

Then another and more. They're berserk for it. But that weren't all. After that, I'd pick a girl from the crowd. Up onstage, dance with her. Then I'd plant a kiss. The roof lifted off.

'Hey, Tex! Quit that or I'll sock you in the jaw!'

It was at the Toledo Civic Auditorium, Brett. This girl, happy to up and do it. But yonder chump, boyfriend or brother, tries for the stage, swingin' every fist he's got. Bouncers pin this dimwit, but me, I don't need them. I'm boiling hot for it. Heck, I'm the star of the show here, not some lumpy kid!

Wasn't but a second split three ways before the tour manager stomped out on to the stage. Closed the show. Backstage, he cussed and profanitised. But his foolishness I chastised.

'It's *me* they come to see! Freakiest beast *ever seen outside a circus cage!* They can't get enough!'

'Well, I'm a baboon's red ass if I can see what the *what* of *enough* is,' he says.

'Why, that's easy, hoss,' I said. '*I am sex itself.*'

Now, Brett, that baboon's red ass went and prattled, but Dick Clark had a full fix on who was packin' out this big top. He let it slide. But down the road, other disturbance.'

Yeah, well, surprise me, Proby, I'm thinking, through the blur of daily Probywatch.

'It was in Louisville, Kentucky. Now, Brett, Kentucky makes the finest bourbon in the whole round world.'

'It is acknowledged and honoured thus, my man.'

'But the thing of it is, they make it in these certain counties.'

Oh, Christ, Proby. You hear the truck comin,' but...'

'Dry ones. No booze may be osmoted in for purposes of consumption.'

'Sober up or your days on this bus are over, Jimmy.'

Hello, Harlan County lockup. Smuggling hooch across the state line. They go all steam and whistle on me.

'Your bail comes out of your check, Jim. Now, we've about sold out this tour. So you're not indispensable. You hear?'

'Why, gentlemen,' I said, 'those kids will stamp you flat as the Great Plains of Texas if you can my ass off this travellin' show.'

And fixed 'em with a pearly smile.

'Now, children!'

Cumberland College, Baptist U, Williamsburg, Kentucky. Ten thousand kids going ape.

I held up a hand like it nursed a cigar, make-believe.

'You know what I'm holding in my hand, don't you?'

'Yeesssss, PJ!'

'Well, this is not Bull Durham, is it?'

'Nooo, PJ!'

'Well, if it's not Bull Durham, children....*what is it?'*

This big pep rally chant started up, stomping their feet, as one.

'Mar-i-jua-na! Ma-ri-jua-na ! Ma-ri-ju-ana!'

They went bananas and further. For their messiah was among them.

Jimmy! What were you thinking?'

'Nuh?'

I'm jarred from my slumber. It's Dick Clark himself.

'Out there! About reefer!'

'I didn't say it, Dick. The kids did.'

He lunged forward as if to start swingin'. I held up my hands to stay his.

'Dick.'

I feigned chuckle to disarm him.

'Those lyrics. Cajun *patois*. How could Baptist kids perceive what such lexifications signify?'

'Well, Jimmy. Here's what they signify for *you*.'

'Verily you must be shittin' me, Luigi.'

Marcucci told me. My being bumped off that tour, bad, right enough. But now, news of that motherhumper Neil Diamond. Top of the bill. In *my place.*

'Bob. Leave it with me.'

'Leave what with you, Jim?'

Bob calls a couple days later. In a mighty fury.

'That Neil Diamond sings even worse than he writes for those Monkees.'

He reads over the phone my words to the newspapers.

'And as for them, they'll only last until the public finds out who they really are, who really plays on their records, all that fakery.'

Bob swore at me in Italian. Said no-one would book me, or have me on TV, doing that to other acts. I had to explain it was just to get a feud galloping. Like with Tom Jones. Shame ol' Neil didn't rise to the bait. Nor the Monkees. Oh, well. Time to seek out new fishin' spots.

CHAPTER FORTY-SEVEN

*Z*ero connections at Channel Nine. Pure cold calling.

'He's an international artist. Big in the '60s. I imagine he might be of interest to Ray Martin's Midday Show.'

I didn't expect to hear back in a hurry. I mean, Proby's been MIA twenty odd years. And deep in such pondering, the phone rings! A segment producer.

'Brett, we're very interested. Now, how about *Good Morning Australia* as well as *Midday?*'

'I'm sure Mr Proby would be delighte...'

'Both of those but nothing at the other networks. Alrightie?'

We're back in centre ring. *Bang.*

'I don't do morning TV.'

I might have known. You've just lined up two telly shows. One of which requires we be there at 0630 hours.

'Look, Proby. I get it. I've *seen* you in the morning. But we *are* doing it because that's how it works. Fuck you and not doing it. We are doing this, Proby, and we are doing it on this date.'

He says nothing at first. Slow as a wet week. Sitting, processing fuck knows what. Freakin' unbelievable what he comes up with.

'So Nini, we have to sit up with him all night.'

'Drink him up so he goes beddy-bye good and early.'

'Correct weight, Warwick Farm. The coma hits. We camp there. Try and stay conscious. Then the tricky bit. You wake him. Not me. He'll go off at me. Four hours before he normally does but he can't know that.'

'Has to think he's just nodded off for a bit.'

'Fine and dandy. So you snake charm him. We get him, don't matter how dead, into the taxi they're sending.'

He kicked up again that night. *I ain't doin' no mornin' TV,* usual dance. Enter Nini. He drifted off. We set up our vigil. Stayed awake. Never mind how.

'It's OK, Jim. You've just nodded off. *Just for a moment.'*
Nini. Not speaking, purring. He don't go off. He's *buying it.*
'Here's your beer.'
Massaging as she goes.
'We're off to the studio today. I'm coming with you. Don't want to miss this.'
Bang. He's hypnotised. I flash a six pack at him.
'Got these for the cab.'

'We're goin' to Channel *Nine!'* says Proby to the cabbie. Nini's got his motor running.
'Yeah,' says drive. Looks back through his rearview. Doesn't freak him out, thank fuck. Nor the grog in Hazmat's paw.
'You're a guest on the show, then.'
'Yeah. I'm PJ *Proby!'*
'Oh, *yeah.* I remember *you!'*
A fan. Bonus. They start raving. We settle back for the drive. *Top result.*

*

'Oh, I like her. So she's interviewing me.'
'Yeah, Proby,' I say. 'So don't ...'
'Oh, I like her.'
GMA presenter Liz Hayes keeps her cool when she eyeballs Proby, undead and no-one home. Nini and me cover as best we can. All teeth and smiles and love your work. The floor crew flash *Enter The Dragon*

stares. Fair enough. I mean, who fronts at dawn with a frosty in one hand and five more in the other?

'As a general rule, I do my own.'

'Do you, Jim?' says the makeup gal. Sweet as.

'Yes. I come from a theatrical background.' Hoists and sucks a beer.

'Yes, I can see that,' she says. Flashes me a glance. *You got a live one here, mate.*

'Brett. Where's the Green Room?'

Just two stubbies left. *Oh fuck.*

'I'm not sure, Proby. I'll find out.'

Pig's arse I will. Just as the producer rocks in.

'Righto!' he says. 'All set?'

Then Proby sees Liz Hayes going by.

'Oh, Liz!' Proby calls out. 'Where's the Green Room?'

'Oh,' says the producer. Looks at me. 'Not open till eleven.'

Shoots me a death smile. *You need to hose down your mad mate.* And just like that, Proby flips.

'I've been fuckin' all over the *world!* I been *everywhere!* I don't *do* morning TV! I don't *do* this shit! Whaddya*mean* the Green Room's *not* ope...'

'Jim.' Nini. 'You've got two beers, it's alrigh...'

'I want a real drink!'

Then he sees Liz Hayes again.

'The Green Room's not open, hey, *Liz!'*

Without a word, she wheels on her heels, producer in her slipstream. Nini gets to work on Proby. Producer comes back. Signals me aside.

'Liz is not doing the interview, mate.'

His eyes would glow red if they could.

'Steve Leibmann will do it. Liz says no way.'

Nice one, Proby.

Nini's got him to cool down. They plonk him on the set. The weatherman, Brian Bury, in front of his little map of Australia, doing his rave, hears this from the couch.

'Who *are* you? Who wants to *know* if it's gonna rain? Who *gives* a shit?'

Bury, smiling, to camera, don't drop a beat.

'That's PJ Proby you can hear. He's our next guest.'

They go to an ad break. Proby sings out to me.

'There's no *Green Room,* Brett.'

'Well, what do you want *me* to do, Proby? I can't open up a TV network's Green Room!'

I'm trying to keep it down. They're all chuckin' me looks like *I'm* nuts too. Which, it's fair to say, may well be the case at this stage.

'Liz is not doing the interview!'

'Well, Liz is not doing the interview because you come across as a fuckin' *creep!*'

'No, no, no, no...'

The producer shooshes everyone. Leibmann's here. Here we go, in *five, four, three....*

'Orbison, Johnny Cash, Scott Walker, Elvis...'

'Even Elvis?'

'Yessir. All of 'em. Stole my whole act...'

Leibmann's straight into it. Shoots a few Qs. Mentions Proby's Elvis demos. This sets off his Presley whinge. Entertaining, I'm sure. Viewers ain't heard it three hundred times like we have. They talk of his ponytail. The Beatles.

Leibmann says with a smile that the split pants back in '65 might have been a stunt. Now you'd think Proby would have a snappy comeback, twenty-five years down the line, but what we get is verbal shredmix. A diss on Jack Good. Zero context about who he is.

Then Leibmann invokes the name *Tom Jones.* Oh, no, *no, don't mention the war, no, don't...*

'Hadn't been for *me,* Tom Jones would still be doin' workingmen's clubs in Cardiff, Wales! He would not *exist!* A nothing. Can't even *sing!* Can't fight, either, you know,...'

Leibmann heads him off. A query about gigs. Fortunate that he has the facts to hand. Answers it himself. Proby sure can't. He thanks him for stopping by. Throws to the news. Floor manager swoops.

'Right, mate. You can go now.' The eyes. *Before I set the dogs on you.*

'I *told* you I don't do morning TV.'

'Come on, Jim.'

Nini takes Proby's arm.

'People here got work to do. We're in the road.'

He's blown it, into the next world blown it, but I turn to the producer. I need to show Proby what he's done.

'So, er, who do I see about *Midday?*'

Dude's all sunny and smiles. But the eyes, dialling triple zero.

'You're not *serious,* are you, mate?'

I come back at him all sheepish. Let him know I get it.

'Nah. Just checkin'.'

Then a voice, from far away.

'Say, friend. Can you get me on *Neighbours?*'

'So,' said Proby, taking his drinks from me, 'I'm off Dick Clark's tour. Bad press. I, portrayed as drug addict. Clubs won't book me. Nor TV shows.

That said, Skip and John from Canned Heat had a new venue. Old movie theatre. Called it Kaleidoscope. So I played a gig there with 'em. The Doors, too. Mike Bloomfield, Al Kooper.

Then Marcucci called around. With what he'd pledged in the first place.

'It's a western, Jim. Shooting in Italy.'

Yes, by glory. No luck round Hollywood, but Bob scared up this whole other deal. These producers bypassed LA. Pre-shoot to post, did it all in Italy or Spain. Bob teamed up with Roy, Steve Rowland's daddy, to get this baby bankrolled.

'It's called *Johnny Vengeance,* pardners.'

This to the bar I'd just bought for.

'And you're lookin' right at him!'

'Jim.' Marcucci at my dadgum door again. 'More great news.'

The hero's name, and the movie's, now *Django.* I liked it well. And to go with all that, a theme, for me to sing.

'Well, Bob,' I said, 'this affects my asking price. Double my fee.'

'Jim, it's your first feature, *mi ragazzo. Madon'.* First timers don't get to...'

'Don't *but* me, Bob. Just get *on* it.'

'What do you mean, *bumped?*'

'Jim, it's complicated.'

'Well, here's what we do, Bob. We pay this Franco Nero a call. Convince him that...'

'Jim, Jim. They've decided to shoot in Italian. Overdub the English. Franco, *lui parla Italiano,* he can talk the talk.'

He threw up his hands.

'*Mi dispiace, alora.* You can't.'

'And what of the theme song? Surely they cannot...'

'Another American. Based in Roma. Rocky Roberts. Big in Europe. It's a co-pro with these Italians, *bambino.* And they're the serious money.'

Franco Nero. Only scored the part because he was bangin' that actress Vanessa Redgrave, and her daddy being Michael, the Limey star. This Rocky fella singing the *Django* theme came on the car radio a few months on. They must have said *sing it just like Proby*. My voice, my precious gold mine. Now plundered, by every thieving drifter passin' through.

'Well, sir, you need to get here quick.'

Phone call for me in a bar on Sunset. Neighbours must have said try here. It's the fire department. I called my neighbour, Bobby Darin.

'Robert, will you look to see if my house is still there, please?'

'Well, no, it sure isn't, Jim. A lotta fire engines, but no house.'

'My dog died in that fire. All they found was this grease mark. An explosion, they said. Could have been anything, Brett. Or anybody. Judy Howard. Liberty Records. Or some termagant took exception to my Nymphets Club.'

He's got a head on like a beaten favourite now. Having a rough trot and no mistake, was the Proby, but with him it was always this bizzo that everyone's put the mozz on him, never that these things might just be square-ups for crap he's hung on *them*. And no point laying out how things he saw as just jake might be sized up as less so by others. Somewhere back there, he'd lost all grasp of that. A mind that couldn't make no sense of all that made sense.

'Notice of bankruptcy now served, even as I raked the ashes and bones of my home. I'm unable to work Stateside. Against the law for bankrupts.

Hello, Tito. A proposal. Quid pro quo UK work visa, I'd proffer Her Majesty any assets I could, for sale, and slave all the hours the Redeemer sends, to meet that debt.'

'Alright then, Jim. A result, sunshine.'

A tourist visa. A work visa, well, conditional on my presence there to discuss the terms I'd advanced, they said. I flew BOAC. They got Special Brew.

CHAPTER FORTY-NINE

'*Tomorrow*, Tito? Where?'

No sooner make it out of Heathrow, Brett, than I'm sent back there to fly out again. While I was mid-flight, Tito had secured me a spot at a festival, MIDEM in Cannes, France.

Did the first night. Me, Diana Ross And The Supremes, Procol Harum, Sandie Shaw and Julie Felix. Orchestra to back us all. New numbers here. I did a medley, *I Think I'm Going Out Of My Head* and Little Anthony And The Imperials' *Hurt So Bad.* And *A Day In The Life* off of *Sergeant Pepper.* Slayed 'em.

Great gig, but I'm rankled. I wasn't top star. That went to Sandie Shaw. See, she'd won the Eurovision Song Contest in recent time. Diana Ross and The Supremes on before me, so I went all out on 'em. I do so love those gals. And they came to play. But I came to win.

So now a party, on the Riviera, in a town that never takes a disco nap. Playing here for this MIDEM bash, Long John Baldry, Petula Clark, Canned Heat, the Moody Blues. And one other. Of this galoot, I spoke to any press who'd listen. Words not of peaceable nature, and me in fightin' trim. Yeah. Tom Jones was on here, but not for three nights hence. And me, a record date in London tomorrow. Curses. Ol' Tom Fraidy Cat would have to wait.

CHAPTER FIFTY

'So, boys. We do what we did like we used to.'

Les Reed and Barry Mason, EMI's inhouse hit machine. Did it for Lulu, Petula, that troutmouth Engelbert Humperdinck, Herman's Hermits. And, it pains to recall, *It's Not Unusual* for Tom Jones. Now, numbers crafted for me, conceived as if from *West Side Story*.

'I want *Abbey Road!*'

I cared not for this Wessex Sound Studios. Some old church hall in dadgum Highbury.

'And *George Martin* to produce!'

Well, they said, the Beatles were cutting at Abbey Road right then. For some stretch. Talk of a double album. This here noise factory, they said, their own studio.

'Designed to get the sound you hear on those hits, Jim.'

These songs before me now, all possible singles, they said. A string of Number Ones be their design. Well, then.

'Let's make it majestic, boys.'

Pressing cause for action chartside, Brett. My new *entente cordiale* with Her Majesty's allowed them to pillage as if rampaging Norsemen with horns on their helmets. My home, antiques, cars, yachts, torn from me for quick sale. I contented myself with modest lodgings in Notting Hill and the company of my dogs. And took to fresh amusement that didn't cost a penny.

'Anytime, any show, any TV network. That's the challenge.'

This, issued at a press conference.

'I can beat Tom Jones in a sing-off. Is he man enough to accept?'

Then an ad lib.

'I could beat him on the street, come to that.'

'*Oi.*'

A voice. A hand on my shoulder in the Bag O' Nails this night. I turn about. Why, it's ol' Tom himself.

'Right,' he says.'You've been bad mouthing me. Three fucking years. But now, here, there's no press around.'

Jerks with his thumb, *outside.*

'Out there, not a soul,' he says. 'So why not step out and sort this?'

Well, I had cause to ponder his challenge. The Bag, full tonight. Some big names in here. McCartney. Eric Burdon. That new group Traffic.

'Well, Tom,' I say. 'What's the point of *that?*'

I saw the Page Ones. *POP STARS WILD BRAWL!*

'Outside! No one to see it! Tom, I only do it to get in the paper. I don't have thing one against you.'

Stood. Doffed my hat. My jacket.

'*So let's do it right here.*'

But he feared for his candy-ass image. Or a lickin' in front of our peers. He wagged a finger, *we are not done with this.* Left only fairy dust in his wake. I never did fathom his upsetment. All I said was just for publicity, Brett. For him too, not just me.'

I find that rather hard to believe, Proby, thinks I, but maintained diplomatic silence. To keep the peace at the Hopetoun Hotel. And me from being barred.

*

'Well, Brett, Tito insisted. A message to ol' Tom, to broker a cease-fire. To my surprise, came there an invite to the London Pally. Tom playing there, him and the Shadows.

At the stage door, they knew me right enough from when I'd headlined there myself. About my person, a gift presentation bottle of Jack Black. A pleasant greeting exchanged. Tom invited me to watch the show from the wings. Then, a drink backstage. Had a good talk. I'm offered a ride home. Both fried now. Tight like old war buddies.

'Now, PJ, mate. Careful when you shut the door. The glass in the windows of this Roller is brittle. Could break if you slam the door. So...'

'Oh, sure, Tom. A great, great night. Forget the bullcorn. PJ Proby and Tom Jones. The *two* greatest singers in the world!'

Then slammed that sucker with all the might I had. It cracked in four places. Tom, he goes for the door, to bust out and take a swing. But his driver plants the gas. Roared away. Damn.

'Jim. It better not be true, what I hear.'

'Oh, Barry. That Welsh blowtop been squawkin'?'

'You know what you've *done?*'

'I don't much care for your tone, mister.'

'Jim. I'm producing a new show for ITV. From which you've just been *bumped.*'

'What the what?'

Well, now. Seems ol' Langford had got me on the pilot of his new weekly program. With Peter Sellers, Lulu, Bee Gees, Moody Blues. A music and variety show hosted by and called *This Is Tom Jones.*

So Barry railed till he ran dry. But I'd no need of Tom dadgum Jones. For back at Wessex Studios, why, Brett, a six-pack of Number Ones, radio ready. We moved on to the flipside.

'I ain't singin' this. Next!'

The music sheet I held high by thumb and finger, that they see it from the control room. Dropped it to the floor.

'Jim, we wrote this one for you as a single. And EMI feels the same way about it.'

The subtext, no choice. Terms of my contract. But this tune, alongside its siblings here, the countenance of a red headed stepchild. So I made it sound like what it was. A tote sack of guano. Single? That dog didn't make the album. Not even a B side. Road I chose, the gallant one. What did betide subsequent, irks me still.

'Jim. Three bottles a day some days. Have you thought...'

'Yet I remain standing and a gentleman, Tito. What you got for me?'

Europe. King size tour. And TV shows. *Beat Club*. Two spots. For the first one, I'm in a sleeveless jerkin, it being summer. I looked hot as Ecuador but, I'll concede, not all there for a mime to *Ling Ting Tong* from *Phenomenon*, introduced by compere *strudel*sweet Uschi Nerke. Gone to glory, I be. Schnapps. Missed my cue. I heard me singing on the monitors but just stood there, gazin' dazed at the cameras. Out of synch, go to whoa. Hell, the Krauts didn't pay it no mind. I to them, the business. *Verrukt im kopf! Das Beste! Mach schau!*

'What new single?'

I'm back at *Beat Club* a week on, between live shows. EMI decreed I must perform *What's Wrong With My World*, my new 45, it seems, lifted from the recent sessions.

'Hell, news to me it's even out.'

Mine not to reason why. For TV and gigs now, I'm all in white. Bejewelled belt. Years before Elvis. Like as not he stole that from me too.

To wind up the tour, I played that casino, Montreux in Switzerland. That one that burned down. And me, just about to do the same.

CHAPTER FIFTY-ONE

'Y ou think you can hornswoggle PJ Proby, you got swill for brains!'

Here was treachery, Brett! For Reed and Mason took *Delilah,* that song I sung bad so they'd can it – and gave it to Tom *Jones!*

'And now it's bustin' up the charts!'

A headed for Number One hit.

'No need to fret how to finish this disc, fellas. Ain't your concern. Because y'all are *fired.'*

No word from EMI for a week. Then on the radio, from the sessions, *It's Your Day Today.* My *new* new single. See, it sounded a portion like *Delilah.* It made 32 in week one. Thence to its eternal rest. Same week as that noise in Memphis. Martin Luther King and all.

'Ever hear the term *embalming,* son?'

Bob Reisdorff calling. Boss of Liberty in London.

'You mean for funerals and such?'

'It's a record business thing. You're alive but no-one can see you. Or hear you.'

'So you're breathing but might as well be dead.'

'You're a quick study, Jimmy. Yeah. Frozen in time in your deal.'

'You tell them I will stand fearless in the face of any foe who...'

'No other label can give you a deal.'

'Is that all? Why, I...'

'And you're banned from TV, radio airplay. Your catalogue deleted. And can cut no new records.'

'Says you. And then what?'

'An injunction on you performing live. Transgressors prosecuted. World steps over you in the street, boy. As you lay dying.'

Bob, a producer before he made suit city, assigned me three numbers. Al Martino and Ed Ames had hits off *Mary In The Morning*. So Bob squeezed that lemon one more time. Of *I Shall Be Released*, every clown in the three-ring was cutting Dylan round then. My take, based on the only one worth a damn, Nina Simone's. *Cry Baby,* by Bert Berns and Jerry Ragavoy. A Garnet Mimms Number One back in '63.

To fill up this LP, one of my own. *Judy In The Junkyard.* A sayonara to wife the second. Yeah, about that. I thought we were done. Not so, as I'd soon find.

'What do you mean, it's in the stores?'

Tito called. They'd rush-released a new album, *Believe It Or Not,* off all those sessions. I'm not even notified, Brett. No launch. Like they *wanted* it to fail.'

Crikey Moses. Now and then you'd get next door to droppin' a tear, all that tit for tat they dropped on him, but he never twigged. I mean, it's the freakin' music business. *Short fuses and long knives.*

'You see, the Beatles, Stones, Hendrix, Cream, Dusty, Simon and Garfunkel all had new releases out now. Their labels got behind them. *Believe It Or Not* a wallflower that no-one asked to dance. Then, after the fire and the flood, the famine.'

CHAPTER FIFTY-TWO

'That's what a manager is for. I will not fall alone for the larceny of others.'

I'm forced to the London Bankruptcy Court, Brett. Insufficient effort to satisfy tax debts, they bugled, despite sales of my goods and all. Debt now 84,000 pounds. Assets, way my lawyer told it, 59 pence. Income, just 25,000 pounds per annum. All this, down to swindles by record companies and managers, we said.

Well, they didn't buy the single or the album of it. Declared me bankrupt. All I had left, such as it be, naked now to government muleskinners and chattering auctioneers.

'Well, take it or leave it, chum!'

Tito. Scored me some dates, but liked not my chiding for his accepting such a low price.

'I need real money, Tito! Or my world is gone! Down to *you!*'

Took 'em anyway. July nineteen and sixty-eight. The first, as five minutes to showtime replacement. Pitney, fallen ill, or more like, coming off a three day drunk. This beanfeast, a Czechoslovakian festival, the Bratislava Lyre. Here, Millie Small from *Around The Beatles.* Cliff Richard. Julie Driscoll and Brian Auger. The Easybeats too, but couldn't be found when sought out for sums owed.

Then West Germany. Clubs. Krauts dug me good. Stood me Jagermeisters. In double fistfuls. I did more TV on *Beat Club. You Can't Come Home Again* and *What's Wrong With My World.* I'm ragged as Washington's troops at Valley Forge. *Weltsmerch,* the Germans call it. Tired of living. Beyond consolation. For such was I.

'Still owe them *what?*'

'Well,' said Tito, 'according to EMI's lawyers, two long playing records.'

'And they are become calamitous?'

'Well, chum, they word they said to drop on you was *embalming*.'

EMI nickel and dimed us. No orchestra, they said. A pretty pass. Then ol' Steve Rowland came to mind. Based in London, a producer now, he'd cut some hits on Dave Dee, Dozy, Beaky, Mick and Tich. Had a group, the Family Dogg. And we both Texas-raised. So we took the crumbs brushed from EMI's table. Booked time at Olympic Studios.

'Well. How do, how do, how do?'

Steve lined up a stringbuster name of Alan Parker. Hawk Hawkshaw, piano and organ. Amory Kane, catgut guitar and cello. John Paul Jones, bass. Clem Cattini's drums. Family Dogg singers, backups. Five of 'em. And I brung to this moondance twelve cases of Carlsberg, with a big side of that hot red o' be joyful. To teach EMI not to mess with Tex.

'Got but three days,' said Steve. 'Let's get this got done.'

Hangin' From Yor Lovin' Tree, a Jim Ford tune Liberty wanted for a single. *The Day That Lorraine Came Down* for another. Then *Three Week Hero,* by John Stewart. He wrote *Daydream Believer* for those damn Monkees. By this time I'm up to both eyeballs in JD. My vocal for this next baby, on purpose, like Cousin Cletus the hillbilly hog banger.

For a Lee Hazlewood thing, *New Directions,* I talked it, like a story. As told by Huckleberry Hound. Rendered it unsaleable, Brett. No Caruso The Pirate here. Only Jethro Bodine. Moonshined to desecration.

Roger Cook's *Today I Killed A Man I Didn't Know* I did render as a cartoon Johnny Cash. I'd show those boneyard thieves.

Amory Kane's single *Reflections In Your Face* I cut a cover of, as a favour. And *Little Friend,* a number about some bitty dog. We couldn't afford no big dog song.

'Jim, we're about to do our first album. So this'll be some studio practice for the band.'

242

The Family Dogg's split the scene. No more EMI bread to pay 'em, and we're shy a full side of long player. Just a half day left. But ol' John Paul Jones, he has a new group with Jimmy Page and this drummer, Bonzo Bonham. Singer Robert, a fine line in harmonica. Called the New Yardbirds. Jimmy in ye olde Yardbirds, so took the name when they foundered.

Remy Martin played the music. Maker's Mark wrote the words. Steve rolled the tape on me *a capella*, an improvised lament on the trials of a coloured man. Like those old blues hollers. A minstrel show, clowning for white folks voice.

The band kicks in. A slow blues. Liquored up good, I roll out any words that occur to me. Then Jimmy, JP and Bonzo shift into double time. George Wallace, the segregationist governor of Alabama, running for president then, so I took the lyrics right off the day's news.

'We still lack about eight minutes.'

Steve. Wasted so bad, he's clutching at that soundboard, to stop the control room revolving.

So the band broils up this 2/4 country feel. Ol' Steve and Proby, we just talk it through. Introduce the group, they all solo, like a live show. Forty miles of bad noise. Called it *Mery Hoppkins Never Had Days Like This,* after Mary Hopkin, a singer McCartney had recently made a star. I sent that record and EMI to hell. The only way to fry.

'We'd love to, Jim, but we're about to go on tour ourselves.'

I took considerable to JP and Jimmy's new group. Asked 'em to be my touring outfit. What might have been. Save the dumbo name they switched to. What kind of group calls itself *Led Zeppelin?*

Three Week Hero EMI called it. Released alongside the Beatles' *Abbey Road,* the Stones' *Let It Bleed, Blind Faith,* a supergroup sired and damed by Traffic and Cream. And *From Elvis In Memphis,* Presley's first good'un since forever. I, first casualty of this contest. Record buyers fancied no meat, white nor dark, from this turkey. Vengeance was mine.

We met at the Scotch. Vanessa Forsythe, an actress on TV. *Coronation Street, Blackmail,* TV movies. Straight up ring-fingered engaged, Brett. Mutual besottment. News photographers came. Shot pics with my dogs at my new home in West Hendon, and holding an old musket.

But the yellow press set to howling of impediments to our nuptials. One, that 84,000 pounds sterling owed the taxman. And that I'd not divorced my ex-wives. But, hell, Brett, gelignite publicity. *Kablooey.* So who cares?'

This yarn would make the freakin' moon weep. The way it coulda shoulda been and what had come to pass. Alas, poor Proby. Gone as mad now as those who made him that way. Couldn't see nothin' as it is. Gone into the hall of mirrors and smashed 'em all.

CHAPTER FIFTY-THREE

'Could I do an on-air with him?'

Tony Biggs from Triple Jay. A top show. Top *rating,* too. Its presenter, a massive 1960s Britpop fan. Biggsy digs Proby. He gets it.

'He's right over here.' Biggsy lobs at the Hoey. 'Tee it up with the man himself.'

Proby's having an off day. Low in the water. Borders on rude. But DJ Biggsy's a charmer. Bought him a beer. Greased his ego. A smile on his dial all the while. Me, stoked. A drive-time show. Beats pre-freakin' dawn.

'Listen, Proby. Some bad news.'

Clyde and me heard it on the car radio. Jim had said they'd been pals back in LA.

'It's Del Shannon,' I said. 'The mail, he's, well, he's taken his own life.'

Shot himself. Figured that Proby, they being mates and all, would take it hard.

'Oh,' he says. 'Another one down.'

Raises his VB to the cosmos in a half-arsed way. Zones back into dazeland. All the way weird. All the way Proby. We roll on, up William Street to the ABC. Near the Coke sign. The jaws of the Cross.

'Wear the ears, man. Old-time Americana. It'll pep him up. Call up his inner Disneyland.'

Biggsy used to wear these Mickey Mouse ears on his show. I gave him a caution too.

'Never know what you're in for with this one, bwana. Could be a degree of difficulty.'

'Oh, yeah. But I'm looking forward to it.' He winked. 'After all I've heard. Oh, Brett, can you give me a list of gigs so I can...'

Oh.

'Well, there's Newie. Carrington Inn. Paddo RSL. And, um,...'

Look, best bet, I said, just say more were being set up. Just as a song kicked in on the station monitor. Stone Roses. *Fool's Gold.*

So Proby raves. Of Elvis, Beatles, Led Zep, as prompted. Then Biggsy gets to it.

'Jim, did you know Del Shannon? It's very sad to hear of his passing.'

The Proby just about starts weeping. Then this:

'Oh my goodness. No-one told me Del had passed.'

Clyde and me glance at each other on the other side of the glass. *What the f...*

'Del's been battling his own demons.' His voice trembles. 'I knew him well. Worst thing he ever did was sober up. I told him this AA shit could kill ya! It's his own fault.'

'No, we're not going crazy,' Clyde says to me.

'We told him and he didn't give a shit.'

What an act. No business like show business.

*

'Well, Brett, as night fell on the Sixties, I'm adrift like flotsam. Nought but clubs would have me, for wages paltry and mean. I did get me on a bill at the Empire Pool Wembley. A charity event, the Annual Stars Organisation For Spastics, as they styled the disabled then. But I'm close to bottom of the bill, only slot the organisers would countenance. Had to go on before most of Cliff Richard, Spencer Davis Group, the Amen Corner, Dave Dee Dozy and all, Chris Farlowe, Geno Washington and those dadgum Easybeats. I gazed glum at my dead man's hand, those aces over eights. Braced for a bullet in the back.'

246

'It's a rock opera, Jim. Like *Hair* or *Tommy.'*

Well, now. A record album project of which Tito had heard tell. These fellas, Tim Rice and Andrew Lloyd Webber, auditioning singers. A musical of the Gospels, they say. Tito and Steve Rowland put my name up. The Jesus part.

'Yeah, Jim,' said Steve. 'They offered it to Lennon. But he said he doesn't believe in Jesus.'

'Rowland, that boy never did have a shavin' of common sense.'

Well, they took warm to our advances. Sent the libretto, demos of the songs. Then, news of more gladsomeness.

'A three week season', said Tito. 'Best nightclub in the ruddy country, son.'

Chequers. Sydney, Australia. Barry Langford as tour manager. Swing-a-ding-ding.

It's just days after the moon landing. Barry and his wife Shirley with me, she a dancer and choreographer. We busted some moves for the press at Heathrow. Massed like crows on a hanged man's bones, they cawed their gibes as ever. This time, that touring Australia meant only one thing. *You're washed up everywhere else.* Their barbs I disregarded. Of the rock opera thing, I said nothing other than I was saving a big ol' surprise for 'em on my return.

*

'I have the script with me. Let's just say we're considering each other.'

In Sydney, I gave the press the skinny about the Jesus record. Also of an offer to play the Saviour in a film of His life. This a stretcher, I'll grant you, but in our business, Brett, it's build a boat or be drowned.

'You're looking at the new Clark Gable, boys and girls,' I told 'em. Brett, who's the guy they call the Lanky Yank, what's his name...?'

'That would be Don Lane, Proby.'

'Yeah. I sang on his show.'

I recalled seeing it. Proby off his chops, but my punt, this possibly not of his making alone. Aussie producers back then often got the talent munted in the Green Room, to gee up a bit of on-air argy. Ratings, all that mumbo.

'Ol' Don Lane brought up my split britches, Brett. He claimed I meant to do it. My response, that it'd be as smart as having a million dollars, taking it to the top of the Chevron Hotel in Kings Cross where I was accommodated, and throwing it off.

Now no sooner I hit town than a call comes in. Movie producers. Made motion pictures right here in Sydney. Local cast and crew, fly in one American as the lead. Semi-big names. Vera Miles, Barry Lansing.

'It's big, Jim.'
    We met, at the Rex Hotel, if I recall right.
    'A four-picture deal.'
    Fine and well. But I had conditions, Brett.
    'Y'all are casting me as a villain. But you're looking at a leading man here. Only way you'll get me.'
    And proof was required, I said, that these were international pictures. First release hardtop screens across America. Not drive-ins, kids fuckin' in their surf wagons.
    'The world is my market.'
    Then I told them my price. They were never heard from again.

*

'Whatever these jaybirds were playing, I couldn't make north nor south of it.'
    Chequers. Opening night. Reviews agreed. Proby and the house band, giving separate shows. My guess, ample and more of the great red spirit pre-gig. Proby, I mean, not them. By showtime, well, ...

'Time to blow this hot dog stand, Barry. For better offers. Play all the cities in the nation here.'

248

People were calling, Brett, with just such proposals.

'Jim,' he said, 'it's an exclusive deal. Chequers only. They'd sue us if we...'

I'd have him rethink this coward's resort.

'You heard me, Barry. Upgraded to the penthouse in this here Chevron or no show tonight. That clip joint Chequers can afford it. Jiminy, they serve that KB Lager in silver buckets!'

Yessir. Foment havoc, that they cancel the season. Set me free, to tour. Twice the paydirt in half the time. I took to rumbling over anything.

'This is *domestic champagne!*'

Howled like a grey wolf at room service this night, I entertaining two young ladies.

'Remove this hogswill at once. Bring Dom Perignon!'

'How dare you humiliate me, sir!'

Dadgum night manager. A-knockin' at four in the AM. Guest complaints. Noise. Mess of people I've brung from Kings Cross. US dogfaces on R 'n' R leave from the Vietnam conflict. Two girls for every boy.

'Why five men do the same job?' he said one day. He meant the horn section. 'One man good, no p'oblem. Four men, not needed.'

Chequers manager, this fella Denis Wong, now mounted a counter-attack.

'Barry,' I said, 'that charlie pulls but one player off the stand, expect no-show, every night, until they are reinstated.'

Well, he fixed it. But then this Denis said the bass player had to go.

'He and the other man, boom boom boom. Same thing.'

He meant the drummer. Again, it was made clear. No bass player, no *show*. Barry fixed it. Heck knows how. Not my cross. Not my hill.

'This amount, over and above the fee, cash, each night, then I'll go on. If not, well...'

I suspected I was being underpaid, so I told Barry what was what the what.

'Tell you what, Jim. I fucking quit.'

'Say what?'

'I'm having a bloody nervous breakdown. I'm off.'

'No, you don't. Y'all don't quit. Y'all is *fired.*'

The season ended before its time. But worse awaited me, like the steel teeth of bear traps, across the seas.

FIFTY-FOUR

'My fiancée Vanessa answered not my calls, Brett, nor the door. Her Dear John, when it came, said I was not ready to wed. Maybe she was right. Third time lucky has scant credence in my philosophical domain.

And now Tito Burns let me go. We fell to dissidence. He stuck me in the frame for his difficulties now in booking his acts, he of the view that this was down to me. I contested this assertion, but he said he'd not do diddley more for me, short of behaviour modified.

So I took to booking myself. My terms, way past reasonable. Meet my price, three thousand pounds, I'd make the date. If not, I wouldn't. A hit record comes to pass meantime, price goes up. Seven thousand pounds.'

Somebody call a freakin' ambulance, I thought.

'Sparse catch from these nets, to my dismay. Then I recalled Sinatra and Lucky Luciano. Went fishin' once. With Tommy guns and hand grenades. Well, Brett, I took heed of their method and now applied it.'

So Proby shirt-fronts Liberty and EMI. His deal's up for renewal. So he tries it on, goes the piss and vinegar. A cash advance before he'll even sniff at a contract. I mean, fair enough, this mob's been short-changing him from the off. But now he's gone and woken the cave monster. They give his paperwork the once-over. Turns out *he* owes *them* one more album! Yeah. *Dense* don't even come close.

'On budget pitiful, Brett, the producer's job went to Emile Ford. He had a million seller back in '59. *What Do You Want To Make Those Eyes At Me For*. More off the back of that.

We used Emile's group the Checkmates. My aim, get it done in one day. All that record co deserved. So our selections, doo-wop, R 'n' B classics we all knew. *Blue Moon, Cherry Pie, Bop Ting-A-Ling, Caldonia. Tomorrow Night,* waymore better than Presley did it. *Hound Dog,* the Big Mama Thornton take, not that milquetoast Elvis one.

Heck, I did that retro trip years before Lennon cut *Rock'n'Roll* with Spector. And ol' Alvin Stardust, Gary Glitter, all those 1970s Limey greaseballs. Ol' PJ. First westward with the wagons. As ever.

We cut just nine tracks. On purpose. I get a call from those dippers. *It's three shy of an album.*

'Well, ain't that a daisy?' I said. And no more would there be till my due from all past sales be forthcoming. Cash moneys.

Well, they dug up some old Jett Powers cuts to make the weight. Called this biscuit *California License.* That's LA slang for a tattoo on a woman's lower back. A permit to get your rocks off. Front cover, my California driver's license from '62.

The last of it with Liberty. Some ride. Some road. At every bend, set upon by brigands and jackrollers.

*

'I can do something with you, Jim.'

This fella Jeff Kruger called. He'd owned the Flingo back when. Now, toured US acts in the UK. Stevie Wonder, Gladys Knight, Marvin Gaye and such of that feather.

'Does that feature making records, Mr Kruger?'

'Well, my son. After Glen Campbell, who else but Jim Proby?'

Kruger had a label, Ember. Glen couldn't get a UK release, so Kruger took him on. Made *Galveston* and *Wichita Lineman* hits in Limeyland. Ditto coloured acts in same predicament.

Kruger really dug Presley's 1968 Comeback Special. His plans, a TV show and album.

'We'll call it the *PJ Proby Comeback* show.'

'You'll do no such like, Kruger. The Proby has never been *away.*'

To the fire down below with that, I said. Made me look a dadgum has-been.

'But, Jim, old son. It's the only way with any hope of success.'

The face he serves me, *take it or leave it.* And he be the candyman here, so...

'Months ago, and not word one. I want that part. Fix it.'

I told Kruger of that record album, *Jesus Christ Superstar* the press now calling it. Meanwhile, Kruger used Drury Lane Theatre for touring Marvin Gaye and Gladys Knight. And so it would serve also for I, Proby. And he paid for a makeover. Bespoke tux. Edwardian shirt. Frills on the bib.

'Ponytail got to go-go, baby,' said Kruger. 'Deny the press their sordid orgy, sweetheart.'

Yessirree Bob. No ammo would they have, this mischief of rats fixin' on a string-up.

For the show, *Maria, Somewhere, I Apologise.* New numbers, *They Call The Wind Mariah* from *Paint Your Wagon. Put Your Head On My Shoulder. Mary In The Morning,* bein' that Presley was doing it in Vegas. On top of that mess, *Only You* and *Twilight Time.* Rehearsed till the dots fell off those charts. It was showtime.

'You were warned not to call it a dadgum *comeback!*'

The box office, well, we filled the stalls. That is, when those few in the cheap seats moved down ten rows for a broad choice of vacancies there. Kruger's aims for a TV show, abandoned off this blowback. Christine Perfect, the support, must bear some cut of the blame. Went on to join Fleetwood Mac, that one. Got lucky.

Of the VIP guest list, some did make the scene. A passel more didn't. In my dressing room with the press, I received Diana Dors. Also Vanessa Forsythe, we no longer engaged but still friends. My new squeeze here too, Dianne Craig. Fun while she lasted. And someone else.

'Jim! My wayward rover. Sen*sational!*'

'Great God! Who let *you* in here?'

Bygones called as bygones, we set to talking. Jack Good's musical of Othello, *Catch My Soul,* at long last had a backer. Himself.

'Dear boy, you'll be Cassio. Reimagined as a drunk from Baton Rouge, Louisiana.'

'Jack, that's as close to me as it gets, any which way you dixie-fry it.'

No word on *JC Superstar,* said Kruger. Way Jack saw it, this news of *Catch My Soul* would clinch me the Jesus part. What revived Jack's interest was that he'd seen *Hair.* Boffo box office, he said.

'Broadway, West End smash. Million-selling soundtrack. Talk of a feature film.'

So he'd refashioned *Catch My Soul* in the manner of *Hair.* Relocated *Othello* from Venice to the Deep South. Two fistfuls of songs for me, plus acting between 'em. Right over here, world.

This fella Lance Le Gault, Jack cast as his Iago. He'd been a stunt double for Presley in his dadgum D pictures. And wrote a song I'd cut, *Good Things Are Coming My Way.* Only good enough as filler on an EP. Yet a lofty self-regard, as if a true star.

'The whole world's heard of the Proby,' I said. 'The same cannot be said of you, hombre.'

Thus established, who's boss on this cattle drive. For Desdemona, a creature of beauteous splendour. Welsh gal, Angharad Rees. On British TV, in *Poldark.* And Jack's Bianca, like me, a pilgrim from America. PP Arnold had hits in the UK with *The First Cut Is The Deepest* and *Angel Of The Morning.*

Playing Othello, well, now. Jack a stone wizard at showmaking, but meagre facet as thespian. And his makeup, blackface except all over, that ol' jessie naked save loincloth and Mexican hoodoo armbands. Well, his dime. Co-star PJ Proby kept his verdict under his rolled brim cowboy hat.

'Surely you shit me, Jack.'

This was not Jack's first pass at *Catch My Soul.* He'd staged it in LA the year prior.

'Jerry Lee Lewis? As Iago?'

'Yes, Jim. But you can match, nay, even better, the Killer.'

I had every intention, Brett. My guy Cassio, three solo numbers. *Drunk,* my bravura moment. Plus duets with PP, Anghared and Lance. Yeah. Up against *me*. That football game, over before it started.

To Manchester for rehearsals, and to open there.

'Ten nights, dear boy. Birmingham the same. Oxford, twelve shows. Thence to London, three week season.'

That same day, news. The Jesus part, the *JC Superstar* album. Went to Ian Gillan from Deep Purple. His stylings, well, guess who he hooked it all from, Brett. And still sounds like a steer with its wang caught in a ranch gate.

Rehearsals, a trial. Jack made us do stretching and breathing every morning. Nevertheless, a flipside. He hustled a TV crew to come film us. A segment for a show called *Aquarius.* That day, I wore tight floral pants. Split 'em in a dance routine. I made great flap of covering balls and ass, and fleeing the set. Stole the show when they screened it on the TV.

But impecunious times. Reduced to Boone's Apple Farm wine and Merrydown from the flagon. And cast members griped to Jack of my demeanour toward them. I paid this the heed it deserved. Zero.

We opened in Manchester, University Theatre. Last weeks of '69. And our host there, the 69 Company.

'Sixty-nine,' an ad lib from my Cassio on first night. 'Breakfast of champions.'

Now this Lance de Gault, we had a duet, *Cannikin Clink.* He, most of it. Me, but a few lines. Opening night, at the end, I continued singing, his lines and mine. Bid the band keep on rockin'. Sang that creampuff right off the stage. Swiped his applause and spooked him from first pitch of the series. And with Anghared, I'm soon entwined. Hot romance.

'Well, there's only room on stage for one PJ Proby, kitten.'

PP Arnold quit. Of our duets, she'd got uptight about my remarks on-mike during her lines.

Reviewers called *Catch My Soul* 'dire.' Hell, Brett. It wasn't down to me. To replace PP, Marsha Hunt from *Hair*. Makin' whoopee with Marc Bolan, it was said. Later, Jagger. Said to be the subject of *Brown Sugar*.

At Birmingham's Repertory Theatre, I missed shows. Waylaid by drinking pals. A guy from the chorus had to fill in as my Cassio. Most asked question at the box office, no surprise.

'Is PJ Proby on tonight?'

See, Brett, Jack needed to know who was pullin' the hayseeds to this tent show. So I did this to show him.

Jack did a live recording here. Pye Records mobile truck. He released an album of it later. Never told me, Brett. Made millions off of it.'

I doubt it.. It's freakin' unlistenable. Not even mixed or mastered. Straight off the sound desk. But this frazzled minder not about to contend such with Hazmat here.

'*Catch My Soul* rolled on to the New Theatre in Oxford. Yeah, Brett. College town. On vacation for Christmas. So no audience. Mad Jack. Never wargamed anything. Impulsive choices. Bore no fruit nor flower, only the thorns of consequence.'

Sounds like someone else I know, Proby.

'Christmas of '69, the Roundhouse Theatre, Camden Town. Jack counselled we pay our critics no heed.

'In fact, children, wish them well. These bad reviews will lure the curious.'

Yet these curious dwindled right quick. We had to shift to the somewhat smaller Prince Of Wales Theatre in the West End.

And now the funniest thing. Michael McClure, this rambler from Kansas now based in London, cast me in his new play, *Spider Rabbit*. About a rabbit turned into a spider. Amanda Lear as the Angel who saves him. My makeup, somethin' else. Half my face like a rabbit. The other, an evil spider.

The Soho Theatre, just the upstairs in a pub. Shows, afternoons. So matinees with *Spider Rabbit,* and *Catch My Soul* at night. Amanda Lear, the word on the mojo wire, had undergone a sex change at a Swiss clinic. Some broad. Or dude. Heck, you tell me.

In this play, I had to devour vegetables dipped in ketchup and food colouring, to simulate human guts. And run about, a chainsaw buzzin' and smokin' in one hand, cauliflower soaked in ketchup in the other, for fake brains. Then dash out among the patrons with that three-foot Black And Decker and swing it around. Maybe why houses dropped off so fast.

Well, Brett, no curveball to me that *Spider Rabbit* was reviewed as 'crude and hard to swallow.' Didn't make a lick of sense. Meantime, of Anghared Rees, I asked for her hand. But Fleet Street damned it all to Hades when they heard tell. So her family declared there'd be no match. Their blessings denied me.

Catch My Soul died quick. Jack talked of more seasons, but he's whistlin' in the graveyard far as I could see. Anghared and I quit the show. And then she quit me.

Jack did a return run of *Catch My Soul* the next year. In time, a movie. No invite my way for either. There went my movie career. Snatched away as if by Pancho Villa's raiders.

CHAPTER FIFTY-FIVE

'Listen, Clyde. I need a break, my man. For the sake of my own cerebral stability.'

I'm jack of Proby. And hardly driving cab shifts no more. Down to seeds and stems in every sense of that Commander Cody phrase. And to drink and drive on Probywatch jeopardised my taxi license.

Kenny Starr's name came up. Big unit. A soundo. Don't mind a drink. Likes to sit around, talk shit. Free for Proby patrol and up for it. Perfect pick.

'So I got a bead on Kenny,' I told Clyde. 'He's in Melbourne.'

Yeah. No biggie. Just a day away. But there's a bit he don't tell me. This is just as magnum force St Kilda wild man Fred Negro breaks up with his wife. She shoots through with their kid Rowdy. If you don't know Fred, his bands' names, like I Spit On Your Gravy, The Fuck Fucks, 57 Pages Of Pink, tell it best.

So Negs, best solution he can come up with is go on the biggest bender he can. And with who else but Kenny Starr?

'Oh, Fred's in a bad way, Brett.'

Kenny calls from the St Kilda Bowlo bar phone.

'Just give me another day or so.'

I call two days on. Same place.

'Oh, that. I can't come up now. Spent all me money drinkin' with Fred.'

'That's cool,' says Clyde. 'We'll send you the money.'

They drink it. Clyde sends more. Yeah, I know, loud and clear, but we couldn't find no-one else. Among our mob, Proby now too well-known. No starters. Sure, I'll wear it. Engaging the Kenny not the smartest move. But this is how rattled Proby could make you. Trying to discern between the static, the tantrums, the whims. The weirdness.

'Righto, Kenny. Alls you gotta do, just talk to him. It's mostly listening anyway. Drink with him, keep him topped up. Don't leave him on his tod till you freight him home and he flakes. Too easy.'

So Proby meets Kenny. A how do and the Proby's back into his life and times. A long way yet to tumble.

'Now, Brett, this Kruger signs me to his Ember label. Then without so much as howdy nor doody, goes and cuts these tracks with some orchestra he's hired. And now he tells me I must track vocals for these.

'Not one breath, Kruger. First, the surety of an advance.'

His counter-offer to my upturned palm, that he'll book no live work for me until these vocals are laid down. So off all this gunsmoke, an LP on ice and we at stalemate. And as I dust off from that roll in the dirt, a telegram.

It's from EMI. Read the fine print, old cock. One last single. Past due, they said. A posse of lawyers should I object. Well, Brett, how many contracts have *you* signed that you set a spell to read first?'

Dude had a point, it must be said.

'Well, I started down the road of sayin' hell would ice over before...a crate of Special Brew, they said, and a soldier straight and tall of Jack Black would be waiting at the studio.

It's Goodbye sounded mighty like *Delilah*. But abrim with their hospitality, I gave all I had in the tank. Then I sprung one on *them*.

'Do as you fancy for a B side. But I won't be cutting one.'

They broke out some Jett Powers outtake for that. *It's Goodbye* didn't sell doodly-squat.

A *Delilah* stunt double. The rubes only get bit once.

'Well, Jim, he pulled a gun on us in the studio.'

Fowley was in London to cut an album on ol' Gene Vincent. Gene got riled when Paul Rothschild, the Doors' producer, and John Densmore, their drummer, dropped in to rubberneck a session not goin' so sweet. Gene objects, with a handful of blue steel. So anyways, Fowley's called me up on another matter.

'I called the organisers, Jim. I said we want a lot of money. And a lot of women to fuck.'

'Sounds about right, Fowley.'

It's just days away. No time to get a band. Just my guitar and Fowley his. The Festival Of The Midnight Sun. Europe's answer to Woodstock, they claimed. At a race car track outside Stockholm. Chuck Berry, Canned Heat, The Byrds, Dr John, the Crazy World Of Arthur Brown, The Move. Blue Mink, a pre-fame Elton John at the piana. Woodstock it weren't.

'You see, Fowley, this is what happens.'

Like many festivals back then, publicised poorly. This birdbrained hippie notion of 'build it and they will come.'

A bare five thousand of the hundred such expected showed. Dismay among we performers. We'd been gypped. We set upon the promoters. They said it had been paid into our bank accounts, that they couldn't lay hands on cash weekends anyway, banks closed and all. Can't recall if we ever got it. Nor the set with Fowley. Nor if we played one, come to that.

CHAPTER FIFTY-SIX

'Not a dime to show now, Brett. On a tip from Fowley, I had a doctor vouch for my ailing health. This fetched me sickness benefits from the NHSS. Yet despair roiled within me. No balm for it. My wish now, go home to Texas. To die.'

Well, backstory like his, I could feature why he'd feel that way. He often talked of going out in speccy style. Once to a bunch of us at the Hoey. Take a supply of liquor out to the Australian desert, he reckoned. Dig a hole. Prop up a pile of rocks with a stick.

'I'll get in the hole. Have me a drink, get good and throwed. Then kick that stick away. Crushed by red boulders right there in the outback. I will show them all.'

Yeah, righto. *Show them all what?*

'I looked down from the plane. The lights of LA. Chose to stop a spell, say adios to friends. I'd brought my guitar, a good one. If needed, to hock for beer or stronger. Returning to my room at the Chat with booze, I espied the guitar case. Clasps unclicked.

Ford.

Inside it, a shitbox guitar in place of mine. And a note. *You'll get over it.*

Ford I found in the Jack Rabbit Inn. Said he needed a good guitar for a record date. And that he was buying, to show his gratitude. Some bars later we encounter Tom Baker and Michael McClure. Baker and Jim Morrison, best buds. Baker had a threesome going with Morrison and his girl Pamela, Ford claimed.

These hombres were making a movie. About Bongo Wolf, no less. Offered us parts right there. Paid in booze. I of no mind to refuse.

Yeah. *Bongo Wolf's Revenge.* Bizarroville. Mike Bloomfield did the music. The script, improvised. A fashion at the time, Ford said.

'Not a crumb of sense to it, Ford,' my reply, 'but give me this day my daily booze and I'll remain a gentleman about it.'

It was about then that Jim Morrison was busted in Miami. Flopped his doodah out on stage, police claimed. He's facing down hard time and the group, its end of days, a situation which would come to affect me.

The Bongo shoot wrapped. Again enswirled in melancholy, I hit the blue highway. Stuck out a thumb. That's how I got to Houston. Aiming for the Chihuahuan Desert, in Big Bend Country, West Texas, there to lay me down. But hold. There's booze at my daddy's, and this boy's hurtin'.

Not at home, his housekeeper said, but on his way. I had at his desk drawers for liquor or cash. Amongst legal papers, a handgun and such, this leather-bound folio. Newspaper, magazine clippings. Of *me.* Page after page. I felt a presence. Looked up. Daddy. Looking at me looking at him.

'You old buzzard,' I said. 'I thought you spurned the road I chose. And now I find...'

I was overcome. We embraced. And he had Chivas. Well, that desert would still be there, tomorrow and all the days beyond it...

A tranquil interlude, holed up there. I paid a call on Mama too. Daddy 'advanced' me, he called it. A banker. Could not bear to call it a gift.

That desert thing I let slide. Rode the skinny dog bus back to LA. There, my career I could rekindle. Lodging could be had with friends. Or strangers, well met in the bars of Hollywood. Bido Lidos, It's Boss, all them. Pat and Lolly Vegas had a group now, Redbone, themselves and other proud First Nations boys. They still ran gigs on the Strip and the Boulevard and sent some my way. Fine fellows. Never gave up on me.

*

Such a night. Forgot where I parked my ride. It's after a gig Pat and Lolly gave me. All my ID misplaced in post-show revelry. Money all gone to boot. So I'm walkin'. To a friend's pad, North Hollywood, seven miles from here on the Strip. A favoured stop on my sofa circuit.

'You know the drill, shithead. Hands on the wall, legs apart.'

He kicked them out to assist in the latter endeavour. LAPD prowl car. Me, no ID nor cash. Cuffed me. Vagrancy. A night in the tank.

Just about that time, the Doors' last ever show. New Orleans. Morrison now said he was quitting the group. Yeah, Brett. Oldest fable on the face of God's green. I'll bet the ranch he was fired.

'You'd be crazy to, but a pile more not to, pilgrim.'

This the view from Ford, and Baker and McClure, they now working on screenplays in which they planned to star Morrison.

'We talked to the other Doors, Jim,' said McClure. 'Your name came up.'

Around the tenth drink, it grew to be a fine idea so I followed up on it. Their label called back three days on. Fixed a time to come on in.

'You can never replace *that* son of a gun!'

This I shouted at the moon. At Sunset Recorders, they'd bid me wait. A red light on over the studio door. A take in progress. Do not enter. Then it went off. I stood up. And walked right out, Brett. No way to make that skin fit. I could not sing for this group. And anyway, I heard there was this other guy trying out. Fella called Iggy Pop.'

Yeah, I dunno. I could see Proby fronting the Doors. Also, opposite me in the beer garden at the Cricketer's Arms, why the move might have had its shortcomings.

CHAPTER FIFTY-SEVEN

'Oh, fuck. What's he done?'

Clyde glances at me. He's fair dinkum spooked.

'It's reception at Bondi. My Amex. He wants to charge seventeen hundred...'

Nini weighs in. Doesn't miss a beat.

'Give me the phone.'

Righto, Nini. No arg from me.

'Put me through to Mr Proby, now, please,' she says. Waits a couple of ticks.

'Janine here, Jim. Now. What's going on?'

He starts burbling defences. I can quote 'em all verbatim by now.

'Now listen,' says Nini. 'Has the deed been done?'

'Oh, no, *no,*' I hear. Then a plea for clemency. He won't get none from Nini.

'Right, stop,' says Nini. 'Put the girl on.'

They chat. She's from one of your more toney knock shops. An establishment in Surry Hills.

'Okay,' says Nini. 'So the deed hasn't been done?'

She shakes her head at us, *no, it hasn't.*

'Well, you won't be getting paid,' she says. 'So just leave. If you're from an escort agency, any concerns, here's the phone number here. Got a pen?'

Gives her the number.

'If there's a taxi fare or show-up charge, we'll cop that, but no services shall be rendered to this man. Now put him back on.'

I hear Proby protesting.

'Now, Jim,' says Nini. 'You're an idiot. I'm disappointed in you.'

Then Clyde double-takes it.

'Wait on! Kenny Starr's there! How the hell did he...put him on!'

To Nini, motions, *gimme that phone.*

'Now, Kenny,' says Clyde.

'Oh, mate. Proby told me it was *cool*, mate. Says youse do this all the ti...'

'No, Kenny!' Clyde. 'This is *not* what we do. And *seventeen hundred dollars?*'

'Well, yeah, it did sound pricey, mate. I told 'em he was a pop star, PJ Pro...'

'You *told* them that? And wonder why the price jumps? Fuck, Kenny! Use your *brain!*'

We never heard from them. Did wonder if Proby might cop a visit from strangers in the night. *Or if we might.* Yet we kept Kenny on. The break from Proby so good. I mean, in his defence, the Kenny had no clue what he'd dropped himself into here. And let's face it. Neither had we.

Sunday now. Just two more comas to first gig. Surely nothin' else could hail toads on this rock'n'roll circus.

*

'I ain't doing no road trip. No *chopper,* no *show.'*

I've stood Kenny down for the day. Nini along, to get Proby vibed up for the drive to Newie. And now it's a whirlybird or he's a late scratching.

'I'm gonna take a shower now, hoss,' he says. Twists the top off a VB.

'That 'copter best be lined up pronto or...'

I said nothing. Waited for him to emerge.

'I made a few calls, Jim.'

Pig's arse I had.

'We can get a chopper, not a problem, my man.'

'Well, best get to it and let's go pickin'.'

'But they don't allow alcohol on board.'

So he's on the sook but in the car, lured by six pack. We'd booked a motel, an overnight stay in Newie for Clyde, Nini, Proby and self. I mean, feature it. Proby getting the horrors post-midnight, halfway down the Pacific Highway, two thousand warm beers from home.

'I want a *real* drink!'

Just shy of halfway. Gosford. No doubt payback for failing to scare up a chopper with a wet bar on board. It's right on opening time. We look like we're here to do the pub, says the barmaid's face.

The band, no accom for them. Budget's long blown. Six hour round trip. Roll home under the stars, dodging B-doubles. And lug-in, soundcheck, show, lug-out. Clyde paid them full whack. Been through that flesh grinder himself.

'They will sell them, Brett, at handsome profit. And not dime one for me.'

The room's full. Not jammy but a good large crowd. A lot of your greybeards. Warpainted chooks. Long faces, tired eyes. Bearing old Proby LPs for his autograph. He wouldn't be in it. I was the only human on that tour who got my Proby vinyl signed. Took days to convince him I wouldn't sell it and not sling him a slice.

'It went off, Proby. Deadset!'

A herogram after the show. *He killed it.* We had to write charts for his lyrics. He read 'em off a music stand. Not a real flash look. But he sang so good it didn't matter. Smiles among the band as they sailed through the set. The way they played 'em spurred Proby to dig deep. The crowd called out for more and got it. Doc the lighting dude of legend did his party trick, stood on his head, as Doc does. It all bode mighty well for Paddo. Still only Tuesday. But felt like almost Saturday night.

'I want to go back to Bondi!'

Couldn't last. Even after a blinder gig. Had to be fluffed to billyo by Nini till the stupor blew in. Morning, he's rolled back down the hill. Flat. Morose. As if last night never was. One strange cat.

CHAPTER FIFTY-EIGHT

'Well, Brett, I made the premiere of *Bongo Wolf's Revenge* at the Cinematique Theater. The picture, unwatchable. And upon me now, a more pressing concern. News of Liberty. Word along the Strip, a goodly number of their artists were riled. Never paid royalties, not since Si Waronker got out in '64. And Al Bennett, no longer here. Tipped out in some takeover.

'I've seen my stuff chart at both ends of the Atlantic and the Pacific. Saw *Niki* go gold.'

'Jim,' this junior under-vice president says, 'we don't owe you a thing. And don't wish to conduct further business with you.'

'I'll not quit these premises 'til I get what's mine.'

From memory, this pencil dick spotted me a Jackson to make me go away. I believe it was someplace 'twixt Sunset and Fountain Avenue I came to later. In that De Longpre Park.

*

'I would horse-trade this day, *hermano*.'

Back to London. An offer I made now, in good faith.

'Kruger, fetch me bookings, and I'll ruminate upon cutting that album you so crave.'

'Well! What brings you here, Mr Wayne Fontana?'

'Same as you, Jim. The bar is open.'

Kruger booked me this gig. Stockport, near Manchester. And here he was, ol' Fontana. Companion of misadventure past. I did not refuse his invite to party on at his home after the show. Nor his offer to stay the night.

One thing led to a whole string more. At Wayne's behest, I relocated there, with he and his wife Suzanne. I'd no place in London, no funds for one, so this, pure kismet. The clubs Kruger booked, all here in the North-West anyway.

'Ford! I am coming for you and we are going out on a drunk.'

He was in London. Si Waronker managing Ford now. Had flown him in to cut an album.

So then. Wagons ho. See what could be had for ol' Proby.

'Si says it's the only way we can make money, since I can't hack it playing live shows.'

Ford's at Olympic Studios with this group Brinsley Schwarz. No sign of Si, but a whole lot of Ford and all that travels with him.

'I had 'bout this much again,' he said. 'But I got on a party at the airport, waiting for these boys to come pick me up.'

Brett, I never saw such bulk for personal use only. A big round fishhooks box full of cocaine tied on Ford's belt and a sack more down his pants comprised the half still unconsumed. Danced through Customs like Fred and Ginger, this in spite of powder on his bib overalls from jolts in the plane's restroom.

First day, not much got cut. Every time they rolled, Ford recalled no words nor chords.

Yeah, all of a sudden, how 'bout that? See, Brett, in LA, he'd go the length of Sunset, all the publishers. Sell the same songs five times. Some, not even his. Ripped off from Pat and Lolly Vegas. So, this day, a stillborn session.

Second day, no better. The next, the last. Ford wouldn't finish or even start a take. The Brinsley Schwarz guys quit. Si flew in. Brought in Joe Cocker's Grease Band. They quit too. Ford has that effect on people.

*

'Hello, Jim? It's Nick Lowe. From Brinsley Schwarz.'

These boys, fans of mine, he told me. So Si elects that if Ford won't sing his songs, then Yours Truly might could. At Olympic, we captured *I'm Ahead If I Can Quit While I'm Behind, Ju Ju Man* and a third, maybe called *You You You*. My favourite Bluegrassers along to help us out. Ol' Jack D and Jim B. Precluding further recall of that session.'

You don't say, Proby. A yarn's been going round for donkey's about that schemozzle. The plan, a PJ Proby country album. Songs by Ford and Nick Lowe and his bandmates, the menu. But Hazmat lobs on the day off his dot. Went to smash from there. Brinsleys bailed.

So it rolls and on rolled Proby.

'Well, I don't got 'em, Kruger. You go get if you want.'

His claim, I'm signed with his label so those cuts were his. He did try and purloin the masters by such petition, but this scofflaw's play was met with the response it deserved. And while about it, of the cuts, the studio opined, well, the words 'useless' and 'disaster' featured.

'He followed me home, Fontana. Can I keep him?'

Took but five days. People in London looking to kill Ford. He's stealing drugs and running up lines of credit on such, no means to settle. Best he take refuge in Manchester, I explained.

Well, Ford and Wayne got on right enough, but Ford and his frolics abraded Wayne's wife somewhat. Powder, pills, bringing home all manner of lowlife, all that rumpus. Then Suzanne said she'd call the police, tell them the all of it, if Ford wasn't gone by close of business that same day.

So for that Kentucky bear, home to LA. Then Wayne and wife had words. Voices raised. The outcome of this exchange, I'm re-situated, from main house to garden shed. Back gate only for comings and goings.

Kruger called. Cabaret shows. Clubs. The Midlands, Birmingham, Coventry, Darby, Wolverhampton. Also in closer reach, Newcastle, Liverpool, Manchester, Leeds. Not too swift, Brett. I'm on bills with singing dogs, end-of-the-pier stand up comics, exotic balloon dancers.

These scrubbers, as the Limeys style 'em, they'd pop all the balloons they were wearing. Next door to nekkid underneath.

'An apposite metaphor, Kruger,' I said, 'for the music business.'

I was barred hither and yon. One place, I having been refused service, they claimed that theft from the bar fridge had occurred. Elsewhere, I'm banished over offers to fistfight hecklers. And there were no-shows, I now pilloried as *PJ Probably*.

Kruger, after a time, couldn't hardly get me bookings at all. So I took it upon myself. Clubs, pubs, bars. Singer and guitar. Pay in booze. The sickness benefit still came. I engaged in no fraud, despite press claims. Due to their persecutions going back to '65, I was unwell.'

If you say so, Proby. Sure, bang on, the Texan had been fitted up, perp-walked and exploited to buggery by these tabloid gronks, for purposes less than kosher. But this mook don't see that he feeds that same pack of dingoes with punts like this. These sickie slings he blags, for your squareheads, that spells bludgers and dodgy doctors pulling swifties. *He goes and jumps without a parachute 'cause that gets him down faster.*

'I had a walk-on about now in a movie, *Die Screaming Marianne.* I'm in Brighton for two shows. I said hell yes, to leading man, Barry Evans, when he came upon me at my gig. Shot the scene in my best loud and wild, that more parts follow. Pink and purple poncho, John B Stetson, snakeskin boots. They bought a celebrity cameo for a mess of beer.'

A mess of beer for a mess of what the fuck.

'Alright, Kruger,' I agreed. 'For all the cash you can bear to part with. Today.'

I haggled a hundred quid with a side of Kentucky neck oil. In the studio, I sang on three cylinders out of eight, those that I assayed he'd paid for. The LP he called *I'm Yours.* Our business concluded, I declared. But we'd meet again. And it would not go well.

And now the labour exchange declared me fit to work. Cut off my benefits. Compelled attendance as a janitor. Office building, Shepherd's Bush

Road, Hammersmith. Opposite the Palais, where once I'd headlined. But this not yet the worst of turns, Brett. That gang of *pistoleros* lay in wait down the line.

'Why, Jim! So nice to see you again!'

No clue how she found me, but loony gooney ex Judy Howard's here, at my bedsit door. Her manner, warm. Eyes, blue ice. Seeking a divorce. That she might remarry. Well, now. She'd near put holes in me. Twice. Caused me much ado and upset.

'This will require a fee, *gringa.*'

A smile I threw in for free. Her gold, a goodly sum. She lit out for Hawaii with her beau. Some weeks on, news. Took her own life. Only one she ever did, for all her shootin' iron foreplay. Left two notes, one on either side of the bed. Neither for me.

I'm showing up at work late or not at all. So no more job. And forbidden back on benefits. I called around. Every face I'd met on the way up and down. But I was knockin' on doors already slammed.

CHAPTER FIFTY-NINE

'Well, Jim, I too hail from the great nation of Texas. So here's your boots back. Now *git.*'

Shaken down at LAX. My dishevelled presentation. Fortunate, the provenance of this Customs feller.

My burned-out Hills home foreclosed upon now, so I rented an apartment. Troy Donahue's pad, in fact. Next to the Whisky on Sunset. Ol' Troy's moved to NYC to shoot some daytime soap series. I caught up with Fowley, Ford, Pat and Lolly. Dennis Hopper. Other crazies. Found gigs on the Strip and further.

Then I had to vacate the Troy place, so I moved to Malibu. I roll home one day. Something cooking. Smells like a dadgum hospital on fire.

'What the hell you doing, Ford?'

'Here, Jim, take this.'

A pistol. *Mine.* He's tossed the damn place.

'Now I'm gonna try this,' he said. 'It's like to make me go insane. You may need that iron.'

'Not sure I savvy.'

'I may try to kill you. You'll need to shoot me.'

He had a good toke on that meth when it was done. An hour on, it's just as he'd said. Except *he* wants *me* to shoot *him.* Well, he had deputised me to do what needed doing, so I clubbed him upside the head with that sidearm. TKO. When he came to, his first remark no less than you'd expect.

'Gahd daaaaamn. That sure was a trip, maaaan.'

'Sly calls me the baddest white man on the planet.'

That mess Ford brewed up was for two new pals, Sly Stone and Bobby Womack.

'I'm spending a whole piece of time in his home studio loft up in Bel Air.'

Sly had rented this mansion from John Phillips of the Mamas and the Papas. Here, he and others did meth and that south of the border stardust while helping Sly cut a new record album, *There's A Riot Goin' On*.

Ford was playing guitar and co-writing with Sly. He had Ike Turner, Billy Preston, Bobby Womack up there laying down stuff. Miles Davis one day. All manner of cats.

Cynthia Robinson, the trumpeter, and Jerry Martini, sax man, the only other Family Stone members there. Lived on the premises. Gregg Errico, the drummer, quit some time into those lunatic sessions. You see, Sly had this new-fangled drum machine thing, a Maestro Rhythm King. But it didn't sound like any drums I ever heard. Other Family Stones would come by, lay down bass, drums, guitar. But Sly would just re-record those again over what they'd done, play the part himself.

'Proby,' Ford said, 'I feature we cut a record on you this way, from scratch, a mess of different players.'

Many the plans of which Jim Ford waxed, Brett. Few made the journey from word to flesh. I guess we're all made a little that way.

For all our disputations, Ford oft sought my company and this was welcomed. Had me up to his own domicile one night for dinner. Claudia, Ford's latest girlfriend, was there. Ford had no idea about women. Once their fire was consummated, he'd begin to disregard them. Grow disparaging. Hard to figure. For here at this table, a sprite of beauty celestial. Reminded me of someone. Way she looked, talked. All of her.

'Oh, daddy's alright,' she said to Ford's inquiry of her father. 'But, you know, hassles. The network, his TV show. And Frank. And Sammy.'

Why, this was *Dino's* daughter. Well, this must be done. She'd made eyes my way all evening.

I sent a gift sparkling and bright. A note with it. Said what had to be.

'Hi, Jimmy?'

Claudie calling. Well, then. Diamonds are a dude's best friend. Here we go, stud.

'Why, how do, angel mine?'

'Jimmy. That ring you sent me.'

Whoa. She sounded scared.

'Ford found it. He's coming to shoot you down.'

I got my roscoe out. Made a call. Waited to see who got here first, Ford or the cops. All the while thinking *there might could be a song in this.*

'Claudie? I'm still standing. Ford, he'll be alright. I'm watching it all go down here.'

From my window, vantage of the street. Cops drew their gats on him, he still in his Peugeot. They knew it was him, informed as they'd been of his Frenchy car. He had a thing for 'em.

Judge denied bail. Unlicensed firearm. Outstanding warrants. Handed Ford a piece of time. *You'll get over it.* Me, I hired a U-Haul. Had Claudie come abide with me, in sweet sin.

*

'It's no sham showbiz deal either. Write that down.'

These press dogs needed a firm hand.

'This one's for keeps.'

Early nineteen and seventy-two, our engagement. LA's new showbiz couple, seen at all its toney chowdowns. Stefanino's. We're on the wall at Chasen's. Dan Tana's.

'Best sit-down groceries on the West Coast,' I assured the LA press. For each and every of 'em, *quid pro quo.*

'I am moved to hear of your burdens. I have known such myself, sir. Respect to you.'

Claudie and me as item, at first to Dino's discomposure. But he was soon charmed, by my renditions of old songs he loved well. And my empathetic ear. He's going through his divorce with Jeannie. And just wrapped on a B Western, *Showdown,* with Rock Hudson. Strolled right off the set when he could bear it no more. Didn't want to play Vegas any more either.

'One show a night, I said, Jim. Not two.'

Unheard of in the Big V. Also, *The Dean Martin Show* in straits. The press. Demanded it be axed for its crudity.

'It's a sippin' liquor, Jim. Don't guzzle.'

He'd not abide mixers. Well, no impost to take my JD neat, to win favour. Dino had a new squeeze, her age way south of his, Cathy Hawn. And had dyed his hair russet, a most unnatural shade. But my putative father-in-law, so these things went unremarked upon.

'Jim, you two are a perfect couple. Seeing Claudie happy, I'm the happiest man alive.'

His blessing. We set the date. November first.

'Claudie, honey. Our nuptials may need postponing, I fear.'

Stones in my passway. Clean forgot I'm still wed to Marianne. But Dino said he'd assist. Have her come to terms. No objection from me. Nor questions asked.

*

'An early wedding present, baby.'

'Oh, good God, Claudie! This is entirely wonderful!'

Dino's TV show. She asked him to have me on. Good got better. *Secret Love* his favourite song, said Claudie. I'd cut it on my LP *PJ Proby.* Pepped up some, but she said he'd dig it all the same. Liberty were called for permission and a tape of the backing music, so's I could sing live over that. A pure formality.

'What do you mean, *no* and *no?*'

The only Proby number viewers would recall, they said. These Wall Street tyre-kickers now running Liberty insisted I do *Hold Me,* not *Secret*

Love. Protest was made. Sing *Hold Me*, their response, or they'd sue. I fell into despair. Before the taping, a good drink. Only way to endure it. My rendition deemed unprepossessing. Never went to air.

From high and fine to hell now, Brett. My taste for hard liquors, ruffian companions and freebootin' ways, now less to Claudie's liking.

And Dino's home grew to feel unwelcome. He's tight-lipped now of the wedding for which he'd said he'd pay. Divorce from Marianne came through. But Dino now making obnoxious asides, of my contrary attitude to matters of career, my failed marriages, of the company I kept. These, he suggests, injurious to fitness as husband and provider. A fine thing, coming from *him*. For now, I endured it.

But over there one day, his living room is full of cash. Tote bags. Paper sacks. From the *Showdown* shoot and Vegas, he said. Insisted on payment in such manner. The same from the showrooms. Well, I'd had all I could abide of his disrespecting, Brett, so I felt it meet to respond with everything I had.'

Oh, give me a break, Proby. Now he blows it. Incurable drongo.

'All this cash,' he says.'You are connected, I perceive, with the Mafia. So, Dino, do not be pointing the finger, or anything else, at me.'

Not hard to pick what followed.

'She didn't even leave a note.'

CHAPTER SIXTY

'Bottle of Jack inside me. Another in my hand. And in the other,...'

It's two months on. Proby's out in Hollywood. Motoring along. Clocks Claudia with new boyfriend. Plants the brake. Reefs out a shooter.

'That I might attract their attention and meet with them, Brett,' he says. 'But I failed to notice I'd parked my ride opposite a police station. Next I know, there's a .48 in my ear, a Remington shotgun at my chin, a Colt .45 in my other ear. Hell, I wasn't but discharging a fully licensed firearm at the sky.'

So, yeah, the Proby pictures it as per but the LAPD saw different. Reckon he took aim at the couple as they fled.

'Well, they cuffed me. Popped the trunk of my car. Here, sixteen baseball bats. I'd taken on a job, managing this little league team in the Hills, for some walkin' round money.'

Or to meet baseball mamas and their daughters, maybe.

'But me knee-walkin' down the street, bottle in hand, shootin' off a pistol, well, I didn't look like too much of a sportsman. The bats, way they saw it, likely weaponry for outlaw bikers. Drugs turf war, such of that nature. I'm charged with DWI, affray, and the stepdaddy of 'em all. Attempted murder.

'From here,' they said, ''it's San Quentin. Twenty-five to life, Tex.'

Four killers in here, Brett. Waitin' on a train to Death Row. I sang for them to temper their ire. Did three months in that glasshole, as we called it. Counsel got that attempt murder beef dropped. I'm cut loose.

My old pad up in the Hills, for sale now. Boarded up. I jemmied the door with a tyre jack. Out in the yard, there it was, behind the rabbit hutch. A gallon jar of whiskey. Soon, all became clear. And the only thing that could be did was done.

*

'The reviews damned it to exile at earth's icebound end.'

So Proby decides that back to London is the you-beaut option. Lobs there as *I'm Yours* is released on Kruger's Ember label.

'Brett, that platter went to hell and stayed there. I'd no taste for further of Kruger and his pesterations. Yet my need was clear. To this end, I made my availability for live shows known via other means.

Jimmy Savile these days had a Saturday night BBC TV show, *Clunk Click*. The name, from his TV ads for safety belts. He, most amenable that I come on and sing *What's Wrong With My World*. For this would reap ratings.

Savile's taste for, well, flowers in first bloom of feminine wile, not abated any. Behind the scenes at *Clunk Click*, it was the same as had been at *TOTP* but for their now advanced years. Swarms of foxy mamas. Staunch fans of Savile and his guests, we Sixties stars. Flirtation and further with these old boilers, as Savile badged 'em, paved path to their daughters was his *modus operandi*.

Now, Savile's detractors whispered still of brutal penchants. I never saw any such. But can affirm one thing. This pooch was insatiable. Anyway, Kruger saw me on *Clunk Click*. Begged I return to live shows, to promote that dadgum LP. So I did what I must in such straits.

*

The first single off *I'm Yours* was *Put Your Head On My Shoulder*. The B side, *Momma Married A Preacher*, a song Kruger bought off of Les Reed. Of that style Dusty and Elvis did on their Memphis albums. But these Limeys, no clue how to make that sound. Tin Ears Kruger, he'd hired these half-dead players from variety TV. Dadgum elevator music. *Muzak, Jack.*

'Man, Kruger,' I said. 'You sure know how to put the *s* back into *hit.*'

'No, Kruger, this is on you.'

Radio won't play his brokedown record. He puts this on me, my tear-it-up rep. I'd none of it.

'You go cutting inferior material on me, that's your barn on fire, mister.'

Still, he got me gigs. Clubs. Cabaret. The B-towns. Blackpool. Bognor Regis. Bournemouth, Bristol, Birmingham. The summer seaside seasons. Then Coventry, Solihull, Dunstable.

I been everywhere that's nowhere, man.

'They want to hear my hits, dang it. Not this junk.'

Kruger pleaded I do numbers from *I'm Yours* at my shows, to sell his cold and stale biscuits. But I paid no mind. Had grief sufficient without he made me the mule of his burdens. See, Brett, my earnings, now garnisheed by Inland Revenue. Work visa could be had only as a trade for this brutal caveat. Again I put it to these dadgum trimmers to pursue EMI, the Delfonts, Grades, all my managers for those tax moneys. But it cut no ice with these icemen.

It was my Robert Goulet period. Tux and moustache, baby blues and deep purples. Work came and went in '73 and '74. On the Continent and crisscrossing England's foggy shires. The Winter Gardens Theatre in Blackpool imposed a ban. The state of me onstage. But I'd only had Special Brew. Ain't even a *real* drink. Refused to pay me. Breach of contract, they said.

One weird scene, Brett. We singers, what these clubs called the 'talent.' The band would come on. Dinner music. Then standards. Then me. Before us or in between, spoons players, ukulele singers, plate-spinnin' dogs. Thus did I eke out my days in numbsville.

The best TV shows, *Old Grey Whistle Test* or *Top Of The Pops* or *John Peel's BBC Sessions*, liked Kruger's record about as much as I did.

So that left just morning TV for promo options. Or local shows from the regions. *Wheeltappers and Shunters Social Club* one such, from ITV Granada. Set in a fictional club for railroad workers. The compere, this unfunny comic Bernard Fanning. Interjections as I sang, from club manager, a fella called Colin Crompton. I sing *I Don't Have To Tell You* while being heckled by this flat-capped Limey shitheel who slanders me as 'Mr PJ Probably.' The song, from Richard Harris. Yet another who swiped my act.

'That liquor, Kruger, was *not* stealing.'

My alleged crime, to seek payment from behind the bar. My fee, this club said they'd not pay. This, down to my dishevelment in concert. Waylaid by security, I swung a bunch of fives which found only air. Those doormen served me hard, fist and boot. Yes, bookers all over bellyached now. Of tardy arrivals. No-shows. My turbulent conduct. I told Kruger to cram it.

*

Between hell and sunrise, a phone call. Some honch from Sydney. In advertising, if I recollect right. His pitch, the clubs there, money plenty if your road be skulls and bones.

Hold that plane.

*

'Just *three shows?*'

The news on touchdown in Sydney. Nine or ten dates promised. Only these remained. Slow ticket sales. A good drink on the flights, but I'm now fatigued. And the promoter, all beered up. Blaming me. Relations soured right there in his Rolls Royce at the airport.

'Hell, hoss. For an ad man, you ain't so hot at selling your product, I discern.'

The temerity of his responses prompted my desire to return home at once. *Turn this car around, driver.* And, well, a blackout after that.

Next day, a trial to recollect which country this was, peering out the window with eyes gone red. I'm all set to lam it. But then I spy the mini-bar. Stuffed to bustin.' A pause then, to sample of this bounty.

I believe Melbourne was first. Dorset Gardens Hotel. September nineteen and seventy-four. Some clamhead in the crowd, or such as passed for one, called me drunk. I decamp the stage, take my passage across the tabletops. Bear down on this oppugnant, swingin' windmill punches. Security tackled me, dragged me away. I cannot feature why patrons demanded refunds. Hell, not after a show like that. Bareknuckle boxing and all.

Next, Adelaide. Joint called Countdown. Word was this place and others on this Hindley Street strip, torched from time to time, the band here told me. Insurance grift maybe. Or they'd upset some friends in the cement business.

Now Melbourne had been right after that London to Sydney flight. So by now, I'm in no shape. I sought a postponement.

'Here is the news,' when they said *nope.* 'Right now, a cash advance on top of the fee. Or I'm gonesville. Right out of this so-called dressing room not fit for man nor hog.'

Well, I weakened when a passel of young sweets sought audience. Only a churl could refuse such entreaty. So, then. A fine, fine backing band here. Told them so when we were done.

On to Sydney now. The where of it escapes me, Brett.'

Some reckon Revesby Workers. Others, Marrickville RSL. No-one knows for sure.

'Claims here of a barkeep sucker-punched for refusing me service. Then that promoter grew lippy again. I responded. Bouncers pinned me. Surely my last go-round in this neck of the world.'

He tipped his hat.

'Then you boys happened along.'

CHAPTER SIXTY-ONE

'Emile Ford came upon me, indigent and disarrayed. Pitied the ragamuffin before him. He lived in Spennymoor. South of Newcastle, England. I stayed with him a piece.

In deleterious state of health, I'm now back on benefits. But a six mile walk each way each week to get it, at the nearest DHSS office to Spenny. So Emile advanced me. A used white El Dorado for sale in the vicinity, Brett. A rusty, smokin' ride. Yet a Caddy for all that.

Spenny had its charms. Like the Top Hat nightclub. Here, I traded songs for booze. And met the mother of a girl attending Durham Road Secondary Modern. Mama's a PJ fan from right back when. Keen to be on intimate terms. Her daughter, too, I perceived. So some effort now in quest for a little high school confidential when mama's out, she a cashier or something in daylight hour.'

I didn't ask if this was straight up. And hoped to fuck it wasn't.

Spenny was a coal mining town. Boys worked 'down pit' as they styled it. I was made offer of wages there. But I'd no time for drudgery. Why, I had a new show to plan. Collaboration with Emile was mooted, but he wearied now of my loosey goosey ways.

'I'll none of it, lest there is payment. I have guns and dogs here!'

The press found me in Spenny. Came to gorge as vampires on fallen pop idol PJ Proby. And Emile fell to bickering and yammering of this and that. I heard that highway callin'...

I had a gig every year come summer. The casino at Blackpool. This moon in June, two things made it too sweet to depart at run's end. First,

I relocated here at invite of local resident Cyril 'Ciggy 'Shaw, from the Rockin' Vicars. We'd done shows together way back. Their stringbuster was this fella Ian Kilmister.'

'Later Lemmy from Motorhead,' I said.

'A fact uncontestably veracious, Brett. The other reason, well,...'

'I've been a fan since I was thirteen, like. I saw you on *Around The Beatles!*'

Dulcie Taylor. Twenty-one, to my thirty and seven. Mine still, the twinkle to make 'em tingle. She, a croupier at the tables here. We were soon betrothed.

'A bride of such allure,' I declared, 'should wed in no less than Westminster Cathedral.'

I told the press of my wish. They might could see a story in it, I figured, use the swing they had to set it up. Alas, not tempted. So we man and wifed it at the registry office in Bury, north of Manchester. Made a home of Stockton-On-Tees.

Shang-ri-la for a stretch. I told Dulcie it was well that she found a croupier's job at Houndsworth Workingmen's Club in Stockton. For I needed to create sonic magic at home, in solitude. Write a hit. Get an album out, too. Thence tour it to glory.'

Yeah, Proby. You don't say. Write? Pickled by half time each day. Hard pressed to write his own name. In piss in the Manchester snow.

'Jim, ya canny bastard, ya!'

A call from Hughie Green. An old drinking bud, Brett. Host of *Opportunity Knocks,* the new faces talent show, since long about William the dadgum Conqueror.

'I might have a job for you, son!'

He was in Manchester, filming *OK*.

'I want to get off this bloody show, Jim,' he said at my gig at the Fagin Club. 'Had a better offer to do it down in Australia.'

A hundred and fifty pounds was paid to all performers on *OK*. This and a side of Jack D's Old Number Seven, sealed a deal I could not pass by.

Come the day, *OK* viewers were treated to a song by an unknown even less known than the other unknowns on the show. See, he wore a mask. Superhero style. Just across the eyes. Introduced as the Masked Singer. By far best in show, yet ran second.

Hughie believed he'd be bounced, his contract paid out. As he desired. Pro singers forbidden on *OK*. So ours, a major breach.

'And, Jim,' he said, 'your career will roar again!'

Two days on, photos of me in the press. In that Zorro mask, on the show. The Masked Singer, declared disqualified. And so, unpaid. Whole deal went sideways. I, portrayed as a cheat. And Hughie, they didn't fire his ass. They raised his salary! Only loser in this game of thimblerig, Yours Truly. Circus left town without me. Again.

'Keep your keks on, Jim. Zip up your fly. I can't be mithered with all this'.

Dulcie had tired of me in matters of intimacy. My belief, she's been stepping out with younger studs, fellow casino employees. And she took issue with me as a provider.

'It's dead hard, it is. I do all the graft and you spend all the lolly.'

Time to get a job, she said.

'I am writing *songs*. I have no time for *donkey work*.'

Then she reminded me of her brothers. Hefty miners, not averse to taking blows and even less to delivering them. I'm served news of my new quarters, there to better contemplate on my options. As a rule, goes by the name of the back seat. *Clunk click.*

'Well, if y'all don't call it a sheep ranch, what dadgum title *do* you affix to it?'

A wool-growing farm. My job, move the flock about, to different paddocks. For shearing, lambing season, drenching. That, and distribution of fertiliser. *Muckspreading,* these Limey crofters call it. The company of working dogs. Preferable to most people, Brett.

Tardy to my labours was how it went soon enough. Or I didn't make the date at all. The pub, its fireplace, easy beats over wind and rain. Why, some as might call it, this designed to provoke dismissal.

'Gold is where you find it, dear boy. Before some other blighter does.'

Well, this was a bewilderment. Jack Good made contact. We at cold war since *Catch My Soul*. Presley had passed on, not two days past. Jack planned a show in memoriam. But salutes to dead stars, Brett, well. In America we call this *ridin' the coffin wagon*. And I'd known Elvis as a good and dear friend.'

Yeah. With Proby, the past was always three different freakin' countries.

'But I considered further. Someone's gonna do this anyway. My druthers, that Elvis be shown as he really was. And that someone who knew him to do Presley this courtesy.

Elvis The Musical had three singers. Guess who as Older Elvis. Shakin' Stevens, a retro rockabilly act, Middle. Some kid, Tim Whitnail, did for Young.

'You see, Jim?' said Jack. 'Just like the old days. You'll cause a sensation, dear boy.'

And I did. And how.

*

'But, Jim, *PJ Proby* on the marquee will get the punters in.'

'I must be billed as James Proby, and that's final.'

Jack press-released *Elvis The Musical*. Quick as speckled kingsnakes, with scalding tar and feathers am I plastered by the Fleet Street rags.

'If not, Jack, y'all can start this hootenanny without me.'

So *James Proby* it was. This, a levee bank to stem the torrent, to signify the vulgar britches buster now all growed up now and refined. Jack had TV people film the rehearsals. And set up interviews with we three Presleys, for a short documentary, televised just before opening night. Some TV chat shows as well. Thereon, I acquitted myself with decorum despite the provocations of inquisitors.

'Not exploitation. More an Irish wake,' was how Jack parried the killjoys. We opened at the Astoria to the mock and scorns of the critics. And so did Jack go bold and nimble, jinking our adversaries across a mess of TV and radio.

'And our top star, James Proby, knew Elvis,' he reported. 'Worked with him, sang his demos. Indeed, played football with him in LA and oft a guest at his home.'

Ticket sales began to rise. And a great fortuity showed its face, agrin like a demon's.

'Dear boy. The marquee says *Elvis The Musical,* not *PJ The Musical.* Stick to the script, do.'

Jack took exception to improvements I made. I talked of my times with Presley, between my numbers. This, not in the script. But, see, Brett, people were coming to see *me,* not Presley. I slipped in a song, too. Told the band that Presley had sung *Hold Me* back in the times. They knew no different. And during *Burnin' Love,* I dropped in *Niki Hoeky.* Took to regaling patrons of how Presley hired me as a demo singer so's he could steal my style. The show claimed to be of the real Elvis, so that's what they got. Hecklers could expect no mercy. Received none when some grew prickly. But from Jack, it seemed, nor could I.

'En garde! Pistols or swords, varlet!'

He I now challenged, my replacement, one Bogdan Kominowski. To a duel. Jack says I'm off the show, but I want back in. So I walk right up into that dressing room. Slap ol' Bogdan's face with a glove as they set the bruisers on me. Exit swingin' and singin'. *Lord Almighty, feel my temperature risin'...*

*

'A faithful wife does not keep such hours. Devilry is afoot!'

Dulcie, she's working extra shifts, she claims. Yet refused to show me her paychecks, and here she be, coming in at four in the AM.

'Who will the next fool be, Dulcie? Who's been fishin' in my pond?'

She handed back as good as got. But her sass could not be endured. To hand, one of the Bolton farm's air guns. Liberated for my own self-defence.

'Jim, you shot Dulcie six times.'

My lawyer was perplexed.

'Oh, dang it, man! It's an air gun! A slug gun. A dadgum toy!'

Brett, she was wearing Levis. That and ample hindquarters, so no harm to her person.'

If you say so, Proby. Geezus.

'Bail granted but I had to report to the cops daily. Passport seized. Trial to come. My woes I confided to drinkers in a pub nearby. Warm weather now. They'd been fans back then. Gave me shelter, their coal cellar being vacant.'

'Dulcie wants you put away, Jim.'

The charge, upgraded. *Attempted murder.* But the judge said it wasn't a real gun. Just a pop gun. His Honour a sporting shooter, it transpires. Pheasants and such. Hence my acquittal.

I scored some shows off that commotion. Even TV spots. In part down to my new secretary, name of Pamela Baglow. We'd met at a Fagin Club gig. Bedazzled, she made offer to take on this task. Like many I met now, a fan from back then. Hustled for me on the phone. Walked my dogs. Grocery shopping.

Yet a happy union for but a short piece of time. I'd lost a three-night club season in Birmingham after just one show. The grounds they advanced, beyond my ken to hark back to, owing to inebriation at the time, I expect.

So Pam's bought groceries. Spent all she's got till next payday from her day job. But I lack funds for refreshment. And I am run dry.

'*Damn* your *profligacy!*'

She ran out into our back garden when I took up a hunk of wood. Then I saw the axe. Hefted it up but tripped over that ol' chopping block as she escaped through the gate.

'Plead guilty. You'll get off with a fine,' said the duty solicitor. Sure enough, my imposition but a slap and ticket, as she had no wish to appear in court.

My finest quality suitcases, now found to be equal to any rigour. Bounced intact off the pavement, flung from the upstairs bedroom. Of my proposal we wed, she'd grown disinclined.

CHAPTER SIXTY-TWO

'Chim. Are you busy right now?'

We'd first met in the Netherlands. Thijs van Leer had this group Focus. Big time for a short time before a bustup. Reforming now but their stringbuster, Jan Akkerman, declared *nee*.

'And sho, Chim, I thought of you.'

I fly in. This Dutchy sprung for it. Our purpose, cut a new Focus album, me as guest vocal. He lived in Brussels. We're up all night learning songs. Then he fetched a case of Heineken.

'Why, thank you, amigo.'

'*Ach*, Chim. You'll need it.'

That box of beer, conditional on getting in his car right there. A three hour drive to Amsterdam. To cut that biscuit. This day.

'*Nooit,* no way. You're too well known round here, Chim.'

Last thing Thijs wanted. Me out around Da Wallen, the 'dam's red light district. Not after last time. Or all those before that. So what does he do? Locks me up like it's Alcatraz, in the studio! Booze laid on, but confined to base. I slept under the piano.

Focus Con Proby was not a success, Brett. Thijs had talked of taking it on the road, but now nixed that idea. Why, I cannot feature.'

Well, I'm gonna take a wild guess here, Proby.

'I don't recall what it sounded like. Sure, there was Grolsch and red spirits. But not near enough to kill me.'

Proby was still working live come 1980, he said. Europe, anyway. In the guts of that, this German label, Palm, put out an LP. Hyped as brand new Proby product. *The Hero,* they called it. Cover's a 1980 Proby head shot. But hold the freakin' bus. The gear within, twenty years old. Demos from Liberty in LA.

The lurk merchants who'd got their clammies on Liberty must have sold their Proby masters to this Deutsche mob. I didn't ask, lest he chuck a mental. His freakouts, by now troublesome to my own state of mind.

Back in Manchester, landlords let him sleep it off on pub floors after *time, please.*

'Or I laid me down a pallet in squats around North Manchester, or Brompton Street in Oldham. Derelict old factories and slaughterhouses.'

It was about now Proby met Dave Britton and Mike Butterworth, the fun lovers from Savoy Books. A club gig in Harpurhey. Proby's hair now in two bangs, either side of his head. In a tough Manc drinker. These two, dragged up in this hood, blown away by the move. And that this ratbag's still alive. Their aim, write his life story. And, they'd heard, best get in quick.

These two bods not exactly your Penguin Books. The specialty of their imprint, so gruesome and explicit it was banned even as it hit the stores. Proby reckons the meet didn't go so good. He puts the arm on 'em for a monster advance they didn't have. But they were believers. They'd be back.

The only TV shows Proby could get his head on by now, those 'where are they now' setups. Hits and memories. Like this Channel 4 turn, *Greatest Hits.* Proby's take on the 1980s, twin ponytails, sprouting out the sides of his head. White headband. Red shirt. S'pose he knew what he was doing. Even if no-one else did.

Another one of these he did round then, *Unforgettable.* Prompted the press to go the cut chook on how long the Texan had to live. Proby reckons a journo asked what he'd like on his headstone.

'So what did you tell him, Proby?' I asked. A rare time he smiled.
'I'd rather be here than with you, cocksucker.'

*

Producer Bill Kenwright gave him the Pharaoh part, he said. A West End run of *Joseph And His Amazing Technicolour Dreamcoat*. But Proby bailed. After the first act. Opening night. Scrawled in lippy on the dressing room mirror as he went. *I will not work with homosexual dancers.* You tell me. A take on the world full as a goog with phobias and neuroses, this hoedad. The mind fair boggles.

'So, Brett, impelled by this turnabout, a return to that harder master now. In Haworth, West Yorkshire. A sheep ranch in Huddlesfield, where it's said the Bronte sisters had lived. My bed, in Charlotte Bronte's old barn. Well, such is what they claimed so. My boss, this farmer, Gerald Hardy. And then along came his daughter Alison.'

Oh no, no, Proby. Don't. Please. Don'...

'Mayhap fifteen, sixteen when we met. Still in school. Not a whole peck of time before we formed mutual attraction. And moved toward consideration of romantic liaison.'

You don't say. Had to wonder why he wasn't planted two feet under somewhere...

'Her daddy spoke sharp to me. Of what might could obtain, given his disapproval. This fella, access to troves of firearms. Ol' Gerald not just a farmer but a gun store proprietor. Round these parts, handy for *pest control*, he said.

So we eloped. She's sixteen by now. Made for Gretna Green In Scotland, to elude her daddy. Got wed there on the QT. February '84. Fleet Street went nuclear. To evade our pursuers, we relocate to Bronteville. Then the landlord at the pub there wised me of two hombres in town. Lookin' to have words. My apprehension, substantial. Maybe Inland Revenue. Or the DHSS about my benefit. Or associates of my bride's daddy. But no...

'Jim,' said Dave Britton, 'can we have another chat?'

Well, they'd come all the way from Manchester and they were buying.

'Your life story. Bestseller, no risk. A big drink in it for you.'

'One hundred thousand pounds,' I said. 'And that's just the advance.'

Well, they had not that kind of money, but all they asked, they said, was I talk with them. For all the firewater my belly could hold. They'd do the writing off our pow-wows.

So we had some sit-downs. But it summoned sour memories. Moonrise found me in ill temper. On a drunk. Quick to affray. And other than victor in some of those combats.

News of my wedding brought requests. TV interviews, all that medley. So I did it if I had gigs to promote. And spread word of this memoir now in development.

'It's all in the book,' I'd say when the questions grew curly. Some shows had an in-house pianist. I did *Green Green Grass Of Home,* just to beat the squelch out of Tom dadgum Jones. Or *Hurt,* the Timi Yuro classic.

A few shows were national. Like the BBC's *Time Of Our Lives* with Noel Edmonds. I sang *Hold Me* for Alison in the studio audience. Her parents had spoken to the press of late, in mean and rapscallious terms. Edmonds got right into it.

'How long have you been married now?'

'About three months.'

'And that was a much-publicised thing, with parental opposition...'

'She was only ten.'

Brett, it was meant as but a jest. But Edmonds comes back with this.

'You might be telling the truth there, actually.'

England didn't see the joke. I went on *Jameson Tonight* on Sky TV. Wearing these big ol' shades, having acquired a pair of shiners and a lump on my forehead the night before. After the show, a floor manager, tasked to hold up my lyrics up for me to sing *Love Letters,* said I'd mauled her right there on TV. No truth to it. It was Sky TV's hospitality. A request for Carlsberg and JD in the Green Room, not met. Verbal chide was all I served. Naught else.'

Well, I've seen that clip and beg to differ, my man.

'Getting back in the clubs, this was the payoff for doing all that TV. And I'm spared those dadgum sheep. I took to speculating how long before one of *them* went bawlin' to the press that I'd had my way with 'em.

And I was booked for this Rock'n'Roll Legends tour. Swingin' Bluejeans, Helen Shapiro, Billy J Kramer. I said I'd do one show only. Manchester. And at a fee of my stipulation. These terms they met, on condition that I talk up the gig on Manchester's *AM* TV show. Heck, why do a whole tour if you can get the same price for just one show? And all in glass and cans.

'My book must read like this one. *The Moon's A Balloon*, David Niven's book.'

But the boys from Savoy, discomfited.

'Jim, we need the good times *and* the bad if you want an earn off this.'

'Mister, I have *done* no *wrong*. All that bunk, the lies of malefactors and rivals. The good stuff. That's the story. The only one you're gettin', *hermano.*'

So it fell by the wayside. But then they came back.

'Jim,' they said, 'how'd you feel about some recording?'

'Things have changed a lick in studios, boys.'

This joint looked like the flight deck out of *Star Trek*. And these machines here. Drums, bass, strings, horns, alchemised with these dadgum electronic keyboards.

'Fakery. I'll have none of it.'

'We had a feeling you'd say as much, Jim. But...'

'I need an orchestra. And a five piece rhythm section. Finest first call players in England.'

They demur, so I'm all set to up and out of there when they bring forth a box of Carlsberg.

'And plenty more where we got that one, Jim.'

'I ain't even heard half these numbers.'

'Oh, come on, Jim. The stars of today. Bowie. Prince. Phil Collins. Iggy Pop. Sex Pistols, Joy Division. Your new mojo.'

'I can't listen to all that slop jar.'

'We don't *wan't* you to. Go in cold. We'll get a fresh take on the buggers.'

Fresh? Hell, Brett. I made those dadgum songs wish they'd never been born.

'I ain't cuttin' here. I want Olympic or Abbey Road or....'

'Jim, the Gang Of Four, Teardrop Explodes, Joy Division have all recorded here.'

'I never heard of no Teardrop Explodes.'

'They sell a lot of records.'

Suite 16 in Rochdale in Manchester, their preferred sound factory. Built by Peter Hook from Joy Division, they told me, and of some renown. We'd cut here to turn music business heads, they said. Get me noticed.

'The sound of now, Jim,' said Dave. 'They'll never know what hit 'em.'

*

'I heard this on the radio. Sounds like a Dear John letter. From another damn John.'

Soft Cell's *Tainted Love* had been a hit, they countered. And our cut on it could be too. They proffered ale and better that I be persuaded.

'It's a suck-off song the way they do it anyway, Jim,' said Britton. 'You show 'em how it should be. Like with *Somewhere* and *Maria.*'

Yessir. Booze in cascade as if from the Horn Of Plenty itself, so I kept on comin'. Next, they cut Bowie's *Heroes* on me. Must've had a semi-truck, ol' Davy, to haul away all that he thieved from me.

Unease with Alison of late. Press likened us to Jerry Lee and his thirteen-year old cousin Myra. And she's pouty. I spent no time with her, she alleged. Well, she could not come to licensed premises. My God, she was underage!

She split the day we cut *Heroes,* while I was out. I did not give chase, mindful of her daddy and his firearms emporium. That said, in my heartbroke state, I told the Savoy fellas I planned to shoot her and then myself. But by the morrow I'd cooled on that notion. The shoot *her* part at any rate.

'My God, David! What cavern of hell *is* this?'

Screaming guitar from some sallow kid. Fast shuffle from the drummer. On every song. Only dadgum beat he knew. In the studio, this deadbeat band they'd engaged.

'And no bass player! What kind of outfit...'

'We'll overdub the bass parts with the synth, Jim. Relax, mate.'

But there was no sense of event. *No glory to be had.*

'With *these* three poltroons?'

Britton had booked a PJ Proby gig, hence this rehearsal he'd called. The band, that ghost boy on guitar, that same drummer. And no bass player. Just this other milk-white kid.

'Son, you look like you died and they dug you up.'

He played a de-tuned synthesiser, this one. For that end of days noise to which these Limeys are so in thrall.

The gig, a new pub in Manchester. Looked like a dang airport. We did not fare well.

'Matters not, Jim. We'll get B-sides for the singles off this,' said Britton, recording this mess. Then I found Dave had told those three freshmeats they'd be my band on tour.

'I need musicians who can read. Not you popeyed palefaces.'

Rehearsal. My box of beer, empty. They'd helped themselves, at no invite from me.

'You think you're going on tour with PJ Proby, you can take that down the road!'

Disgruntled, they fell to scrapping. One put another on his ass. I called it a day. Pubs closed in one fast hour and my thirst needed slakin'.

'Vengeance on this vapid industry will be yours, Jim. No bad song goes unpunished.'

Our *Tainted Love*, all mixed now. Opened with my scream like to freeze the blood of a tiger, a salutation to Little Richard. To give it a push, Savoy did a promo booklet, *PJ Proby: The Survivor*. Tales of a swashbuckling outlaw. I liked it well.

'We'll get this to the press before we release,' said Mike. 'Get 'em all drooling.'

But interest was slim when it was sowed across the land, other than the music press. And further sessions now, despite that radio would not play our *Tainted Love*.

'Lose that dadgum band,' I said. Well, they did. But at our next session at Pink Studios in Liverpool, there was no band at all.

'It's band or booze, Jim,' they said. 'We don't have the ackers for both.'

These synthesisers would more than suffice, they averred.

'For the sound of civilisation burning down.'

They had me cut one of my own songs, *The Mugwump Dance*. This word *mugwump* from a Native American language, meaning 'big chief.' But I didn't care for their production stylings on it. Mashed my prime rib into dadgum hamburger.

And now they had me track TS Eliot's poem *The Waste Land*. One strange campfire story, that one. So I made it even more so. Did voices from Richard Burton to Strother Martin in *Cool Hand Luke* to Orson Welles to Vivien Leigh as Scarlett O'Hara. Then round that bend came a runaway train.

'Boys. Reckoning for my misdeeds is now upon me, and eternity near.'

Attending for repeat scripts of anti-anxiety, mood-stabilising and sleeping medications, my physician concerned at symptoms reported. Tests. A diagnosis. Stomach cancer.

CHAPTER SIXTY-THREE

He granted my request that I pass on here at our home. Yet my daddy's new wife, all rancour and suspicion. She obtained a referral to a specialist in Houston.

Well, now. The tumour but an ulcer.

'There is no place for you here, Jimmy.'

Handed me the air ticket.

'Your poor father. The turn of his life. These false tales of terminal illness.'

I, a threat to her, I perceived. Claim jumper, the only name I could ascribe to her aspirations. Daddy, gruff in farewell, said little. Taken ill himself of late.

Wicked thoughts tempted me, Brett. Of a sporting rifle. Planting her out in the Panhandle. But prospect of daddy's grief and my apprehension on capital charge stayed my hand.

On the plane, I set down on the tray my shaking handful, the half-spilled first of the day. Dropped a straw in. To minister without mishap.

*

'Hey,' I said. 'All my hits got girls on 'em. Why don't y'all get some on here?'

Back at Rochdale, Steve Buckley the engineer fetched up Denise Johnson and this minx who went by just Rowetta. Went on to do stuff with Primal Scream and Happy Mondays, I recall. Here, backups on a Phil Collins number, *In The Air Tonight*. Some others. And cut two of their own, *Shoot Yer Load* and *Golden Showers*. They knew me well.

Next, *Anarchy In The UK*. Sex Pistols. I'd never heard it. So I read the words off a sheet. Actorly voice, like Peter O'Toole or Richard Harris. *I'm On Fire*, Springsteen, we cut that too.

For a B side to *Heroes*, an Iggy Pop number, *The Passenger*, they said.

'Boys, never listened to it, no plans to. Next!'

Its case, pleaded with gift of Wild Turkey, that it could be recited as per *Anarchy*. That's how *The Passenger* got did, including that *la la la la la-la la-la* bit. Next day, I quit.

'For I am come down low.'

'The time has come to join my father in the sky.'

This to drinkers in a pub close by the studio. News. My daddy's passing. From his widow, no reply to entreaty for airfare. So, then. Next best thing.

'They use 'em for pest control on sheep spreads hereabouts. Do the job, no messin'.'

To any here who cared to listen.

'Stick it in your ear and pop goes the weasel.'

But right then, some work rolled in. A gig at Wooky Hollow club, Liverpool. Distraction from my sack o' woe. But once done, little more to be had. Nor muscle jobs. My name among farmers around these parts, now a poisoned village well.

*

So I go back to Savoy, Brett, at their urging. Payment in lager and harder, as before.

'But conditions apply now, Jim.'

They'd only cut on me between two and four in the PM, when the pubs were closed. And booze only at session's end. No cash, lest I get rabbit in my blood. My persnickety ways had cost 'em a deal of money, they claimed.

'Sing it like Bowie, Jim.'

This got my dander up.

'Bowie stole it all from *me*, motherfucker!'

This for *Love Will Tear Us Apart*. Their idea of great songs, well. Of such I'd grown wearisome.

'Everything y'all think is fun,' I said, 'I think is *boring!*'

We got kicked out of Pink Studios. Maybe it was the mess on the sound board. I poured white wine on some Chinese take-out, to lap up that Charlie grub like a dog.

'Too bad if that offends y'all,' I said to their yappin.' 'Only way I'll eat this chop suey.'

Again, I said I was through. But they brung me apple wine. Compelled me to backslide.

'Jim, you know of Bobby Sands, the IRA hunger strikers, right?'

A big news story then. A studio in London's East End, the Strongroom, this time.

'I don't know any of these dadgum numbers.'

A list of Irish Rebel songs.

'I'll just talk 'em like last time.'

For *The Old Fenian Gun*, Peter Hook added some fuzz bass from Joy Division's *Blue Monday*. To what end, only hell and its hounds know. On *Kevin Barry*, a disco beat behind me. A military march on *Bobby Sands*. Lyrics by Bobby himself. I talked in a dead man's shoes.

'It's illegal to record it unauthorised,' they said. 'We can offend everyone.'

We did *God Save The Queen*. Not the Sex Pistols. The national anthem. But for all that yak of outraging the nation, to this biscuit, *Savoy Digital Angst*, little mind was paid and sales were few.

More live shows now. Just me and backing tracks from the sessions. Small pubs. I dressed up like Iggy Pop one time. Shirtless. Blonde wig. Mascara-blacked eyes. Like a panda bear. Or an old boxer come off second-best.

Dave Britton fell bleak now, at the passing of his mother. Her home in Saddleworth overlooked the scene of the Moors Murders. Five children. Here, we did conceive a whole new mission. The most shocking record ever made.

Hardcore M97002 we called it. Britton's prisoner number when his ass was in stir at HM Prison Strangeways. For publishing pornography. This record, grotesque. Sure to make the news. Raise awareness of my Savoy catalogue. Launch a thousand hits.

Opened with a creepy synth humming. Me bawlin' *Ain't no such thing as rape / When you're wearin' a Superman cape / Hi ho fuckin' Silver, I am the man with the twelve-inch gun, / I am PJ Proby.*

More along these lines. Had Denise or Rowetta, can't recall which, repeat every line. Also did simulation of sex acts, the screams of murder victims. Fifteen minutes of it.

We released it as a twelve-inch single, Brett. Me with ex-wife Alison on the cover. She, not nekkid, but most of the road there. Back cover, me again. With a ten year old girl.'

Well, Proby's done it. A grand tour of the mansion. And now he's tellin' me what's under the freakin' floorboards.

'*Hardcore* made the news, bigtime. So now the press were told that the studio had been decked out like a porno set. Red velvet drapes. King size bed. Acts of love thereon. That we'd rolled tape on these. Making all that wail thereon, a star gone incognito, we said. Madonna was touring England then. Our story, that she'd made time for us special. That she'd wanted to record with me for years. And not just record with me.

Well, those press chawbacons ran all this like it's true as due north. Then we sent the single to the radio stations. To ensure it would be banned.

Yet we sold zip. Britton, in a last bid to shift biscuits, told reporters I reminded him of Dennis Hopper's Frank Booth out of Hopper's movie, *Blue Velvet,* displaced to Manchester and on the loose on the Yorkshire Moors.

'You don't know Dennis like I did in LA. Hell, I was no Dennis Hopper,' I told them.

'I was far worse.'

A portion of sunshine off all that. Promoters called. But at the *Rock 'n' Roll Legends Festival* in Epping Forest, they say I fell off the stage during the first number, then did two more but finished neither. Demands for refunds and such clangour. At a music fest in Heaton Park, Manchester, I made it through *On The Road Again,* a speck shy of only just. Crowd let me have it. And I found that I did not care.

The seaside towns, but one show that year. Blackpool. Did it slumped against the drum kit. Well, the part that did get did. The last gig I recall, Brett, before you and Clyde here flew me out, I did at the Fagin Club. I quit the stage thirty minutes into my act.

'I'm sorry,' I said. 'I cannot continue. I am suffering from gonorrhea, more popularly known as the clap.'

Well. I had an image to uphold.

CHAPTER SIXTY-FOUR

'My faith is strong. All will be schmick, my man.'

My call to Clyde. Then I see Proby's condition when Kenny's mate Bill Burbon delivers the pair of 'em to the show. But the band has it nailed. And in Newie he'd sung as in days of wonder. I kept my distance. Didn't want Hazmat doing his block this close to showtime.

A tiny dressing room at Paddo RSL, just off stage right. Here he sequestered himself with room temp beer and box wine in a spooky, shutdown state. Now Kenny Starr's gone AWOL. So not at his post when Proby locked the door from the inside. Then refused to come out.

Supports 50 Million Beers and Christa Hughes have done the bizzo. It's showtime. And he chooses now to have a freakin' out of body experience.

'Where the fuck is he?' from the crowd.

'Oh, here we go,' I say to Clyde. 'The fun lovers are restless.'

From the moment they lobbed. Whingers. Ticket price. Drink prices. How far they'd had to come. The Hendo's *Bandstand* mob. Fans from all the way back. That codger bogan's impatience and ill-will. And here it came, right on cue.

'I want me money back!'

Slow claps. Croaked curses. Bunched up on one side of the room. A ghost coach party.

Kenny Starr has a pass at wheedling Proby out. But he's on the shitlist too. He let Nini and Clyde pull the pin on his hooker, after all.

So enter Nini. She don't ease into it. Hands him a big serve through the door. No other way. See, we forgot to tell Kenny to keep a firm hand on the Texan's pharma intake, like Clyde and me had been doing. So now, he's off in some unknown cosmos. Those pills, its moons and stars.

'When you're near me I feel so romantic...'

Nini's done it again. The Proby shows his mug just as the band belts out his walk-on music for the third time, an overture Scotty Saunders cooked up of *Gone With The Wind,* the *Godfather* theme and *Maria.* That first tune says it all. But the mob goes berko, both halves of the room, the *Bandstand* miserables and the kith and kin of Sydney's rock 'n' roll stayers.

Proby's clobber, a red and white zip-up parka, *LA* emblazoned on it. Black strides, boots. Weird, given he's lugged all them you-beaut cowboy outfits, Savile Row suits and whatnot all the way here from a houso in Hatfield Road, Bolton.

So he rips into *Hold Me.* Shaky start. Perched on the Probythrone. More mobile in Newie, but we had the whip hand on his pill trove there.

Proby tries to peel off the parka as the band blazes on. Gets his arms out of it. But can't untie the drawstring. It's hanging off him now. Bunched around his legs. He stands up. Steps out of it. I got no idea what this is in aid of. A pass at his strip show moves of old. But he looks less wack now at least. Black jacket, white braces, red shirt.

Hold Me winds up. Big finish. Proby aims his finger at the crowd. A sweep across the room. Yells into the mic. *Bang. Bang. Bangbangbangbang.* In a zone known only to him. Some applause, but heaps of urging, mob turned cheer squad.

'*Go PJ! You still got it, PJ!*'

Band kicks into *Mission Bell.* Speedy scoops up Proby's parka lest he trip over it. Nini, in all black and beret, turned the pages of his charts. He read as he sang, glasses on his nose. Finger in his ear, trademark move. He'd promised Clyde he'd be full bottle on the words by showtime. But the grog, the gobfuls of poppers on board...

Our backup singer well across Proby's vocal cues, so he took his from her. Well, when he realised she was there. He did pull off a speccie vibrato note at the end. Mob went nuts.

Then some knob sings out for *Danny Boy*. Proby, lost in a mist, forgets the set list, in place and running order, rehearsed thus, to keep him from crashing the plane. Starts singing the bugger. Acapella. *Not on the list. Not rehearsed. Not good.* Can't find his key. The words fail him.

Scotty Saunders has his arm up. Circling his finger in the air. A signal devised in rehearsals to cue the band into the next number, to drag Proby back down when he drifts. They tumble out the intro to *Hurt*. But he tosses his specs aside just where he should come in! Then this:

'Sorry, ladies and gentlemen. I can't do it without the words.'
Which are right in front of him on the stand.
And now he grabs *them*. Slings the sheet into the air. *Elvis has trashed the building.* Nini sweeps and swoops. Props it back up. She points, helps him find his way in. He makes it to the end, coming good too late. Riotous applause.

'C'mon PJ!'
It's then I see he's weeping.

Nini and Speedy bring him his hat and guitar for *On The Road Again*. He kicks off, lyrics and chords in different places. Band try to lock in but falter. Then drop in at some point they've tracked on his sonar. Four square got his back now. But he's blubbing again.

'Stop cryin' and get on with it!'
From the *Bandstand* cabal. The band jumps into *Niki Hoeky*. Proby shucks his jacket. Means business now. Yet zero from the pipes. Lyrics up in smoke in the burning library of his mind.

Then, *oh shit*. He heads to front of stage, down the steps. *What's his freakin' game?* Nearly trips over his mic lead, tangled round his boots. The band, comping *Niki* all the while. Proby plonks down on the steps. Faulty Batman Villain is the look I flash on. Red shirt, white braces, black hat. The waxy face just seals it. He stands up. Crams a finger in his ear. Out comes *Niki*.

'Down in Louisiana, down in cajun land,...'

Well, some of it. After one line, gone. Reefs off his hat. Stabs at a chorus, all he can summon.

'Niki niki niki hoeky, daddy's doin' time in the pokey,...'

More tears. He's twigged what we all have. We're watching a dude skin himself alive.

Listless hand gestures now. Meant, I think, to be his arms outstretched, handflicking routine from days long faded. Points at Teddy and Ged, *solo*. They oblige. Band still riffing, Proby starts in on the fake joint routine from back in '66. Takes a hit off an air spliff. Offers it to a head in the crowd.

'One for you. One for PJ.'

Then the same to another.

'What about you, hoss? And one for PJ. This ain't no store-bought cigar I'm holdin' here, children. What do you think it is?'

But no-one here has a freakin' clue what he did back then. *Fuck's this about?* It's excruciating. And the Bandstanders won't cop none of it.

'Sing a song!'

'Get off!'

'Get on with it!'

Back on the Probythrone, he mutters non-sequitirs. Waves his hands about. Rips again into *Niki*. Then *Land Of A Thousand Dances*-well, the *na nananana nananana* bit anyway. It's just asking for a pile-up, so the band kills it. Stops dead on a dime.

Someone calls for *Let The Water Run Down*. Connoisseurs, I'll give 'em that.

'Come on PJ, give us somethin'!' honk the Bandstanders. Dissing each *other* now. Half of 'em giving the Proby heaps. The rest, taking to task for it these very grizzlers of their own crusty clan.

'What's the fuckin' P stand for? Poofter?'

'Up yours, carnt!'

'Why'd ya fuckin' come to Straya anyway?'

'Up yours!'

Speedy hands Proby a fresh lyric sheet. Then out it rolls.

'The most beautiful sound I have ever heard...'

Now this is what it's all abou...He loses his place. He don't know the words. To freakin' *Maria.* More passes at it, between sitting, shaking his head. At the finish, delivered by the band like a mercy killing, he takes a punt. That top note of legend. Yeah. Misses it. By waymore than that much.

And oh, yeah. We couldn't talk him out of it. Gropes his way now into that Julio Iglesias cheesefest, *To All The Girls I've Loved Before.* Well, it shuts up Hendoland, a welcome bit of shoosh. It's right up their dead end street, straight outta Rooty Hill RSL. He reads off a sheet so most of the words get a look in. But the song stays round too long. Crowd sags. Precisely why we'd said to give it a miss...

'Play something we *know!'* and worse, 'Play something *you* know!' from the hooters and shouters. His response, *Love Letters Straight From Your Heart.* Yeah. Two ballads in a row. A never never move. But try tellin' that to a flip who showers with a beer.

He rolls into *I Apologise.* Rallies a bit. For *Somewhere,* the backup singer has to do the first verse entire on her Pat Malone, as cues to grab on to. By the end, he's back on the stage steps, holding some gal's hand. He sings her a few of the lyrics, four bars behind the band. Somehow they all finish together.

They ride into *I'm On Fire.* But he's not in synch with his players. First class falsetto fragments, but a deadset desolation about it. It fair clubs down the sizzle of the moment.

Nini comes on with Proby's jacket. Drapes it over him, a la James Brown. Takes his hand to lead him off. Damage control move. He baulks a bit. Tries to bow. She hangs on to him so he doesn't totter off the stage. He smiles. Like he's got away with it. *He thinks it's been a top turn.*

He looks back. Nini shepherds him off, firmer now. He waves again. To some awed crowd that ain't even there bar in his own mind.

Now he's gone. The band winds up *I'm On Fire.* Clyde grabs a mic on a stand.

'Ladies and gentlemen. We have survived.'

And now the mob wants an encore! He don't waste no time taking them up on it. Rips his shirt off. Not smart. Beer belly. Twig-thin arms. Life size squishy toy. They reprise *Somewhere.* Rock into *Proud Mary.* Close as it comes to goin' off.

Proby tells us to drive safe. Blows kisses. Royal waves. The crowd howling, stoked. Maybe convincing themselves he'd been worth it.

Then it goes Biblical. The mob splits in two. Left of centre, barflies from the Hoey, musicians, singers, JJJ crew, music journos, aficionados. Laughin' like kookas. Entertained. How could you not be?

To my right, the surly squares of Bandstandland. Clutching old Proby LPs, now never to bear his autograph. Not after their dissin.' They move for the doors. Some swerve back as they go. Sling a last bit of abuse at the empty stage. One, I'll never forget.

'You're not PJ Proby!'

This unit, and a bunch of them now the seed's planted, think we've sold them a horse of a different colour, a ring-in. Paint come off in the rain. *Oh fuck.*

Sally G and a pal of hers, our door sentries that night. Money changers and wrist stampers. The swarm turns on 'em. No security about at all. Sal and offsider take it on the toe to the manager's office. Lock themselves in. Yeah. Top night.

I see from the middle distance, two of these tools giving Ged our guitar player a hard time. Flashing badges at him. Off duty cops, as it happens. On the stomp and shout for refunds for all and sundry. Their mob trying to barricade everyone from leaving, noising up about this fake Proby. So now me and Clyde have to disperse *them.* Convince them they've just seen the one and only. Not that it falls under their freakin' purview at any rate. We hose down the verballing they're trying to hang on us and get them to understand they ain't been gypped and that pile-up they've just seen, the ridgey-didge article. They'e not happy but they wear it.

'See ya later,' I say as they move to leave. One of the cops looks back. Chucks me a smile with a sneer in it.

'You never know.'

Those bookers from the big circuit pubs who'd fronted, well. A sweep of the room tells me they've all shot through. As for staging the Proby at smaller joints, Max's, the Lansdowne, the Annandale, that option now lay gasping, bleeding out in a bomb crater.

'I take it there's no business plan still standing,' I said to Clyde as we tallied the takings.

'Far as I'm concerned,' he said, 'only plan now is have we got enough here to get him on a plane, and how fast can we do it?'

CHAPTER SIXTY-FIVE

Sunday morning comin' down.

'Oh, I know I've been bad, y'all.'

The stench hit me first. Hadn't seen the Probycave for a week. Squalid then, but now...filthy, sordid. Dead cigars. Spills. Takeaway food boxes. Bottles, cans, left where they'd rolled. What looked like a chuck splat on the carpet. And this bad dead odour.

'Sorry doesn't barely cut it, but I truly am.'

Weren't no sense breaking out a peace pipe. He just didn't get it. No offer to play a few pubs. To sober up. To get some of Clyde's money back. No *I'll come good and do a tour.*

Clyde booked the first that Flight Centre fished up. *Bang.* We kept this from Proby. Best apprised as his Kingswood to the airport stood blowing and smoking out in the street.

*

50 Million Beers playing the Hoey. Sunday, sundown. Proby's noticed their George Jones and Merle Haggard numbers. He's got a request. I ask their singer Charlie. He's stoked.

'On the road again, I just can't wait to get on the road again,...'

Proby's ablaze onstage. A classic and a ripper yarn of he, Willie and Waylon while he's at it. Likely a complete porky but he brings the pub down with it, they go right off. Then *Blue Moon Of Kentucky.* Right on its red tail lights, *That's Alright Mama.* Yeah. *The show he should have done.*

After the gig, a bunch of fun lovers joined him in the Hoey's beer garden. Well, beer deck. Here, tales of how Jack Good ruined him. How Tom Jones stole his fame. His aim to head for the desert to dig a hole to die in. Most here ignorant of our plans, geeing him up to stick around, play some clubs up the Cross. I had to kick Charlie, the Beers' singer, under the table. *Ixnay*.

We waited till chuck-out time. Till all had bailed out on to Bourke Street.

'Proby,' I said. 'You're going home.'

*

'Geezus, Brettski. Turn on the radio.'

Nini on the blower. Fresh horror. The squareheads from the gig. They've called John Laws this morning. As ever, shock jock Lawsy's on the scout for fresh backs for flogging in the village square of public opinion. The battlers' double denim cobber.

'Anyone who wants, refund,' says Clyde. 'That way it's over. Today.'

'Well, hold the phone, my man.'

These blowups have a loud but short life span is my thinking.

'We all took a risk. They saw the same show we did. They're trying it on. Screw 'em!'

But the Bramley insists.

'We need to let Laws think he made us do the right thing. Only thing'll shut him up.'

'Oh, we've just had a call from the promoters. They're very sorry. As disappointed as anyone, they say. They agree Mr Proby was not up to standard. Anyone who feels let down should contact the station. They'll organise a refund. Can't say fairer than that.'

Lawsy's taken the bait. Hung a medal on himself. Now he gets wiggy.

'And as for you, PJ Proby, get on a plane if you haven't already. Get the hell out of Australia. You're a no-talent bum, do you hear? If it were up to me, I'd see to it with my very good friends in Canberra that...'

On the refunds, twelve of those dingbats actually went to the trouble. Now while all this is rollin' round the deck, Ian Rilen fronts. On the prowl. Cash, or a shout, or something a bit tricky. Just as we're setting out for Bondi to square up the bill. Invites himself along.

'Give youse a hand if the cunt gets punchy.'

'Mr Proby will be checking out tomorrow.'

Clyde pays the freight. We head upstairs. The funk, a face-melter. *And now I see what it is.* Seafood. Shellfish. A boatload of it. Crammed in the fridge. Proby must've made Kenny fetch it on a whim, then forgot about it. I just about gag scooping it out to drop in a bin on Campbell Parade, lest Clyde lose his deposit. Rilo pops one of Proby's beers. Jams a traveller in his jacket while he's at it.

'Well, if that's as be, then so be it,' says Proby to the news of his flight. He takes it well, for all that. Vast experience, my guess. Practiced at the art.

'And that'll be twelve hundred dollars, please.'

Words were few and cold in the Kingswood. At the airport, Clyde had to spring for Proby's excess baggage. Paid in silence. Proby lifted a hand in adios. I turned my back. Walked on.

EPILOGUE

No cassette player in the taxi. Sydney radio, most of it shitful. I go for 2CH. Spins good sounds from back then. And runs these rock 'n' roll news breaks. What the stars of yesterwhen are up to now.

That's how I got the mail. Proby's heart attack. Gig at Blackpool, mid-'91. Then three more in one day, in Florida, a few months on. Of working regular again. Being charged with welfare fraud in the UK and acquitted.

That he'd made a record. With Marc Almond, the *Tainted Love* dude. The single charted in the UK a week or two. And he was sober. As back as he'd ever get. I was happy for him.

I still play his records. Six of the great LPs of our times. The ones Elvis should have made. Now and then, a smile at those moments in our midst when he took our breath away and set eyes to shining.

I wonder if he knew.